P9-APD-001

APACHE BLADES

Johnny Pinto feinted his blade toward Duane, but Duane was as tense as a puma about to strike. Then Johnny shoved his knife toward Duane's belly, but Duane danced to the side and whipped his edge through Johnny's forearm. Blood spurted;

the blade had sliced to the bone and Johnny howled. Duane saw three openings, but chose not to kill Johnny at the moment.

Tendons had been severed and Johnny's knife dropped from his numbed right hand. Lips quivering with pain, he picked it up with his left hand. He didn't have to say anything—his eyes told the story. He was prepared to kill Duane Braddock or die in the attempt.

Also by Jack Bodine

THE PECOS KID—BEGINNER'S LUCK
THE PECOS KID #2—THE RECKONING
THE PECOS KID #3—APACHE MOON
THE PECOS KID #4—OUTLAW HELL

Published by
HarperPaperbacks

ATTENTION: ORGANIZATIONS AND CORPORATIONS

Most HarperPaperbacks are available at special quantity discounts for bulk purchases for sales promotions, premiums, or fund-raising. For information, please call or write:
Special Markets Department, HarperCollins Publishers,
10 East 53rd Street, New York, N.Y. 10022.
Telephone: (212) 207-7528. Fax: (212) 207-7222.

THE
PECOS KID

DEVIL'S CREEK MASSACRE

JACK BODINE

HarperPaperbacks
A Division of HarperCollins*Publishers*

If you purchased this book without a cover, you should be aware that this book is stolen property. It was reported as "unsold and destroyed" to the publisher and neither the author nor the publisher has received any payment for this "stripped book."

This is a work of fiction. The characters, incidents, and dialogues are products of the author's imagination and are not to be construed as real. Any resemblance to actual events or persons, living or dead, is entirely coincidental.

HarperPaperbacks *A Division of* HarperCollins*Publishers*
10 East 53rd Street, New York, N.Y. 10022

Copyright © 1994 by Len Levinson
All rights reserved. No part of this book may be used or reproduced in any manner whatsoever without written permission of the publisher, except in the case of brief quotations embodied in critical articles and reviews. For information address HarperCollins*Publishers,*
10 East 53rd Street, New York, N.Y. 10022.

Cover illustration by Paul Bachem

First printing: March 1994

Printed in the United States of America

HarperPaperbacks and colophon are trademarks of HarperCollins*Publishers*

❖ 10 9 8 7 6 5 4 3 2 1

CHAPTER 1

THE DESERT GLIMMERED spectrally in the moonlight, as Duane Braddock rode south to Monterrey. His trail led through the Apache homeland, and he relentlessly scanned shadows for suspicious shapes and movements, his Colt .44 tight in his right hand, cocked and loaded, ready to fire.

He'd lived among Apaches and knew their tactics well. They could be tracking him at that very moment, coveting his fine horse, weapons, saddle, and equipment. And if Apaches weren't enough, the Fourth Cavalry wanted him dead or alive for the alleged killing of a federal marshal in Morellos, although Duane considered it self-defense. Posters displaying his youthful countenance were nailed all over west Texas, and he was running for his life.

He also was alert for lost wandering banditos, cut-throat Comancheros, and the Mexican Army itself.

Constant guard duty and insufficient sleep were making him jittery and anxious. He looked forward to Monterrey, where he could relax in a cantina, drink a glass of mescal, and observe sloe-eyed dancing señoritas.

Duane detected sudden lateral movement in thick cholla and ocotillo to his right. Maybe it was a desert swallow, rabbit, or buzzard, but it could be an Apache setting up a bushwhack. Duane drew his Winchester and jacked a round into the chamber, just in case.

It wasn't the first time he'd noticed possible danger during the past twenty-four hours. While he'd slept that afternoon, his ear pressed against his makeshift pillow, he'd heard muffled hoofbeats in the distance. At sundown, something flashed on a distant ridge, possibly the worn barrel of an Apache rifle catching the last rays of sunlight. And that very night, Duane thought he'd seen movement in dark moonshadows. It could've been an antelope or mule deer, but there was no way of knowing for sure. Duane wondered if a raiding party had cut his trail.

Duane Braddock was tall, rangy, eighteen years old. He wore black jeans, black shirt, and a wide-brimmed black hat, with a red bandanna tied around his neck. He hadn't shaved since Texas, and his only conversations were with his horse, Nestor. "How's it going, boy?" asked Duane, as he patted the black mane of his big russet animal. He'd paid one hundred dollars for Nestor about two weeks ago, and they still didn't know each other well. Nestor was muscular, powerful, with plenty of bottom, but no horse could outsmart Apaches once they picked up a poor unfortunate white eyes' trail.

Apaches were the best trackers in the world, but Duane had learned tricks from the masters themselves. He was about to put the spurs to Nestor when a little voice said in his ear: Are you *sure* you saw something?

The flash of light could've been a lump of mica or malachite that caught the sun, and the desert was full of living creatures that moved about. I've been in the saddle so long, I'm going loco, he thought as he eased forward the hammer of his Winchester and dropped the weapon into its scabbard.

Duane wanted to light a cigarette, but its glowing red dot would be seen for miles. He was tired of eating raw meat, but no trailside restaurants were available on the Coahuilian desert. He hoped he'd reach civilization before the Apaches got him.

During the previous day, Duane had dreamed of a skeleton cowboy in rags, riding a skeleton horse across the endless plain. The cowboy had a feather in his hatband, a Colt .44 in his hand, and a maniacal smile wreathed his skull. There was something familiar about the skeleton cowboy, and Duane wondered if he was the ghost of his father.

Duane's father had been a rancher killed in a range war, according to information that Duane had uncovered. Duane knew who'd paid for the killing: Sam Archer of Edgeville, Texas. Duane planned to even the score with Mr. Archer at the first opportunity, but had more pressing problems. Duane Braddock, alias the Pecos Kid, was considered a threat to every man, woman, and child in west Texas.

Duane jerked around suddenly and thought he saw an Apache lurking in the shade of a prickly-pear cactus seventy-five yards away. The thick desert foliage was still, and Duane wondered if he was imagining Apaches. You've been alone so long, pretty soon you'll see circus clowns dancing out here. You're not happy unless you're worrying about something.

He smiled wryly, aware of his weaknesses and short-comings. Duane Braddock had spent sixteen of his eighteen years in a Benedictine monastery orphanage high in the Guadalupe Mountains. He'd intended to become a priest, but then began noticing pretty Mexican girls who came to Mass at the monastery on Sundays. Shortly thereafter he'd got into a fight with another orphan, and the old abbot had chucked Duane unceremoniously out the gate. In the secular world for the first time, the naive and impractical ex-acolyte had fallen into one serious jam after another. He understood theology and philosophy, but had huge gaps in his practical knowledge of the world.

He smelled water, his nose twitched, and he hoped a stream or well was in the offing. He had a half canteen of water left, as he pulled back Nestor's reins. "Be still," he said softly.

Nestor stopped, his large round eyes glowing luminescently in the darkness. Duane listened carefully, and his Apache ears picked up the faint music of a stream, but it could be wind whistling over cactus spines. There it was again, far in the distance, the *clomp* of an unshod hoof against grama grass. A chill went up Duane's back, because he didn't know what was real anymore. A war party of Apaches might be aiming their arrows at him, or it could be the music of the night.

A row of cottonwood trees lay beyond thickets of cholla and paddle cactus straight ahead. He was headed in a southwesterly direction and didn't think he was lost. To stop at the stream or keep moving on, that was the question for the cowboy Hamlet. The stream

4

was an ideal spot for a bushwhack. Just when he bent over, slurping cool clear liquid, that's when they'd shoot an arrow into his back.

But there were some things an Apache couldn't know, such as which spot in the stream he'd choose. Who am I, what am I, and what do I want from the world? he mused as he rode toward water. His monastic studies had marked him for life, and he measured himself on a scale that permitted no folly, unless it be holy folly, and no dishonesty, regardless of how seductive.

Duane angled Nestor's approach to the stream, to befuddle possible trackers. He glanced around furtively, then bent over Nestor's long flowing mane. "We can't waste time here for obvious reasons," Duane whispered into Nestor's upthrust ear. "Drink up and let's get out fast, okay?"

Nestor twitched his hairy ear to show that he understood, or at least that's what Duane thought. Sometimes Duane had the uncanny notion that Nestor understood English perfectly and communicated in his own subtle language of winks, snorts, neighs, and the movement of his ears, not to mention his hooves. But Duane didn't know what he was conjuring and what was true.

In fact, Nestor understood the situation far better than Duane. Nestor also had pulled a hitch with Apaches, and smelled them faintly in the night. They'd been tracking him and his boss for two suns, but hadn't yet come close. The last thing Nestor wanted was recapture by Apaches, because Apaches rode horses till they dropped, then butchered and ate them, sometimes raw, on the spot. Grisly memories haunted his horse mind.

Duane and Nestor headed toward the stream glittering through thick desert foliage. A bat darted over their heads, searching for mice and rats. Duane held his Colt cocked and loaded, his sharp eyes inspecting every shadow as Nestor trod toward silvery waters. Needles and spines slashed Duane's jeans, and he poised himself to give Nestor the spurs at the first hint of danger. The only sound was a coyote howling mournfully in a far-off cave, except it might be an Apache signaling. Again Duane couldn't say for sure.

Nestor approached the stream as Duane gathered his canteens together. The horse slowed, lowered his great snout, and Duane slid down from the saddle. Glancing around nervously, his mind taut as a guitar string, he plunged both canteens into the cool clear water. Bubbles sang gaily as Nestor slurped cool limpid water. The canteens stopped gurgling, Duane screwed on the caps, then vaulted into the saddle and gave Nestor the spurs. The huge russet beast splashed across the stream, his belly full of water. Skittish and fearful, he carried his boss southward, as night air thickened with the pungent fragrance of Apache warriors on a raid.

Kateynah sat on his strawberry roan war pony and peered into the night. He knew that the lone white-eyes rider on the fabulous horse was out there somewhere, but didn't know his precise location. It was too dark for reliable tracking, and the white eyes constantly changed direction, covering his trail whenever possible, and carrying his pistol ready to fire.

Kateynah and six other Apaches were returning from a fruitless raid on a Mexican settlement, and they'd lose prestige if they arrived at their rancheria empty-handed. It would reflect especially poorly on Kateynah, their leader, but a mount like the one belonging to the white eyes could buy Kateynah's first wife. Kateynah was twenty-three years old, and tired of sleeping with a moth-eaten stolen U.S. Army blanket.

He heard the approach of a rider and held his stolen old army carbine ready to fire. It was Tandor, bristling with arrows, knives, and his silent bow, an ocher war stripe painted horizontally across his cheeks and nose.

"We have lost him," Tandor reported, "but we will find his trail at the stream, I am sure." Tandor was second in command, only nineteen years old, and had thick curly black hair, because his mother had been a Negro captive. "The sun will be up soon, and then he will rest," said Tandor. "Even if he sees us, he will be ours alone. I look forward to receiving his rifle."

Tandor, Kateynah, and the others had carefully surveyed the merchandise. They would've killed the white eyes on the spot at numerous junctures, but he'd been alert, armed at all times, and the horse was unquestionably swift. They'd have to be subtle and silent as a pack of coyotes, which in a sense they were.

Duane saw the dawn's red glow, time for another difficult decision: sleep or keep going. He longed for his simple monk's life, where decisions had been inconsequential. Whether St. Bonaventure was right or Abelard wrong, Duane could always recline on his safe little cot at night, protected by ponderosa-pine log walls and the prestige of Holy Mother Church. But a wrong decision in Apache country could end your life suddenly, silently, irrevocably.

Duane had lived with Sister Death so long, she was

a gaunt youthful ghost dancing before him in a ragged black dress, grinning maniacally, enticing him toward his doom. The end could come in the form of a bear lurking behind that boulder or a rattlesnake about to snap at his leg at any moment. Duane had studied the great Stoics, and it all boiled down to grin and bear it, or as the Epicureans alleged, live life to the hilt, and when you die, have a bottle of good wine in one hand, a beautiful woman in your arms, and one last laugh for the scurrying dark minions of Sister Death. Duane had learned to be hard, because inner pain hurts more than getting punched in the mouth, and he'd had a few of those too. It seemed that whenever he rode into a new town, somebody wanted to mess with him.

The red glow brightened on the horizon, and Duane didn't have endless time to ponder. He was too tense to sleep, but decided to stop for the day. Thick swarms of scraggly desert foliage to the east looked like a good bet, and he steered Nestor toward them, his Colt in hand as he glanced about constantly.

There were no signs of other human beings, and for all he knew, no white man had been in the valley since the dawn of time. It looked pristine, untouched, the desert of Eden being reborn in the first rays of morning. I'll bet it was like this when Christ wandered the wilderness for forty days and forty nights, tempted by the devil, but he held on and so will I.

Duane examined thickets at close range and settled on one with protective boulders piled around and open stretches in every direction for at least twenty yards. If Apaches want to take me, let them try, he thought bravely.

He pulled back the reins, then climbed off Nestor. Should I leave him saddled or not? A saddle would be best for a quick getaway, but if Duane were killed, a saddle could impede Nestor's efforts to save himself. What the hell, Duane thought, as he unfastened the cinch. He pulled the saddle off Nestor's back, then picketed the animal inside a ragged arc of boulders interspersed with cactus.

From the sheltered position, Duane could hold off a sizable war party with his rifle, or so he wanted to believe. He cut some juniper branches and proceeded to cover his trail all the way back to where he'd turned off his main route.

The first red molten sliver of sun lay on the horizon when he returned to his hiding spot by a circuitous route, and Nestor watched him warily, chomping grass. Duane laid out his bedroll, took a sip of water, made sure his weapons were ready to fire, and sat cross-legged on his blanket. The sky lightened, and a gray-breasted martin flew overhead, glancing at him curiously. Higher in the sky, Duane spotted a lone black buzzard circling about, waiting for something, anything, to fall.

If Apaches were out there, they'd get him in the long run, no doubt about it. He opened his saddlebags, pulled out half a haunch of cold roasted antelope wrapped in his green bandanna, laid it on the ground, yanked out his Apache knife, and sliced off a chunk. The antelope was young, tender, raw, and went down quickly. Duane ate with one hand holding his Colt ready to fire. His Winchester lay beside him, next to saddlebags full of ammunition.

He felt like a fool—there probably wasn't an Apache within ten miles—but something didn't seem right, and Nestor had been acting strangely too. Duane ate several slices of antelope, washed them down with water, and craved a cigarette now that it was daylight, but an Apache could smell cigarette smoke miles away.

His eyes stung with fatigue. *All I want is a good cowboy job and a good woman, so how come I'm always on the dodge?* Frustration assailed him, because he hated to be limited. He returned the wrapped antelope to his saddlebag, and his knuckles brushed against a book. He pulled it out and looked at the cover.

THE PRINCE
by Niccolò Machiavelli

He'd found it in the stable of the last big town. It had lain among other books in a box hidden beneath hay and apparently forgotten. Duane let the pages fall open, and read:

> *The prince must adhere to the good so long as he can, but, being compelled by necessity, he must be prepared to take the path of evil.*

No wonder they excommunicated this galoot, Duane figured, *but you just can't lay back and let somebody kill you. Even popes have led soldiers in war, and what about St. Augustine's doctrine of the just war?* Nestor peered intently into the desert as he chewed grama grass. It looked like something was out there.

"What is it, boy?" asked Duane.

The horse made a sound in his throat. Duane might doubt his own instincts, but not Nestor's. The animal was spooked. Something told Duane that he was headed for a showdown. He lay on his stomach, aimed his rifle around the boulder, and focused in the direction of Nestor's gaze.

It was cactus, boulders, and other scrubby desert for as far as he could see. High in the heavens, the same old buzzard soared on updrafts, waiting patiently for desert pie. Then Duane spotted something, and it looked like brown Apache skin flashing instantaneously in the shrubbery. Nestor snorted—he'd seen it too—and trembled all over. The prospect of another tour with Apaches scared him to death.

Duane realized with dismay that his worst fears had been realized. Apaches were out there; he didn't know how many, but they wouldn't stalk him if they didn't think they could take him easily. Oh-oh, he thought as he broke out into a cold sweat.

Nestor gazed at Duane solemnly, and a thought traveled from Nestor's mind to the Pecos Kid's. If Apaches killed Duane, they'd get Nestor. Now wait a minute, Duane admonished himself, as he looked at his transportation. I paid a hundred dollars for that horse, and I'm not turning him loose now.

Nestor continued to peer into Duane's eyes, and Duane's resolve weakened. I should give him a fighting chance, because that's what I'd want. Then Duane caught a glimpse of brown Apache flesh in another direction. It's a war party, and they're maneuvering for position. If I try to get away in broad daylight, they'll run me down and shoot me out of the saddle.

Nestor was silent, although fur twitched all over his body. His head swung from side to side and he tried to raise his front hooves in the air, but the pin held him down. It was time for Duane to make another decision, but this time he didn't hesitate. He pulled the pin out of the ground, removed the halter, and slapped Nestor on the haunch.

"You're on your own," said Duane. "If I get out of this alive, I hope you'll come back and take me to Monterrey."

Don't hold your breath, the horse seemed to reply as he beheld Duane one last time. Then he turned away, broke into a lope, and went crashing through the underbrush, his hooves rumbling across the morning stillness, and then he was out of sight, gone, and useless to the hapless desert traveler.

Why'd I do that? Duane asked himself in mystification. I paid a hundred dollars for that horse! He noticed a red Apache bandanna for a brief moment in a new direction, and now three warriors were tightening the noose around him. He imagined them cursing angrily, because they'd already lost their biggest prize, Nestor. "Come on, you sons of bitches," muttered Duane through his teeth. "You want a fight—I'll give you one that you'll never forget."

Kateynah heard Nestor galloping off and at first couldn't believe his ears. He raised his head for a brief moment and saw the riderless animal streaking toward distant mountains. The white eyes has seen us, Kateynah realized. But why has he turned his horse loose?

Kateynah couldn't fathom the reason, and the unexpected incident stopped him in his tracks. He knew it was a trick, but couldn't divine its purpose. The white eyes had tried to obscure his tracks, but not well enough to fool Kateynah. The white eyes was straight ahead, and the warriors probed for his exact location.

Kateynah searched the foliage, but nothing moved. The white eyes was hiding like a desert rat, fully armed, and Kateynah had to get low like a snake, then crawl forward silently on his knees and elbows, cradling his rifle in his arms. His sharp eyes examined every spear of cactus and blade of grass, looking for the black pants and black shirt of the white eyes.

Kateynah hated all white eyes, because they were stealing the Apache homeland, killing game, pushing the People all across the desert, and committing unspeakable atrocities. Yet he was jealous of their knowledge concerning rifles and pistols. The manufacture of such implements was incomprehensible to his Stone Age mind, though he could shoot a mule deer through the eye at two hundred yards.

He crawled forward silently, sniffing the air, his eyes sweeping back and forth continually. He was confident that he'd find the white eyes before the white eyes saw him, because everyone knew how weak and stupid the white eyes were. Kateynah recalled the rifle that he intended to claim for himself, now that the horse was gone. From the distance, it had looked like a fast-firing new model instead of the single-shot rusty implement of death in Kateynah's hands.

Kateynah heard a shot directly in front of him. A puff of smoke billowed through the branches of a cholla cactus, and a lead projectile smacked into Kateynah's forehead. The Apache warrior's promising career came to a sudden end as his brains blew out the back of his head, and he was gone to the happy hunting ground before his face hit the ground.

Duane withdrew behind the boulder, not certain that his bullet had found its target. It might've been a hawk, the trembling of a leaf, or an Apache warrior with blood in his eyes. The shot echoed off distant caprock escarpments and then faded gradually into the buzzing of insects and chirping of birds seeking breakfast in the desert morning.

Duane sucked air between his teeth and pressed his back to the boulder. The wait was getting to him, and a rivulet of perspiration ran from his hatband to his eyebrow. He wished the Apaches would rush, and he'd fight it out hand to hand till the bitter end. But they were playing games with his mind.

Duane wanted a cigarette and shot of whiskey to steady him, because it looked like he was going to die. Ever since he'd left the monastery, it had been one narrow escape after another. He'd seen many men bite the dust and had helped a few along, but now it was coming down on him. There were too many holes in his defense, and sooner or later an Apache would move into position for a clear shot. Duane wished he had his back to a wall, but there was only the open desert in every direction.

Duane wished he'd stayed at the monastery, and had many other regrets also. He figured that he'd been born under an unlucky star, and life wasn't so wonderful anyway. Glory be to the Father, the Son, and to the Holy Ghost, as it was—

A gun fired, and lead whacked into the boulder two inches from his right cheek. In an instant, Duane was flat on his stomach, crawling frantically to another boulder, saddlebag filled with ammunition hanging over his shoulder. The next bullet kicked up dirt six inches from his left hip, and he rolled over, jumped to his feet, and broke into a run. Bullets whizzed around him like angry gnats, and sharp needles tore his clothes and flesh as he landed behind a bush with shreddy brown bark. He touched his finger to his cheek; it came back flecked with blood; the first shot had hurled splinters of stone through his beard and into his soft flesh.

He propelled himself forward on elbows and knees, keeping his chin close to the ground, hard rock scraping his jeans. He knew they could hear his every move, but they wouldn't waste precious ammunition; they'd advance close like last time and plug him economically with one well-placed shot.

He came to a halt behind a hawthorn tree covered with yellow nutlets. Every time he moved, a needle or spine from a nearby cow's tongue cactus jutted into him. He battled waves of terror, felt as though he were choking to death, but summoned his will, swallowed hard, and prepared to go down fighting.

He knew that he didn't have a chance, and there were at least six of them, to judge from the shooting. He glanced at the desert bower that would become his tomb. They'd rip away his clothes and leave him for the coyotes, buzzards, and vermin that infested the desert. He glanced up and saw the old crook-necked buzzard circling about, waiting for lunch to be served in all its gory splendor.

The time for Machiavelli was over, and the only entity that could help Duane was Lord God Almighty. He reached into his saddlebag, pulled out his Protestant King James Bible, and opened it at random:

And how dieth the wise man? As the fool.

Ain't that the truth, Duane thought. He flipped a few pages.

I shall lift mine eyes up unto the Lord, from whence cometh my help.

Duane looked at the sky, but all he could see was the wise old buzzard preparing his menu. The ex-acolyte realized that he'd lost his rock-solid faith since leaving the monastery, and now was adrift in the Apache storm. He reached into his shirt and touched the crucifix of the rosary-bead necklace that hung from his neck. *Hail Mary, full of grace, the Lord is with thee.* As he prayed, he reflected upon his brief life, admitting that he hadn't accomplished any of his great goals. As he faced his final hour, in the extremities of fear and doubt, one final unlikely image somehow sprang to mind: a tall willowy blond temptress, his former fiancée: Miss Vanessa Fontaine.

Even with his head on the chopping block, Duane remembered Miss Vanessa Fontaine. The former Charleston belle had made a more profound impression on his soft clay mind than sixteen years of Catholic education. Perhaps she'd lacked knowledge of the Nicene Council, but Duane missed her more than his theological mentors as he faced Sister Death for the last time.

Vanessa had dumped Duane for an officer in the Fourth Cavalry, and Duane considered her the most selfish bitch alive. Yet he couldn't evict her from the bedrooms of his mind even as Apaches were lining their sights on him. He recalled her long sinuous legs that she liked to wrap around him, not to mention her naughty tongue and wicked fingers. He could go on endlessly extolling her many charms, recalling this or that clever remark that she'd made, or burning nights in a little Texas town called Titusville. Duane had been ready to die for her, but she married for money and social position, producing a scar in Duane's heart that no salve could mend.

He found himself yearning for Miss Vanessa Fontaine's long slim configuration, although she was hundreds and perhaps thousands of miles away, probably lying in her husband's arms. Duane detested her betrayal, yet would be overjoyed to see her again, as in the good old days (approximately six months ago).

He heard faint sounds of Apache warriors working closer to him. The flora was too thick to see well, but fortunately they couldn't locate him either. Sooner or later one of them would show himself, and Duane would kill him. Then the final act would begin.

He lay with his Winchester and saddlebags and wondered what might've been. It looked as though he'd be killed like his father, surrounded by enemies, and the irony wasn't lost on him. I'd rather die a lion than a lamb, he tried to convince himself.

Something rustled to his right, and he turned silently in that direction. It was an Apache crawling forward, searching for the white eyes, as the white eyes silently aimed his rifle in that direction. But the Apache stopped suddenly, because Duane wasn't as quiet as he'd thought. The Apache slithered toward a nearby pile of rocks as Duane took aim at the Apache's left kidney. He squeezed the trigger, the Winchester kicked into his shoulder, smoke billowed in the air, and the Apache jolted as the bullet found its intended spot.

The Apache screamed in pain, rolled over and clutched his wound as Duane jacked the lever. He lined his sights on the convulsive Apache, but another rifle fired somewhere to Duane's left, and something incredible crashed into Duane's shoulder. For a few seconds Duane didn't know what happened to him, then ferocious pain tore him apart. He gasped, gritted his teeth, and looked at his shoulder. Blood literally poured out; it was a deep flesh wound, and the bullet had cracked his shoulder bone. He couldn't move his left arm at all.

An ocean of blackness fell over him as he reached for his Colt, but his movement was slow and the pistol unusually heavy. Another bullet slammed into his right thigh and felt like a flaming spear. He tried to clear his head as the universe broke apart all around him. A new bullet whacked the ground two inches from his nose, making him flinch as he drew back the hammer of his Colt. Harrowing pain throbbed through him as he recalled an old saloon rat telling him that if he ever got surrounded by Apaches, save the last bullet for himself.

He heard Apaches talking to each other. Sister Death danced among ocotillo and juniper, eagerly awaiting Duane's departure. "I don't want to die," he whispered as his short life passed before his eyes. He saw himself studying in the scriptorium in the clouds, shooting a gunfighter named Otis Puckett in a small Texas town named Shelby, and writhing with pleasure in the naked arms of Miss Vanessa Fontaine.

He struggled to hold his Colt ready for one last shot, but couldn't see any Apaches. Another gun fired, his ribs were smashed, and he struggled to breathe, hit in the vitals. In the distance, he heard volleys of gunfire, or maybe it was thunder, or perhaps even the voice of Lord God Almighty calling out to him.

"Oh, my Jesus . . . forgive us our sins . . . save us from the fires of hell . . . lead all souls into heaven . . . especially those most in need of your mercy . . . such as me."

He wished he could die straight out, but his fighting Texas heart wouldn't let go. He lay still on the ground, struggled to open his eyes, and it appeared that Vanessa Fontaine was standing before him, wearing a white diaphanous gown, peering at him with great concern, as if she wanted to help him. "Vanessa," was the last word he spoke, then black waterfalls spilled

over his eyes, and he plunged into the bowels of the
raging noonday sun.

Mrs. Vanessa Dawes awoke with a start in her
Austin hotel room, approximately seven hundred and
fifty miles away. The former Charleston belle lay on
her maroon velvet sofa, a book open on her breast;
she'd dozed off reading Lord Byron. She closed the
tome, laid it on the floor beside her, and wondered
why she felt uneasy. It was as though something terrible had happened, but often she was disturbed by
nightmares and vague premonitions of doom.

Her husband, the former Lieutenant Clayton Dawes,
had been killed in action against the Apaches during
the summer. His family had been old Yankee money,
and his grandmother had bequeathed him a small fortune in securities and investments, which passed to his
surviving widow, the former Miss Vanessa Fontaine of
Charleston, South Carolina. Now wealthy again as in
the halcyon days before the Civil War, she'd launched
herself successfully in Austin society, which consisted
mostly of ex-Confederate sympathizers such as herself.

In a week, she was scheduled to attend a private ball
at the residence of a wealthy Austin banker. The crème
de la crème of Austin ex-Confederate society would be
there. Vanessa loved to enact the great lady, and certainly never mentioned that she'd been a poor itinerant
saloon singer before she'd met Lieutenant Dawes.

Vanessa was bored with widow's weeds and toyed
with the notion of marrying again. The most wealthy
and presentable men in Austin would attend the ball,
and she didn't hate the opposite sex by any means. To
the contrary, they came in handy for performing escort

duties and providing certain pleasurable pastimes best not mentioned in polite society.

She drew her long legs around and planted them on the floor. Then she folded her hands together and looked out the window at another bright sunny day on San Marcos Street, not far from the former French legation to the Republic of Texas. She lived among others of her kind in a small out-of-the-way hotel, the Arlington, named after General Robert E. Lee's former estate in Virginia. Servants were available for every conceivable notion in the luxurious establishment, while the kitchen on the ground floor produced excellent meals for every occasion. Vanessa Fontaine could lie on her sofa for the rest of her life, be waited on by servants, and read beautiful poetry, but somehow she wasn't contented.

She knew what she wanted, but considered the idea preposterous. Despite her best efforts, she couldn't forget a certain ex-lover who had shared her bed several months ago. In the cold light of logic, she'd thought him too young and unpromising for a lost wandering ex–Charleston belle, and decided to marry instead the dashing Lieutenant Clayton Dawes. Now, despite the lieutenant's untimely demise, Duane Braddock continued to occupy a considerable portion of her waking hours.

The former Miss Vanessa Fontaine was by no means inexperienced with men. If the truth be told, she'd slept with too many gentlemen, rogues, and liars, but she'd been weak and helpless on numerous occasions. There'd been mornings, during her saloon singing days, when she'd awakened next to individuals whose names she didn't even remember and, in the cold dawn light, didn't want to remember.

Last thing she'd heard about Duane Braddock, he'd shot a professional gunfighter named Otis Puckett, plus several other people, in Shelby, Texas. Some said Duane was a kill-crazy outlaw, while others claimed he was a decent cowboy who'd stuck up for his rights. When last seen, according to eyewitnesses, the Pecos Kid had been alive and well and headed for the Rio Grande.

Vanessa's home consisted of three large rooms with a small kitchen. She filled a glass half with water, then opened the mahogany cabinet and pulled out a bottle marked LAUDANUM. She poured a shot into the water, then mixed it with a spoon. The contents rolled down her throat; she returned to the sofa and waited for the opium derivative to kick in.

It was her medicine for whatever ailed her, and she was unhappy most of the time. Sometimes she wondered if she could ever exist in the new Yankee world. Vanessa Fontaine was an unrepentant Southerner, a member in full standing of the great Lost Cause, and she missed the old plantation back in South Carolina, with a colonnade of great oaks leading to white Corinthian columns of the main house, while slaves did all the dirty work.

Poppy juice invaded Vanessa's brain; she saw vast fields of fluffy white cottonballs, dashing cavaliers on prancing stallions returning from a hunt, and the orchestra playing chamber music in the gazebo. The lost paradise returned in all its splendor as she languished on the sofa, a faint smile on her curvaceous lips.

CHAPTER 2

TANDOR THE APACHE SAW THE
white eyes lying cold and still in the bushes straight ahead. The white eyes
appeared dead, the rifle and pistol lying nearby, blood
everywhere. Tandor sang his victory song as he drew
closer to the modern new weapons. No longer would
he have to load a cartridge every time he wanted to
shoot somebody.

Suddenly a fusillade of lead screamed through the
air around him. He was so astonished, his song
caught in his throat, but in the next second he dived
toward the ground. In the distance, a large number of
white eyes on horseback were attacking, sending
forth terrific volleys of fire! Tandor had been so concentrated on the lone white eyes, he didn't consider
that someone might stalking him. He crawled with
his nose close to the ground and peered cautiously
around a boulder. Fifteen white-eyes riders charged

across the desert in his direction, firing steadily, and he didn't like the odds. "Get out of here!" Tandor hollered to his comrades.

He leapt to his feet and sped through the underbrush, heading for the horses. His cohorts joined in the mad rush while the air sang with whirring bullets. Blue Feather shrieked in pain as a bullet pierced his spine; he dropped to the ground, but Tandor didn't have time to gather him up.

Tandor ran fleet-footed across the desert and leapt onto his horse. A bullet zipped past his left ear as his horse galloped away. Where did they come from? wondered Tandor bitterly as he rode toward the Apache camp in the hills. And why didn't we see them earlier? He recalled the white-eyes rifle that he couldn't steal; a dark cloud passed over his heart, and he cursed beneath his breath. Maybe, on another day, I'll be the victor and you'll be running from me, if you're lucky, Tandor thought with a grim smile, as his horse scampered across the cactus plain.

Tandor and his warriors had been attacked by a gang of American outlaws, and their leader was Richard Cochrane, formerly of the Confederate Cavalry Corps. He and his men rampaged onward, maintaining steady pistol fire at Apaches fleeing in all directions.

A half hour earlier, Cochrane had heard gunfire far away and decided to investigate. The Apaches scattered into the desert, but there was no point to dividing his small force and chasing them. Cochrane held up his right gloved hand while pulling back his horse's reins with his left. His men coalesced about him, a rugged dusty lot, sunlight glinting off steely eyes. They'd expected a small band of embattled Mexican vaqueros, but could locate no hint of the gun battle that they'd just interrupted.

"Could be they was just Apaches a-fightin' amongst theirselves," suggested Clement Beasley, second in command, formerly a sergeant in the Ninth Virginia Cavalry.

"Looks that way," replied Cochrane. He took off his smudged silverbelly cowboy hat and wiped his forehead with the back of his arm. A jagged purple scar worked its way up his right cheek, and he wore a black patch over his right eye. "This is as good a place as any to break for dinner."

He climbed down from his horse and let Beasley pass along his orders. Cochrane managed the outlaw band like a line cavalry detachment, with strict discipline and rough punishment for infractions of the rules. They were mostly ex-Confederate soldiers returning from the armed robbery of a west Texas bank, as attested to by packhorses carrying bags filled with loot.

Cochrane sat in the scant shade of a cottonwood tree as his men performed campsite duties. They traveled light as Apaches, with no tents, only grub and canvas bedrolls. Two men dug a firepit while two others prepared food. Another crew cared for horses, and three were lookouts, because no place is home for desperadoes with prices on their heads.

Cochrane smoked a cigarette and examined his map as dinner was prepared. Thirty-one years old, five-ten, he was sturdily constructed, with dirty tan jeans and two Colts in crisscrossed gunbelts, a bandolier across his chest, and a bowie knife sticking out his boot. He and his men didn't believe that the Great Cause was lost, and fought on as highly mobile and efficient mounted guerrilla fighters. Cochrane had dubbed them the First Virginia Irregulars, and they were on their way to their hideout in the Sierra Madre Mountains.

No one sat near Cochrane, who maintained himself remote from the men. It was partially by design, because men won't take orders from a friend, and partially because he genuinely despised small talk. He removed his old brass army compass from his shirt pocket and took an azimuth on mountains on the horizon, then returned to the map. He loved tactics, ordnance, action, and danger. Certain events that had occurred at the Appomattox Courthouse in 1865 didn't change anything as far as he was concerned. The war that broke out at Fort Sumter was still on, and he'd never bow down to the Yankee invader.

Beasley approached his commanding officer and threw a salute. He was heavyset and wore a walrus mustache. "The camp is secure, sir. Walsh's horse has a loose shoe, but that's the total damage."

"Carry on," replied Cochrane. He didn't have to issue more orders; they all knew what to do and functioned like a smooth well-oiled war machine. Beasley sat opposite his commanding officer and rolled a cigarette. "I wonder what them Apaches was up to. They might come back with some of their friends."

"I don't think so," replied Cochrane.

Beasley and the others usually deferred to Cochrane, while the ex-company commander felt no need to explain himself. Who had the Apaches been fighting? he wondered.

Cochrane had more important concerns, such as his next raid behind enemy lines, and then came the cantinas of Monterrey, with beautiful Mexican girls, gambling tables, horse races, and other pastimes to take his mind off the War of Northern Aggression that had destroyed and punished the South.

A strange sound came to his ears as he carefully folded his dog-eared map. "Someone's there," he said, dropping to the ground and whipping out his old Remington New Model Army .44, the same one he'd carried during the war.

The men were all on their bellies instantly, searching for danger. "What's wrong?" asked Ginger Hertzog, who'd served under General Nathan Bedford Forrest during The Late Unpleasantness.

"Something's in those bushes over there," replied Cochrane.

"It's probably a bird," said Beasley. "Walsh—take a look at that bush. We'll cover you."

Walsh was a survivor of Pickett's Charge, and he crawled forward, cradling a double-barrel shotgun in his arms. His head and shoulders disappeared in the foliage, and then he said, "My God—there's somebody here, and I think he's daid!"

The outlaws looked at each other in surprise, then advanced into the thicket. They found a young man lying on the ground, blood everywhere, flies buzzing noisily. "Guess he's what them Apaches was after," said Beasley.

The outlaw band carried a doctor who had lost his license on their roster, and his name was Jeff Montgomery, formerly on the staff of General John Longstreet. Dr. Montgomery, forty years old, wore a black frock coat, stovepipe hat, and gray pants, with high-topped cowboy boots and shiny burnished spurs. Businesslike, he knelt beside the wounded young man and rolled him onto his back.

The victim had been shot in the chest, shoulder, and leg, his face pale, eyes closed, limbs loose. Dr. Montgomery opened his saddlebags, pulled out a small tin mirror, held it to the young man's nose, and a faint mist appeared.

"I believe he's alive, but not by much." Dr. Montgomery pressed his ear against the young man's heart. "Very faint beat." The physician was the oldest member of the outlaw gang, with a short salt-and-pepper beard. He unbuttoned the bloody shirt and saw dried gore around the wound. "I'd say that he doesn't have long to go."

"Is the bullet still in there?" asked Johnny Pinto, twenty-one years old, the most recent recruit to the gang and the only nonveteran. Cochrane had admitted him because of Johnny's raw outlaw guts. Johnny Pinto was wanted for murder, robbery, and assault with intent to kill in a variety of jurisdictions.

"Unfortunately," replied the doctor, "all three bullets are inside him." He turned toward their leader. "Should I operate, or do we let him die?"

"How long will it take to operate?"

"A few hours."

The former company commander gazed at the young man sprawled on the ground. "He doesn't look like he's going to make it."

"He probably won't."

The weapons lying nearby indicated that the stranger had held out to the end, and that weighed the scale in his favor. "Sergeant Beasley—have the cooks boil some water, and please render any assistance that Dr. Montgomery might require."

The campsite bustled as Dr. Montgomery prepared for surgery. He'd served in the field during all five years of the war, but then, after Appomattox, during a particularly difficult period of his life, he'd performed an abortion on a certain young woman brought him by an old family friend. The woman had died from unforeseen complications, and then scalawags and carpetbaggers decided to arrest the good doctor. He wasn't interested in Yankee prisons, so he'd cut out for Texas, met Cochrane in a saloon, and offered his services. Now the former field surgeon was an irregular, too, but one highly experienced at removing projectiles from human flesh.

Cochrane sat nearby, alternately munching a biscuit and sipping from his canteen as he watched Dr. Montgomery slice into the unconscious young man's stomach. The former captain of cavalry understood wounds all too well. He'd been smacked across the face with a cavalry saber in the hard fighting around Yellow Tavern, 13 March 1864. Many of Cochrane's closest friends had been killed in the bloody struggle, while polite and elegant Captain Cochrane had gone berserk on the battlefield, hacking down federal soldiers with his saber, getting shot and cut himself in the wild melee, then he'd fallen out of his saddle from loss of blood and been trampled by horses. Seven years later some corner of his frame hurt every time he moved.

Meanwhile, Dr. Montgomery probed forceps into a hole welling with blood. His patient was white as a lily, heartbeat barely existent. The doctor had to work quickly, but during the war he'd been awake three or four days in a row, sawing off limbs and digging out lead while the occasional stray bullet flew by.

Dr. Montgomery's bright red nose twitched as he caught a piece of lead solidly in his forceps. Slowly, he withdrew the jagged irregular lump from the patient's open stomach cavity. Funny how a little thing like this can kill a man, he mused.

He took one last look inside the bloody cavern, then removed the clamps, took needle and catgut, and sewed the wound with quick deft strokes while an assistant sopped the blood. At the perimeter of the surgical area, guards searched the desert for Apaches while other irregulars cared for the horses, and the cooking crew roasted meat on an iron spit.

The field surgeon cut into his patient's leg; the patient's eyes were opened to slits, but only white showed. His earlobes were turning blue, not a good sign. Dr. Montgomery withdrew the second bullet carefully.

Cochrane knelt beside the patient and said, "What d'ya think?"

"He's lost a lot of blood, and now it's in the hands of God. We'll have to rig out the travois."

"Beasley—get the travois!" ordered the former company commander.

Beasley turned to Johnny Pinto. "You heard him."

Johnny Pinto appeared surprised. "We're not a-takin' 'im with us, are we?"

"The captain said get out the travois."

Johnny Pinto wore tight black pants, a flowing red shirt, and a yellow bandanna. His flat-brimmed black Mexican *estancia* hat sat at an angle over his brown eyes. "But he's as good as dead, and anybody can see it. We're wastin' our time with 'im."

"Do as I say."

"But it's stupid."

At the sound of the last word, Beasley's eyes widened. He hooked his thumbs in his gunbelt, strolled toward Johnny Pinto, and peered into his eyes. "You were told the rules when you jined up with us. If you can't take an order, you can quit right now."

"What do we need a dead man for?"

Beasley was about to reply when Captain Cochrane stepped onto the scene. "I'll take care of this, Sergeant." Then Cochrane turned toward Johnny Pinto. "Do as you're told, or ride on out of here. It's as simple as that."

Johnny Pinto spread his legs and leaned his head to the side. "What if I don't do neither?"

"I'll have to execute you."

Johnny Pinto blinked, not certain he'd heard those deadly words. Then he stood straighter, loosened his shoulders, and said, "What makes you think you can do it?"

"I'll count to three. If you're not on your horse by then, I'm opening fire. One."

Johnny Pinto raised his hand. "Now wait a minute."

"Two."

The young outlaw didn't like bosses and could out-draw anybody in the band, or so he thought. He'd won six-gun duels in the past, and men had told him afterward that they'd never seen anything like his speed. Johnny Pinto tensed for the showdown, his eyes focusing on Cochrane. He saw the ugly battle scar, knew that Cochrane was a Confederate war hero, and remorseless determination glowed from Cochrane's eyes.

"Three!"

"Whoa—hold on," said Johnny Pinto. "I was jest askin' a question—that's all." With a nervous giggle, he headed toward the packhorse that contained the travois.

Cochrane returned to the surgical area, thinking about Johnny Pinto. The ex-officer had known from the moment they'd met that the young killer would be trouble, but an army needs tough fighters. Cochrane's troopers had obeyed his orders without hesitation during the war, but now it was a new world. One of his father's ex-slaves had actually become a state senator in Virginia!

Cochrane was sickened by the drastic transformation of the world since the war. He was a rich man's son who couldn't become somebody's hireling, but money could be found in banks, and he was well versed in strategy, tactics, and the importance of surprise.

Dr. Montgomery sewed the wound in the patient's shoulder, and the ground looked as if a hog had been butchered. "I wonder who he is?" asked the surgeon as he washed blood off his hands.

Cochrane upended the patient's saddlebags, and a variety of articles fell out, but no identification. Cochrane picked up the King James Bible, then laid it on the ground. He noticed the other book.

THE PRINCE
by Niccolò Machiavelli

Cochrane was surprised to find an obscure philosophical work in the middle of the Mexican desert. He opened the pages at random, and his one good eye fell on a passage:

> *Anyone who becomes master of a city accustomed to freedom, and does not destroy it, may expect to be destroyed by it; for such a city may always justify rebellion in the name of liberty and its ancient institutions.*

The book reminded Cochrane of his student years at the University of Virginia, when his mind had been

exposed to the writings of great thinkers like
Machiavelli. He'd loved libraries, research, and the
writing of essays, but then the war broke out and he'd
enlisted in the old First Virginia Cavalry. Harsh lessons
had been taught at the front, such as killing efficiently,
with no moral qualms. Cochrane had planned to
become a learned professor someday, but was professor of robbery instead. What is this kid doing with
Machiavelli? he wondered.

"Time fer eats," said Jim Walsh, the cook.

They gathered around the fire with their tin plates,
and Cochrane cut the first slice. Then the rest attacked
with knives. Dr. Montgomery held his dripping chunk
over the wounded man's mouth and let some of the
gravy drip into it.

They ate as the wounded man lay ashen nearby.
Johnny Pinto returned from lashing together the
travois, then fetched his tin plate, and was left with a
charred end of mule deer. He plopped it onto his plate
and sat near the edge of the crowd.

"He must be a damned fool if he was a-roamin'
alone out here," said Johnny. "Seems to me a feller
generally gits what he deserves in this world."

Nobody replied, because they hadn't yet cottoned to
strange disagreeable Johnny Pinto. Meanwhile, Johnny
Pinto thought they were jealous of his good looks and
fast hand. He was five feet six, with a sunken chest,
nervous eyes, and constant wrinkling of his forehead.
He couldn't understand why they made such a fuss
over a stranger. One of these days they'll push me too
far, Johnny Pinto thought darkly. Then maybe they'll
larn somethin' new.

"Somebody's a-comin'!" said Ginger Hertzog, one
of the lookouts.

The outlaws grabbed their rifles and left the wounded young man with Dr. Montgomery. The doctor held a Henry rifle in both hands, ready to fire.

"I do believe it's a horse," said Johnny Pinto. "Looks tame."

They watched the big russet stallion approach shyly out of the wilderness, and Johnny Pinto figured finders keepers.

"Where the hell are you going?" asked Beasley.

"He's mine, 'cause I see'd him first."

Johnny Pinto swaggered toward the animal, holding out his hand in a friendly manner. "Come here, boy. Let's you and me be pals."

Nestor didn't like the looks of him. He turned away and broke into a trot, crashing through the foliage, and in seconds was gone. "He was skeered of his own shadow, I reckon," replied Johnny Pinto.

"He was afraid of you," said Beasley.

Johnny Pinto shrugged. "If'n he wants to get et by Apaches, it's okay with me."

"But yer the one who spooked 'im," accused Ginger Hertzog.

"You'd better watch the way you talk to me, friend."

"I'll talk to you any way I like, Pinto."

"That'll be enough," said Cochrane. "Pinto, if you want fights, you'd better join another gang."

Johnny Pinto sulked like a guilty little boy. "Hertzog insulted me."

"You spooked the horse. What of it?"

Cochrane's voice had a challenging tone, but Johnny Pinto wasn't ready to take on the former captain yet. *I wonder how good he can aim out of one eye?* mused Johnny. Cochrane walked past him, heading toward the spot where the horse had been seen last. "Come on out," he coaxed. "We'll take care of you until your master gets well."

Nestor listened carefully as he stood behind tangled Carolina snailseed vines not far way. He was alone on the desert, a treacherous situation for a solitary horse, and was scared to death. A pack of hungry coyotes could rip off his legs, or a rattlesnake might sink poisonous fangs into him. There were too few water holes, and Apaches lurked everywhere. Nestor decided to tag along at a distance and see what developed.

Johnny Pinto turned to Cochrane. "Looks like you spooked him, too, sir."

Cochrane didn't bother to acknowledge Johnny Pinto's presence. The former company commander returned to his dinner, and the others gathered around while the guards watched for Apaches. The doctor pressed his ear against the wounded man's chest.

"Is he still alive?" asked Cochrane.

"Just barely," replied the doctor.

Johnny Pinto returned glumly to the campsite. "If I was like that, I'd just as soon be dead."

"Why don't you kill yourself?" asked Jim Walsh.

"Maybe I'll kill you instead."

Cochrane said, "That time it was your fault, Walsh. If you two can't get along, maybe the both of you should leave."

"Everything was fine before Pinto came here," replied Walsh, who had hulking shoulders and a hairy mole on his cheek. "Why doesn't he keep his yap shut, and everything'll be fine."

"Why can't I talk too?" inquired Johnny Pinto innocently. "Who are you to tell me what to say?"

"That's it," said Cochrane stiffly. "Johnny Pinto,

you can leave now, or you can leave when we get back to the hideout, but from now on you're not a member of the gang. If you get into any more arguments with the men, I personally will throw you out of here."

"What makes you think you can do that, sir?" Johnny Pinto asked tauntingly.

"This," said Beasley's voice.

Pinto turned around. Beasley and several outlaws aimed their guns at him. Johnny raised his hands and smiled. "Hey, fellers—I was only kiddin'."

"I wasn't," replied Cochrane. "You can leave now or later—it's up to you."

Pinto smiled uncertainly. "Well . . . I . . ." He didn't know what to say. "I guess I'll stay on."

"Keep your mouth shut, and do as you're told."

"You won't hear a peep out of me all the way back," replied Johnny Pinto.

Silence descended on the little clearing as the men resumed their meal. Nearby, the wounded man lay still, arms at his side, clothing splotched with dried blood. Dr. Montgomery placed his ear against his patient's heart and heard a dull weak thump. We shouldn't move him, he thought, but I guess we have to.

Vanessa Fontaine reclined on her sofa, reading the *Austin Gazette*. Every day the news was worse, with the scalawag governor humiliating former Confederate soldiers at every opportunity. Sometimes she thought about leaving Texas and heading for Paris, because her ancestors had been French.

Unfortunately, the news from Paris wasn't rosy either. The monarchists had taken over the government last April, after the collapse of the Paris Commune.

Now they squabbled among themselves over power, some factions aligned with the Count of Chambord, others behind the Count of Paris, and a few backing the Bonapartists.

Vanessa threw down the newspaper in dismay. Wherever she turned, obstacles appeared. She'd believed that her husband's fortune would bring happiness, but she still felt strangely unfulfilled.

There was a knock, and she guessed it was her maid. She opened the door, and a tall strong-boned Negro woman whom she'd never seen stood before her. "Maxine can't come today, but I'm her sister, and I'll do a good job for you, you'll see."

Vanessa still hadn't adjusted to Negroes who hired themselves for wages and quit whenever they felt like it. "What's your name?"

"Lonnie Mae."

"Why can't Maxine come today?"

"I don't rightfully know."

She knows, Vanessa figured, but doesn't want to tell me. It was the same at the plantation, with slaves scheming and plotting constantly. But Vanessa didn't feel like cleaning the suite of rooms herself. "Has Maxine told you what to do?"

"I don't need nobody to teach me how to clean a house, ma'am. I been cleanin' houses since I could walk. Besides, Maxine told me how you like things, and where everythin' is."

"Where's my office?" Vanessa replied quickly, hoping to trip her up.

"Should be the room on your left."

Vanessa couldn't help smiling. At least this one's not stupid, she evaluated. "Come in. There's a lot to do."

Vanessa retreated to her desk to get out of the

maid's way. She thought of going for a walk, but didn't feel like chatting with society women on the sidewalks of Austin. Vanessa felt more comfortable with men, but propriety had to be observed; she was a lady with a reputation to uphold.

Since she'd acquired wealth, some men seemed afraid of her, while fortune hunters were in constant hot pursuit. Men from the best families gave her a wide berth, because they wanted fresh young virgins for wives, not a worn-out old married lady of thirty-one years.

She fidgeted with a pen and blank piece of paper, fancying herself a poetess of sorts, but language seemed inadequate to describe her troubled feelings. Sometimes she thought she was insane, because of countless bad decisions, and strangest of all was running off with a seventeen-year-old boy.

Except that Duane Braddock hadn't really been a boy, despite his tender years. He was tall and strong as a man, unusually well educated for frontier Texas, and he'd turned eighteen since she'd met him. She wondered what he was doing just then, and with whom.

Lonnie Mae entered the office, dustrag in hand, a spotless white apron covering her black dress. She set to work diligently, wiping everything in sight. Vanessa watched surreptitiously over the blank sheet of paper. Lonnie Mae represented the new free Negro, subject of much controversy. It cost eight hundred thousand casualties on both sides to free them, considered Vanessa, and they're still cleaning houses, just as in the old days. The real cause of the war was damned Yankees wanting to humiliate the South, thought Vanessa, and darkies were pawns in their dirty game.

Lonnie Mae worked her way methodically around the

room, giving every surface a thorough cleaning. At least she's a worker, Vanessa acknowledged. I don't have trouble respecting somebody who does a good job.

Lonnie Mae approached the desk. "Would you like me to pass by while you're here, ma'am?"

"I'll stop." Vanessa arose and walked to the chair in the corner, where she sat with Lord Byron. She glanced over the pages and observed Lonnie Mae polishing the desk. The Negress was tall and strong, with flowing feminine lines, dark brown complexion, and features pleasing to Vanessa's eye.

"Were you born a slave?" Vanessa asked out of curiosity.

Lonnie Mae stopped what she was doing, then turned and faced her employer. She thought for a few moments and then said, "Yes, ma'am."

"Is life very different now that you're free?"

"Yes, ma'am."

"In what way is it different?"

"Because I'm *free,* ma'am."

"But nobody's really free," Vanessa tried to explain. "You're still doing the work that darkies did under slavery. What's the difference?"

The Negro woman replied politely. "It's true that my husband and I still work the same, but our children will go to school, and they'll be lawyers, doctors, and ministers someday. That's the big difference, ma'am. We can work our way up like white folks now."

Vanessa returned to her desk and reflected upon what Lonnie Mae had said. She's got a man and children, she's got something to live for, while I've got my bank account, Lord Byron, and memories of Duane Braddock. Who is the mistress, and who the slave?

CHAPTER 3

A FAINT GLIMMER APPEARED IN THE endless blackness. Gradually it enlarged, changed proportions, and became a bearded man in a hooded robe strolling across the desert, Jesus Christ surrounded by disciples, with halos around their heads. "It looks like he's coming around," Christ said.

The patient struggled to open his eyes. Christ floated in foggy shrouds, while St. Matthew held a canteen of water to Duane's lips, but Duane lacked strength to swallow. He tried to pray vocally, but no sound come. His existence was pain, and he couldn't even moan. *Oh, my Jesus, forgive us our sins . . .* then his eyes closed, and he dropped into endless oceans of sludge.

Dr. Montgomery pressed his ear to his patient's chest. "He's getting stronger, all right. Soon he'll take nourishment."

Cochrane was surprised that the patient had lasted

so long. It was a week since they'd found him, but somehow he was hanging on precariously, bathed and dressed in clean clothes. Dr. Montgomery had been attending him since they'd returned to their hideout, a scattering of adobe haciendas in a spot gracing no maps of Mexico; they called it Lost Canyon.

Located by chance during one of their many dodges through the Sierra Madre Mountains, it was surrounded by crags and deep sudden drops, inaccessible except for three narrow passageways, each heavily guarded at all times. If a stranger drove past, he wouldn't know Lost Canyon was there.

They had a natural well and pond at one end of the canyon, and plenty of grama grass for horses and cattle grazing in the afternoon light. Cochrane returned to his hacienda, lit a corncob pipe, and looked out the window at his little village domain. It was a far cry from Charlottesville, but at least he didn't have Yankees breathing down his back. His irregulars maintained a small farm, and if money was required, there was plenty stashed in a cave. An old tattered Confederate flag fluttered in the breeze in front of Cochrane's house, and he was pleased with all he'd accomplished.

He watched Dr. Montgomery ministering to the wounded young traveler, who lay outside on a cot set up before the doctor's hut. The doctor believed sunlight had healing properties, and exposed his patient's naked wounds to the rays whenever possible. The stranger was feeding off himself, growing thinner every day, the bone structure of his face standing out like a skull.

He's probably an outlaw like Johnny Pinto, Cochrane figured. Why else would he be riding alone across Mexico? But he's an educated man, and possibly we can have a conversation if he recovers. Unfortunately, he might not survive.

Cochrane had learned to hold back feelings. It wouldn't do for a company commander to break down and cry in the midst of battles for hills and valleys that no one had ever heard of before. The young student of philosophy had become a hard, cold, frontline commander who'd literally charged the mouths of cannon on numerous occasions, and he'd led old Troop D in the most massive cavalry battle of the war, Brandy Station. Cochrane had seen conditions of blood and death beyond the ken of most men, and learned that inner strength was the most important characteristic for a frontline officer.

The unnamed young traveler had shown inner strength aplenty, in Cochrane's professional military opinion. Alone on the desert, he hadn't surrendered or blown his brains out at first sight of Apaches. Instead, he'd fought the odds and actually claimed two of the enemy, quite an achievement. The stranger was Cochrane's kind of man, and Cochrane was curious about him. Who's this philosophical outlaw? he wondered.

A young Mexican woman stepped out of the hacienda against which Cochrane sat. "Dinner is ready," said Juanita Torregrosa, Cochrane's woman, and the only female in Lost Canyon.

He followed her through the doorway, watching her tall voluptuous body move beneath a thin cotton dress. She was five-eight, with shiny straight black hair gathered behind her head, and tanned Indian-like features. They lived together in two small rooms, one a kitchen and office, the other the bedroom and riding academy. He sat at one side of the rough-hewn table as she placed the cast-iron pot of stew in front of him.

She'd introduced him to Mexican food, and he'd become addicted to it and her. She was nineteen years old, a rare exotic flower whom he'd met in a broken-down cantina near Hermosillo. Juanita ladled stew into a bowl and passed it to him, as delicious spicy fragrances rose to his nostrils. Then she filled her own bowl and sat opposite him. They reached for tortillas as the sound of horse and rider passed the front of their little abode.

They didn't say much during the meal, because they'd been together two years and knew each other's minds without verbalizations. She'd been working as maid for the local *alcalde* when Cochrane met her. Tired of mopping floors, she'd been searching for excitement, found it with the strange scarred American desperado, and the fact that he was a gringo was no great consequence to her. Juanita tried to keep an open mind.

They communicated mainly through their bodies, and both were fairly content with the arrangement. He wished he had someone on his intellectual level, while she wanted an *estancia* and a family. But life was easy together, and she didn't want to push *too* hard.

Juanita had studied Cochrane well during their time together, and concluded that the war had scarred more than his face. If he really loved me, he'd buy me an *estancia* in Durango.

She couldn't understand why he preferred to be a bandito and live in an adobe hut. Sometimes she thought he was *un pocito loco*, but it was better than being a maid. And in her heart of hearts, she hoped someday God would smile on her and Cochrane would buy her that *estancia*. She'd mentioned it several times before, usually broaching the subject at an oblique angle, like a cavalry troop launching a sneak attack. "By the way," she began innocently, "the roof has been leaking again."

"I'll fix it after dinner," he replied. "Where's the spot?"

"If there was just one, I would have fixed it myself. But there are many of them. If only, for once in my life, I could have a roof of my own that did not leak."

"There you go again," he said gently. "In English, we call it *nagging.*"

It was a word she'd never heard before, and she added it to her growing English vocabulary. "If you are not careful," she complained sadly, "one day you will lose me."

"I'd be sorry if that happened, but we all do what we have to."

She narrowed her eyes. "You are the coldest, most selfish man I have ever known."

"But you haven't met that many men yet," he replied affably.

She felt herself becoming angry, but it was a long way to the nearest town. Sometimes she thought she loved him, and other times hated him.

There was a knock on the door. "Come in," said the company commander.

Sergeant Beasley entered the kitchen, hat in hand. "We've spotted Mexican cavalry about ten hours south of here, sir. Shall I tell the men to put out the fires?"

"Yes, and keep me informed if they head this way."

Cochrane finished the stew, wiped his mouth with a tattered napkin, and rose from his chair as if Juanita weren't there. He looked out the window, saw Dr. Montgomery leaning over the wounded young man, and felt terrible premonitions. He shuddered uncontrollably as images of bloody battlefields arose to his vision. Then he noticed Dr. Montgomery walking toward the command-post hacienda and wondered what the doctor was going to report. There was a knock on the door, Juanita opened it, and the doctor ignored her as he approached Cochrane.

"He came to consciousness again!" the doctor said exuberantly. "I managed to pour some beef broth down his throat."

"Did he say anything?"

"Not yet, but it's only a matter of time, I assure you. The healing power of the sun cannot be denied, and we'll feed him every time he opens his mouth. He'll be walking within two weeks, mark my words."

It was the night of the grand ball, and Vanessa Fontaine dressed carefully in front of her mirror. She'd selected a plain black silk gown, and beneath it wore a black corset imported from New York. Vanessa loved to dress for parties and viewed herself as an actress on the stage of life. Tonight she'd play demure widow, and certainly didn't intend to mention that she and her husband had been divorcing when he'd been killed by Apaches. Their marriage had gone downhill practically from the morning they'd married, because Lieutenant Dawes had been jealous of her former love, young Duane Braddock.

She felt mischievous, frisky, and rambunctious as she placed a dab of perfume on her throat. Eligible Southern gentlemen would attend the ball, and perhaps she'd meet her next sweetheart. He'd better be richer than I, she mused as she applied a light shade of powder to flawless alabaster cheeks.

The upcoming ball reminded her of old Dixie, where she'd prepared for many parties with her innocent heart intact. Then the war broke out, the world turned onto its back, and she'd learned that love can be a weapon too. Her former purity resided in some old party dress grown moldy long ago.

There was a knock on the door, although she generally didn't receive callers during the day. She wondered who it could be as she took a step back from her mirror and observed her visage from all the angles. In the battle of love, the right glance at the supreme moment could be as devastating as cannon fire.

Vanessa became aware of a commotion taking place in the parlor. "Lonnie Mae?"

The sounds came to a sudden halt. Vanessa reached for her red silk robe and was tying the belt when Lonnie Mae appeared in the doorway. It was clear that something terrible had happened, for the maid could barely speak. "Miss Fontaine . . . I wonder if I could take the rest of the day off. I know I ain't givin' you no notice, but I—"

Vanessa interrupted. "What's wrong?"

"My son has got hit by a wagon."

Vanessa didn't stop to think about it. "Go ahead— go home. Come back when you're ready. Your son comes first."

Lonnie Mae appeared struck by lightning, then suddenly she leapt forward and impulsively kissed Vanessa's cheek. "Oh, thank you, ma'am. Thank you so much."

Lonnie Mae rushed to the parlor, and Vanessa followed. Standing near the door was a big Negro male whom Vanessa never had seen. He was six feet four, wore hard-worn work clothes, his skin pure ebony.

Vanessa was stopped in her tracks by the sheer physicality of the man.

Lonnie Mae smiled nervously. "This is Harold, my husband."

He bowed his head. "How do you do, ma'am."

"I think you'd both better get going. Come back when you're ready, Lonnie Mae, and your job will be waiting for you."

The couple rushed away, and Vanessa found herself alone in the middle of the parlor, wondering what had just hit her. So *that's* her husband? she wondered. Vanessa realized that she hardly knew anything about her new maid.

The lonely widow returned to her dressing room, still thinking of her maid's husband. His face had possessed brutal grace, and she'd felt his energy across the room. For the first time in her life Vanessa felt jealous of a servant.

But the former Charleston belle didn't prefer that hazardous path. Instead, she had a party to go to, and reached around to button the top of her dress. It was tricky, because she couldn't see what she was doing. I'll cover it with a wrap and ask somebody at the party to fasten the damned things.

She put on the scarf and looked at herself in the mirror. Oil lamps glowed on either side of her, and she was a statue by da Vinci, but often wondered who she was beneath the facade. Her life made no sense; she'd bounced from one man to another since the war ended and now planned to bounce to another.

In a way, she was sick of men, but womanly needs propelled her onward. If only they were like books in a library, and you returned them when you were finished. Vanessa didn't enjoy passing time with women because women didn't thrill her. And if she wanted to go anywhere, who'd carry her bags, saddle her horse, etc? Duane Braddock had been her favorite thus far, and she found herself recalling him often. Somehow she'd developed a fascination for the notorious Pecos Kid. *For all I know, he could be dead by now,* she reasoned. *Duane Braddock draws trouble out of the woodwork.* Vanessa had seen him in shoot-outs and punch-outs that beggared the imagination. Duane Braddock in an angry mood was awesome to behold.

She made final touches to hair and makeup and hoped no one would notice the tiny lines engraving beneath her eyes. She couldn't wait forever for the right man, and sometimes a lady of a certain age must lower her standards. *I'll look for a gentleman closer to my age on this jaunt. Life isn't over for me yet, or is it? If I can't enjoy the same happiness as my maid, there must be something wrong with me.*

It was evening in Lost Canyon, and Cochrane sat at his kitchen table, perusing maps and puffing his corncob pipe. He was planning another robbery, didn't want to be disturbed, and appeared totally concentrated, as if Juanita weren't alive.

His ability to dismiss her utterly was hurtful to her pride. She threw on her serape, slipped out the door, and saw the full moon glowing brightly overhead. It was easier to walk around the canyon, collect her thoughts, and pray to El Señor than be with Cochrane when he was planning robberies.

She walked with her arms behind her back, wondering what would become of her. Cochrane could throw her away like an old shoe, or maybe he'd be killed on one of his raids, and then where would she be? Maybe she'd have to strike up a liaison with one of the other unattached outlaws.

She knocked on the door of the doctor's hut, and that esteemed gentleman appeared, his eyes brightening at the sight of her. "Ah, the most beautiful woman in the world," he said gallantly. "Come in and take a look at my patient. He seems to be coming along quite well."

She advanced toward the figure lying on a cot. Like most Mexican women, she'd been raised in the Catholic Church, and the patient reminded her of a plaster statue she'd seen of Jesus in his holy sepulcher, after his crown of thorns had been removed. The patient's nose was straight, well formed, and bespoke nobility to her peasant eyes. He had arched eyebrows, pale lips, and tousled black hair that she wanted to run her fingers through. "He does not look as if he is breathing," she said. "Are you sure he did not just die?"

"He's getting better every day. Put your ear to his heart and listen for yourself."

"No, thank you." He looked dead to her, and she crossed herself. If he had color in his cheeks and a few more pounds, he'd be very handsome. She wondered what hue his eyes were.

A moan escaped his lips, and Juanita turned toward the doctor in alarm.

"He's coming around again," said the doctor. "Maybe I can feed him broth."

The patient tried to move, his lashes fluttered, and Juanita saw that his eyes were green. Dr. Montgomery arrived with his pot of broth, sat on the far side of the patient, and held out the spoon, but the patient was so weak he couldn't pucker up. Half the liquid spilled into his mouth, the rest dribbled down his chin, and Juanita wiped the stain away deftly with a towel. The doctor spooned more broth into the patient's mouth; the patient's Adam's apple bobbed slightly, then he made a choking sound. The doctor pulled back as the patient's eyes appeared to be focusing on Juanita.

The doctor leaned over the wounded man. "Can you tell us your name?"

The patient struggled to speak, but his lips barely moved and no sound came out. The effort was too much for him, his eyes closed, and he went slack again.

"He gets stronger every time I feed him," the doctor said. "I tell you—youth can conquer anything."

"Except unhappiness," she replied.

He appeared surprised by her response. "Aren't you happy, Juanita?"

"I have been much worse," she replied. "We cannot always have the things we want, I suppose. This young man reminds me of a statue I have seen of Jesus. But he is probably a bandito, yes?"

"Probably," the doctor agreed. "Looks part Apache."

"He is opening his eyes again!"

The face of the Madonna floated above Duane, love and concern on her face. He wanted to say a Hail Mary, but somehow was unable to move his jaw. Helpless, weak, confused, he felt something warm and delicious on his tongue and struggled to swallow it down.

"Can you hear me?" asked a voice.

Duane didn't know where it was coming from while the Madonna wiped his chin. He saw the roof of a building and a brass lamp vaguely out of focus. It occurred to him that he'd been asleep for a long time.

"What's your name?"

Duane wasn't sure he was alive. He managed to swallow some broth, it trickled down his throat, time moved slowly. He remembered a shoot-out with Apaches.

"Just relax," said the voice. "Try to take as much of this broth as you can."

The Apaches had shot him to pieces, he'd died, and now he was . . . where? He tried to look around, but it hurt too much to move. Another spoonful poked his lips, he worked to open up, and more warm broth poured into his mouth. Common simple acts appeared difficult, he'd never been so weak, and realized with dismay that Sister Death was just around the corner, rubbing her hands together with anticipation and glee.

But the Madonna hovered above, compassion radiating from her soft eyes. "The more you eat, the sooner you will get better," she said.

In his delirium, Duane Braddock was convinced that the Mother of God was administering the very ambrosia of life itself. It rolled over his tongue, trickled down his throat, and regenerated bones and muscles. A halo surrounded her head, he heard the singing of angels, and felt ecstasy within wrenching pain. When her hand touched his forehead, his brain became pleasantly warm.

"The color is coming back to his cheeks," she said.

Duane yearned to understand the conversation, but terrific winds roared in his ears, his guts were boiling in oil, and worst of all, he still couldn't remember his name. Perhaps I'm in hell, he suspected. The Madonna grew fangs, her eyes bulged out, blood dripped from her maw. He tried to get away from her, broth went down the wrong tube, he was racked by a weak cough, and then passed out cold.

"He's alive," said the doctor, listening to the patient's heart, "but looks like he just had a relapse."

"Maybe he ate too much."

"He looked afraid for a moment there."

"Maybe he thought we are the law. I wonder what he has done."

"Must've been awfully bad to make him travel across the desert alone."

"Perhaps he is John Wesley Hardin, no?"

"I've met John once, and this isn't he."

"You met John Wesley Hardin? What was he like?"

"Nicest feller you'd ever want to know. His main problem was he was usually white and right."

Juanita decided not to question further, because the irregulars despised Negritos, and probably, when she wasn't around, made remarks about Mexicans too. It was the least attractive of Dr. Montgomery's characteristics, but otherwise he seemed a good man. Besides, she wasn't sure herself how to behave toward Negritos.

"It is getting late," she replied. "I must get up early tomorrow, for I have very much to do."

The doctor stood beside her, an expression of concern on his face. "How have *you* been feeling lately, Juanita?"

"I am fine."

"But you look so sad at times."

"No normal person could be happy living like this, Doctor."

"You knew what we were when you joined us. Why'd you come?"

"Because what I had was much worse. We are living like wild dogs here."

"You don't understand what we've been through," he replied.

"Let me tell you something. I was born in a very poor town, and a young girl like me, we get two choices. Be a puta in a dirty cantina, or be a maid and let rich people treat you like dirt. So I became a maid, but do not tell me about what you have been through, doctor. I have seen a few things, too, but unlike you, I am not mad at anybody. I just want to be happy."

A cold expression came into the doctor's brown eyes. "If you don't mind, I'd prefer not to discuss this further."

"I am sorry. I did not mean to offend."

She kissed his cheek, and he was struck by the warmth and softness of her lips. There was a swirl of skirts, and she on her way to the door. Dr. Montgomery poured himself half a glass of whiskey while reflecting on the just concluded scene.

Sometimes he thought himself mad to live like an outlaw, but how could a Virginian be happy with Yankee conquerors grinding their boots into the necks of good Southern gentlemen and ladies? Dr. Montgomery could hang his shingle in a town where no one ever heard of him, but it carried the stench of capitulation. Dr. Montgomery hailed from Savannah, directly in the path of Sherman's army. His family's home had been burned to the ground, and his blind sister perished in the flames. Dr. Montgomery couldn't forgive and forget, and as far as he was concerned, the Appomattox Courthouse was a minor and forgettable aberration in the long distinguished career of General Robert E. Lee.

*　　*　　*

Most of the irregulars slept in a crude makeshift shack with double-stacked bunks at one end and a kitchen on the other. At night the old soldiers sat around the table, played cards, read books, drank whiskey, and talked about the good old days. They hadn't accepted Johnny Pinto yet, so that dangerous outlaw preferred to wander alone through Lost Canyon, beneath brilliant stars, with cattle lowing in the distance. He was confident that the irregulars would ask him to join the inner circle after he'd earned their respect, which he determined to do at the very next robbery.

The one thing they admired was guts, and Johnny Pinto would show them what he had. He loved the frenzy of mortal combat; violence was his best friend, and the irregulars provided the most fun he'd ever had. That's why he'd swallowed his pride and asked to remain with them. Since then he'd kept his temper and ambition under tight rein, but it was only a matter of time before Johnny Pinto would blow up like a sack of dynamite.

Johnny Pinto was the son of a long-bearded schoolteacher whose idea of fun was reading books. Bored, restless, and anxious to be respected, Johnny had settled on a strategy of planned physical aggression. He was slim as a whiplash, liked to wear skintight clothes, and his upper lip was obscured by a scraggly black mustache. More than anything else, he didn't want to be a sickly bookworm like his disgusting weakling father.

As for his mother, she'd been her husband's sniveling servant. Even as a boy, Johnny Pinto had recognized that his parents were different from those of his friends. Regular people looked down on his father, because his father had been an Abolitionist prior to the war, but too delicate for a uniform. The other kids had ridiculed young Johnny, and that's when he'd begun his career as a brawler. To his surprise and everybody else's, he'd often defeated bigger boys. For the first time in his life, he'd won attention and esteem. He'd graduated to gunplay when he became a teenager, and it wasn't long before he'd committed an armed robbery in a small east Texas town. He'd been apprehended by a local posse and served one year in a hellish private prison before knifing a guard and escaping into the night. He'd been wanted by the authorities ever since.

The moon floated over the valley as Johnny Pinto headed back to the bunkhouse. He passed the doctor's house and became curious about the patient whom everybody was fussing over. He angled toward the door, knocked, and the doctor appeared, frowned involuntarily, then faked a smile. "Howdy, Johnny—what can I do for you?"

Johnny Pinto's brown eyes spotted the doctor's initial distaste, but he smiled anyway. "How's the patient doin'?"

"See for yourself."

Johnny stepped lithely into the doctor's parlor, where the patient lay near the far wall. "Has he come to yet?"

"A few times," the doctor replied. "I think he's going to be fine."

"He don't look fine to me." Johnny bent closer. "He's white as a sheet, fer chrissakes." The young outlaw touched the back of his hand to the patient's cheek. "I think he's dead already."

The doctor grabbed Johnny's arm indignantly. "Get your hands off him! You can't just walk in here and handle the patients. That's a human being there, not a side of beef."

Johnny Pinto looked around to make sure they were alone. Then he turned toward the doctor and narrowed his eyes. "Let me tell you something, sir. You ever grab me like that again—I'll punch you right through the fuckin' wall!"

The doctor pointed toward his own chin. "Try it."

It wasn't the response that Johnny Pinto anticipated, and the last thing he wanted was a beef with the doctor, Cochrane's best pard in the gang. Johnny forced a smile. "I couldn't punch you, Doc. I like you too much."

"It's a good thing," replied the doctor, glancing down.

Johnny Pinto followed his eyes and was astonished by the sight of a Colt aimed at his belly. "Hey—what's that for?"

"Don't you dare threaten me, young man."

Johnny Pinto raised his hands and smiled charmingly. "But I was only kiddin'. Yer too serious."

"You don't fool me, Johnny Pinto. It's only a matter of time before you get what's coming to you."

Johnny Pinto grinned. "Dinero—that's what's coming to me. Sorry I upset you, but take good care of the patient, and if you need a gravedigger fer yer patient, feel free to call on Johnny Pinto."

Johnny touched his finger to the brim of his hat, then flew out the door. In the darkness, the smile erased from his face. The gang was the closest thing he had to a family, with Cochrane the father he wished he'd had, while Dr. Montgomery was his Dutch uncle.

Johnny Pinto felt more at peace with himself since he'd joined the gang, but it wasn't easy to take orders.

He opened the bunkhouse door, and everybody went for his gun. They relaxed when they saw him, but he said nothing as he made his way to his bunk, sat on its edge, and pulled off a boot. A terrible odor permeated the smoky atmosphere. Johnny Pinto lay on his bunk with all his clothes on, puffed up the pillow, and relaxed.

"Hey—Pinto!" called Beasley, sitting at the table with the old-timers. "Ain't you even a-gonna wash yer face afore you go to bed?"

"What for?" replied Johnny. "They say too much water weakens a man."

Beasley snorted derisively. "I've never been able to understand how a grown man could be afraid of a few drops of water."

The gang at the table laughed, while Johnny Pinto wanted to crawl underneath the floorboards. He hated personal criticism—his father had been expert at it—but this time it was Sergeant Beasley mouthing off, a big fat pain in the ass, and Johnny had to tolerate him if he wanted to remain in the gang. He racked his brain for a clever retort, but nothing came to mind. All he could do was pull on his boots, stroll sleepily past the table, and go outside.

He found the washbasin, splashed water onto his grimy hands and sooty face, then used the common towel. He was annoyed to be meek like his detestable father, but needed the gang more than they needed him. I can put up with anything to get what I want, he decided.

He returned to the bunkhouse, passed the table, and waited for somebody to say something. Sure enough,

Sergeant Beasley spoke again. "You might want to take a bath tomorrow, kid. You smell like horseshit, you know that?"

Johnny Pinto spun around, nearly tripping over his own feet. "If that's how you feel about it, Sarge, I'll take a bath right now."

He continued toward his bunk, searched through his saddlebags, and pulled out an old wedge of soap. Then he headed for the door, hoping that no one would say anything. A grin was plastered on his face as he reached for the doorknob, and next thing he knew, he was outside.

The grin vanished instantly in the cool night air. Why're they always picking on me? he wondered. I don't smell any worse'n any of them. They're jealous 'cause they know I'm a better man than the whole bunch of 'em put together, and one of these days I'll prove it. He who laughs last laughs best.

Juanita gazed at Cochrane bent over his maps. It was all he did when home, and they never took walks or went on picnics like ordinary people. He glanced up as she crossed to the washbasin, then returned to his work as if she weren't there. I'm just the person he sleeps with, she thought, and if it wasn't me, it'd be somebody else. When he says he loves me, it's just words.

Sometimes she thought she should get pregnant, but had no assurance he'd marry her. Accidents happened and she might possibly be pregnant even then, because she'd been oddly out of sorts lately.

He glanced at her. "Where have you been?"

"I saw the hombre who has been shot. He was having broth, and the doctor said he is getting stronger."

"Did he say his name?"

"He could not talk."

"Maybe in a few days he'll tell us how many men he shot." Cochrane laughed darkly as he stretched his arms to the ceiling. "I'm getting sleepy. Let's go to bed."

That's the way it went every night. They went to bed at his convenience, screwed each other's brains out, and would have little to do with each other until it was time to go to bed again. Sometimes it felt like prostitution to Juanita.

They washed at the basin, undressed in the darkness of the bedroom, and crawled naked into bed. He embraced her beneath the flannel blanket, kissed her lips, and she tried to get in the mood. He noticed something wrong immediately.

"Are you all right?" he asked.

"I am not feeling well."

He moved away, trying to gauge her mood this time. She'd been sulking lately because she wanted a husband, family, and an *estancia* to call her own. Sometimes he thought of returning her to the cantina where fate had introduced them, but he'd have the identical trouble with any woman he chose. Besides, he'd grown fond of her. She was a far cry from the giddy giggling belles he'd romanced in Charlottesville during his previous incarnation. He touched his lips to her warm fragrant shoulder. "I'm sorry."

"Your sorrow doesn't help me."

"I wish things could be different, but that's how it is."

"Your army was defeated seven years ago, and I do not understand what you are fighting for. Wouldn't you like to have a son like a real man?"

"I'm a soldier," he replied gruffly. "And soldiers don't make the best fathers. I might get killed on the next raid."

"Then don't go on the next raid. There is no law that says you have to."

"You should've been a lawyer."

"We could be happy if you would stop being a bandito."

"Do you know what the word 'justice' means?"

"We have the same word in Spanish—*justicia*—so what?"

"Don't you believe that people should fight for justice instead of pretending that everything's all right?"

"Please do not preach to me about justice when your country has stolen part of mine."

He'd stumbled into dangerous territory, and all he could do was retreat. "I don't mean to preach, but there's something very important that you don't understand."

"The Confederacy? But I understand it very well, Ricardo. You lost, but you can't accept it."

"And you can't accept gringos annexing California either, right?"

"Wrong. You gringos were stronger than us, you beat us, and I am not happy about it, but what can I do?"

"You should fight back as best you can."

"We could never defeat the americano army in a million years, and neither will you."

He loved her defiance, and her mind was quick as a rabbit. Never had he known a woman with such a tempestuous spirit. What a mother she'd make for a son, he thought. "There are some things you can't forgive and forget."

"Jesus said we should forgive and forget *everything*."

"I wish we could stop arguing so much."

"I am not arguing. I'm telling you the truth."

"What makes you think you know the truth?"

"It says so in the Bible."

"But the Bible was written by men."

"God was talking to them. Don't you believe that?"

He sighed in the darkness. "I don't know what I believe anymore."

He was weakening, for the Confederacy was a mere idea, while she was a warm-blooded young woman. She pressed her breasts against him and touched her tongue to his ear. "If you want to believe in something, why don't you believe in me?"

"I do believe in you," he replied in choked voice. "In fact, I'm in love with you, Juanita."

"All I want is to be with you," she replied. "Is that so wrong?"

She pressed her lips against his cheek, and once again the stalwart company commander was hurled back by the power of a peasant woman. He hugged her tightly to him, thrills raced across his nerve endings, and the great noble rebellion disappeared into the whirlpools of time.

Outside Lost Canyon, hiding behind a stand of cottonwood trees, Nestor glanced around constantly, alert for Apaches. His senses had sharpened since he'd been on his own, and he was confident he'd hear the Apache before the Apache heard him.

He had plenty to eat, coyotes didn't bother him, and no snake wanted to get stomped by a horse. But he was lonely, and it appeared that his two-legged boss had died. The horse felt sad, because his boss had saved his life. Now he wanted to return the favor, but how?

There was nothing Nestor could do to bring his boss back from the land of shadows. Nestor couldn't hang around forever, but neither did he want to become a cowboy's hoss. Born on a ranch, raised by cowboys, he'd always wondered about running with the wild ones, and now at last had the opportunity.

He turned away from Lost Canyon and advanced into the night. The great herds lived in far-off valleys where two-leggeds seldom went, and he'd find them before long, he was certain. *Good-bye, my generous friend. I'll see you in the shadow world when I, too, am gone from this range.*

Strains of fiddles and accordions wafted to the street as Vanessa Fontaine arrived in front of the Cutler mansion. She sat in the cab of a rented black shellacked carriage; the footman jumped down, opened the door, and bowed.

"Wait until I'm inside," she told him as she swept toward the flight of stairs. The door opened, and a butler appeared in a black-and-white uniform, an elegant smiling beetle. "May I take your coat, madam?"

The music grew louder as she entered a large drawing room filled with purple velvet furniture. Fashionably dressed individuals littered the landscape while liveried servants carried drinks and hors d'oeuvres on rectangular ebony trays with inlaid silver handles.

Vanessa felt uneasy in the presence of so many strangers, but no carpetbaggers, scalawags, or other Yankee sympathizers had been invited. It was her debut into Austin high society; she no longer felt the self-assurance of youth, but neither had she lost confidence in herself. The hem of her black gown glided over smoothly polished oak floors as she searched for her hostess.

She passed carefully barbered gentlemen and well-manicured ladies while small children ran about in expensive clothing similar to that of their elders. A bar was set up against the back wall, next to a table groaning with delicacies. The orchestra played "The Yellow Rose of Texas" in the next room.

A figure stepped out of the crowd, barring her way. He was five feet tall, potbellied, probably in his forties, immaculately tailored. "May I be of service, ma'am?"

"I was looking for Mrs. Cutler."

"I'll take you to her."

Vanessa didn't want to hurt the man's feelings, although she towered over him. Side by side they made their way through throngs of guests sipping beverages, nibbling delicacies, and carrying on animated conversations.

"I don't believe I've ever seen you before," the short man said. "I'm Dudley Swanson, by the way."

"I'm Mrs. Vanessa Dawes, and I've just arrived in town."

"From where?"

"A place I'm sure you've never heard of, named Shelby."

"Where is it?"

"West Texas. My husband was in the army, but he was killed in action against the Apache."

"I'm so sorry to hear that," said Dudley, although he didn't appear sorry in the least.

Vanessa hoped to see an old friendly face from

South Carolina, but the guests were unknown to her, with many gentlemen well on the road to serious inebriation. Near the far wall, beneath a painting of General Robert E. Lee, a crowd of guests had gathered about their gracious hosts. Vanessa noticed masculine eyes turning toward her, measuring her long legs, caressing her small upturned breasts with lust.

Mrs. Cutler was a short dumpy woman with dyed red hair. "Ah, Mrs. Dawes," she gushed. "How good of you to come."

Vanessa bent low and let the hostess kiss her cheek. Then Mrs. Cutler proceeded to introduce Vanessa to everyone in the vicinity. A sea of smiling faces passed by as Vanessa struggled to remember names.

"Did you say that she was married to an ex-Yankee?" asked a jewel-bedecked old crone holding a trumpet to her ear.

"She was formerly a Fontaine from Charleston," replied Mrs. Cutler.

"So why'd she marry a damned Yankee?"

Sometimes elderly people believe that advanced years confer the right to be obnoxious, and the lady with the trumpet had embraced this view with great fervor. The room fell silent as all eyes turned to Vanessa. It was her moment, but she had no idea of what to say. Finally she pulled herself together, and all she could think of was, "My husband was sympathetic to the ideals of the Confederacy. That's why he chose a daughter of the South to be his wife."

"What'd she say?" asked the old lady, making a public spectacle of herself.

A kindly niece repeated Vanessa's improvisation noisily into the trumpet as Vanessa continued to receive introductions. She smiled politely and curtsied flawlessly as they'd taught her at Miss Dalton's School in Charleston, but couldn't help remembering when she'd sung in saloons where rotgut whiskey went for fifteen cents a glass, and shootings frequently interrupted her great serenades.

After introductions, the hostess moved on to other guests while Vanessa retreated into the shadows, covered the lower part of her face with her fan, and observed the guests. Young men conversed in one corner, young girls giggled in another, mature couples strolled about, discussing the great fashionable political and cultural issues of the month, while the biggest crowd gathered at the bar.

It was like theater, where ambition, greed, and naked lust paraded before her, disguised by fashionable taste. Curiously, she felt no part of it, although she'd anticipated the party for weeks, hoping to meet somebody interesting.

It all seemed rather dull to the former saloon singer. She'd had audiences of cowboys yearning for a glimpse of the celebrated Miss Vanessa Fontaine, and when she'd stepped onto the stage, they applauded so loudly, she'd thought the walls would collapse. They'd sung old Civil War songs together, but the grand ball was as measured and calculated as a society funeral. Vanessa smiled behind her fan, recalling smoky old frontier saloons from Nagodoches to San Antone. Her cowboy admirers had treated her like the Queen of the Golden West, life had been constant adventure, and she'd even witnessed killings before her very eyes.

I can't flirt like a silly fifteen-year-old sparrow anymore, she thought, and it's never too late to grow up. Dudley Swanson carried two glasses of champagne toward her. She accepted one and said, "Thank you."

Bubbles ran up her nose as she sipped tart effervescence. She didn't dare ask for whiskey, although she preferred its dusky mellow kick in the pants. Maybe saloon life hadn't been so bad after all.

"You look bored," said Dudley. "Don't you like the party?"

"I was thinking."

"Will you be staying in our town long?"

"I'm not sure, because my life is a roulette wheel these days."

"Mine is a cartwheel, because I own a freighting business. Even as we speak my men are moving merchandise all across Texas."

Vanessa had talked to freighters and bullwhackers when she'd worked saloons, and knew that Swanson's hardworking employees were sleeping beneath their wagons in remote territories at that moment, with rainstorms and the threat of Indian attack, not to mention the occasional tornado, while their employer sipped champagne and wore a suit costing a freighter's month's pay.

"When did your husband depart this earth?" asked Dudley.

"About three months ago."

"Ah, you poor woman."

Dudley tried to appear genuinely sympathetic to her pretended woes, but she'd been out of high society so long, she couldn't think of anything appropriate to say. Just then, out of the blue, a deep baritone voice said, "Evening, Dudley."

Vanessa turned to a big hulking fellow with a jet-black mustache, around forty years old, with an insouciant half smile on his sallow face. Dudley shook his big paw, then made the introductions. "Howard Sutcliffe, maybe I present Mrs. Vanessa Dawes."

Sutcliffe bowed, took her hand, and kissed her knuckle. "I was admiring you from afar, madam, and thought I'd come for a closer look."

"Perhaps I'm more admirable at a distance, the greater the better," Vanessa riposted.

"You're too modest, madam. Why, I was just thinking, before I took my first step in this direction, that you were the most beautiful woman here."

"You're very kind to an aging widow, sir." She fluttered her eyelashes in appropriate Charleston fashion and hoped she wasn't being ridiculous.

"Howard is a lawyer," explained Dudley. "He argues cases before the Texas Supreme Court."

"I also have very good ears," added Sutcliffe immodestly. "I hear all the news. So you're the Mrs. Dawes that everyone is talking about. I must say— you're far lovelier than I'd imagined."

She raised her fan to cover her vain smile. "Now I understand why you win so many cases, sir."

His eyes twinkled with mischief. "Some say I defeat my opponents through bribery, perjured witnesses, tampered evidence, and such, but one should not believe idle gossip."

He was a rogue, he made no bones about it, and she couldn't help liking him. "What regiment did you serve with in the war?"

"I served as an undersecretary in the Department of the Treasury, because my muscles are in my mind, not my arm. Care to dance?"

"I'm afraid not," she replied.

"I forgot—you're in mourning. You know, black becomes you. It makes you look sinister. Are you dangerous, Mrs. Dawes?"

"Little me?" she asked innocently, although bloody scandals had surfaced twice in her past. "How can you think such a thing?"

Dudley Swanson tried desperately to assert himself, but the conversation kept moving away. Finally Sutcliffe shot him a glance that said, "get lost." Dudley coughed, fumbled, excused himself, and backed toward the bar.

Vanessa looked at Sutcliffe with a mixture of fascination and disapproval. "That was cruel," she said, her smile becoming a frown.

"I'm don't want to share you, Mrs. Dawes. You should forgive the follies committed for your sake. Come, let us observe the dancers."

Before she could answer, he took her arm and was leading her to the next room. He seemed sure of himself, while she felt uncertain about everything. He obviously was rich, if he argued cases before the Texas Supreme Court, and wasn't that bad-looking, but there was something presumptuous and overbearing about him, as if he could have anything he wanted, including the former Miss Vanessa Fontaine.

They came to the dance floor, a large room devoid of furniture, with a band at one end, and the crème de la crème of Austin's old Confederate aristocracy at the other, performing carefully choreographed dance movements in which participants seldom touched one another. Vanessa followed Sutcliffe to a dark stretch of wall; they turned to each other, and he said, "I don't like to be dishonest, despite my reputation, so I'll confess that I know all you, Mrs. Dawes. I have an affiliation with the law firm that represented your interests in the probate of your husband's will, and discovered a curious fact, to wit: You had filed for divorce prior to your late husband's untimely demise."

She didn't like his manner, the more she got to know him, not to mention the tone of his voice, although he was correct in his facts. "It's not my fault that Apaches killed my husband," she replied. "Despite what you may think, I loved Lieutenant Dawes when I married him."

"Of course you did, although there were certain rumors about another young man. I don't claim to be a gentleman, but I know how to button ladies' dresses. May I?" He reached behind her neck and fastened her garment with deft manipulations of his fingers. "What a lovely neck you have, Mrs. Dawes. Like a swan. Do you think you might like to get married again some-day, after official mourning has ended, of course?"

"Not very likely," she replied, "and thank you for buttoning my dress, but if you ever touch me like that again, without my expressed permission, I'll slap your face. Do I make myself clear?"

He gazed into her unforgiving green orbs, then took a step backward. "Absolutely, and I apologize if I've been too forward. I guess it's the trial lawyer in me, but I know character when I see it, and you've got it aplenty. Poetry isn't my game, and I don't mince words like some you'll meet here tonight. I can't help thinking that you and I would make quite a team. Look at it objectively. We're both shrewd people who've been around the corral a few times."

"I'm not *that* ambitious," she replied, "and unlike you, I adore poetry. It makes life worthwhile, regardless of how many times you've been around the corral."

"Women like you get men killed, because you're too beautiful for your own good. But you're a very fine example of your type, which you should take as a sin-cere compliment."

Vanessa struggled to prevent herself from smashing

him in the face. "The death of my husband was a terrible tragedy, regardless of what you think of me. But your death would be quite another matter."

He smiled falsely, bowed, and strolled away nonchalantly, because he was rich and didn't give a damn. There was no shortage of beauties anxious to throw themselves at a rich lawyer, but Vanessa was rich herself, fortunately. Never, during six years of singing in saloons, had she met such a calculating and insulting individual. He'd be the ideal husband for me, she reflected cynically, except I can't stand the son of a bitch.

She felt like a foreigner in the dancing parlor. Four blazing chandeliers beamed bright golden haze, and young gentlemen danced with their hands behind their backs, while ladies in hoop skirts twirled around them. The former belle of the ball guessed that some unmarried girls probably were pregnant, and a few gentlemen preferred to sleep with other gentlemen. Maturity enabled her to probe beneath the surface, an ongoing disillusioning process. Nothing was sacred anymore, and if a woman didn't have an income, she could end up giving herself to men like Howard Sutcliffe.

A glass of champagne was suspended in her slender graceful fingers as she recalled her recently departed husband. Lieutenant Clayton Dawes had saved her from Duane Braddock, but what was so wrong with Duane Braddock? She'd left him, not the other way around, and broken his innocent heart.

Lieutenant Dawes had seemed reliable, compared with Duane's immaturity and naïveté. Vanessa had planned to spend the rest of her life on army posts with Lieutenant Dawes, attending tea parties and socials with the other officers' wives, but then he'd been killed on a scout, and another dream vanished.

She hadn't known, when she'd first tied the wedding knot with Lieutenant Dawes, that he'd harbored ill will toward Duane, and vice versa. Then the insanely jealous Dawes charged Duane with murder following a shoot-out where Duane had merely defended himself. Duane broke out of the army camp and had been on the dodge ever since.

Duane needed me, but I let him down. Now circumstances have changed, and I can do any damned thing I want, such as buying a ticket on the next stagecoach west and searching for Duane Braddock.

She stiffened in the corner, shocked by what she'd just thought. Search for Duane Braddock! Are you crazy? Indians attack stagecoaches regularly, and stagecoach stops have the worst accommodations imaginable. Don't you think it's time to wake up, after all you've been through, you idiotic Miss Vanessa Fontaine?

"Enjoying the party?" Dudley Swanson, puffing a pipe carved from Turkish meerschaum, stood before her. "Can I get you something to eat?"

"Have you ever been in love, Dudley?"

He was taken aback by her question. "I guess you'd have to define what you mean by love," he replied smugly.

These people don't believe in anything; they have no romance in their souls, but I mustn't be intolerant, she lectured herself. Perhaps my two so-called great love affairs were nothing more than a lost frightened woman looking for someone to take care of her.

"You don't like me much, do you?" asked Dudley, an amused tone in his voice.

"What makes you think that?"

"You're ignoring me."

"But sometimes I think of . . . my husband—you understand."

He lowered his eyes. "Forgive me. You're so beautiful, one forgets you're in mourning. Would you like me to leave you alone?"

"I hope you won't think I'm being discourteous, but . . . yes."

He bowed and backed away as Vanessa took another sip of champagne. Her long slim body had adorned many bedrooms, but her first love had died at Gettysburg, and her second was Duane Braddock, who probably was dead, too, given his natural tendencies. But what if he's alive and alone in some terrible situation, wishing I'd come back to him?

Don't flatter yourself, Vanessa, she reproached herself. He doesn't miss you in the least, and probably hates you for being a treacherous, devious Lady Macbeth. But why, she asked herself, am I *still* in love with that penniless immature fool? Perhaps I should move to the nearest insane asylum, but wouldn't it be a hoot if I ever ran into Duane Braddock again? Vanessa took stock of herself, standing against the white papered wall as the band played another Virginia reel. Why am I always thinking about Duane Braddock? she wondered. Why doesn't he leave me alone?

CHAPTER 4

DUANE ATTEMPTED TO ASSESS HIS surroundings during brief periods of consciousness, and surmised that he was a prisoner of the Fourth Cavalry. His captors had been attending to his every need because they wanted the splendid figure of a man dangling from the end of their rope, to prove they hadn't mistreated their prisoner.

The hanging would be in a public square, with little children watching and clapping their hands as the executioner placed the noose around Duane's neck. They'd hold a kangaroo court to make it legal while the undertaker nailed together the coffin in the next room.

Every movement strained raw flesh attempting to heal, and Sister Death danced eerily around him. *If I don't get you today, maybe I'll get you tomorrow.* Somebody entered the kitchen and lit a lamp. It was the doctor with graying black beard, sitting beside

Duane and peering at him through wire-rim glasses. "How do you feel this morning?"

"Better . . ." Duane said with great effort.

Dr. Montgomery was astonished. "You can talk? Magnificent! What's your name?"

"Is . . . this . . . a . . . jail?"

Dr. Montgomery threw back his head and laughed. "Hell no! We're just old soldiers traveling through Mexico, and we ran into you on the desert. Some Apaches shot you up pretty bad, and it was touch and go for a while, but it looks like you're going to make it."

"You're . . . not . . . going . . . to . . . hang . . . me?"

"What the hell do we want to hang you for? What've you done?"

"I'm . . . innocent. . . ."

"Of course you are, and so are we. I'd say you're about ready for normal food. How d'ya like your eggs?"

Vanessa was covered with perspiration as she opened her eyes. Her arms were wrapped around her pillow, she was breathing heavily, and she'd been dreaming about Duane Braddock. They'd been in bed together, wrestling and scratching each other like wild animals in some lost jungle paradise.

Vanessa reached for a hanky and wiped her brow. Never had she experienced such a dream. In the cold light of dawn, it embarrassed her to recall the lewd and salacious acts that they'd performed upon each other's quivering flesh. She'd surrendered completely, so did he; her dream had been bizarre, uncanny, and explosive, but now she was alone in bed, the cool morning air made her shiver, and her pillow was duck feathers, not Duane Braddock.

She felt appalled to find herself lusting after young Duane Braddock. I know that he's the man for me, so why don't I simply track him down? she asked herself. It's not as if he's a nonentity, and in fact he's well known in west Texas, a minor celebrity of sorts, the Pecos Kid himself. I'll just follow the trail of blood, and he'll be at the end of it.

Wait a minute! she reproached herself. What are you thinking about now, you idiot? You're not going to follow a *man* all across Texas, and risk your skin that you've been struggling so hard to preserve, are you?

Of course not.

Duane sat on a chair outdoors as the healing rays of sun beat down on him. He could see shacks constructed haphazardly in the vicinity, the herd of rustled outlaw cattle in the distance, and purple mountains that encompassed the hideout. He couldn't move his head well, but caught glimpses of outlaws among the buildings, while high in the sky a lone buzzard circled lazily.

I sure cheated you, Duane thought. You'd better find another meal, because I'm on my way back. The Pecos Kid felt considerably stronger following one egg, two slices of bacon, and a few spoonfuls of grits, washed down with a half cup of thick black coffee.

The pain was there, but had substantially diminished. He was sojourning in an outlaw camp of some kind, not a jail, and was anxious to resume his jaunt to Monterrey. Dr. Montgomery had told him that he'd be up and around in another week or two, but it might be a while before he could ride.

Duane could feel the bullet's path through his guts; the impact had shaken him like a rag puppet, but the

worst was over; now he was healing, and he felt opti-
mistic for the first time since he'd been shot like an
antelope by Apaches. He recalled praying to the Virgin
from the depths of his infirmity, and how she'd
appeared above him, a blinding halo behind her head.
She'd been the turning point of his illness, so he closed
his eyes and gave thanks. Hail Mary, full of grace, the
Lord is with thee. Blessed—

Footsteps approached, interrupting Duane's prayer.
Dr. Montgomery and a tall distinguished-looking outlaw drew closer. "Feeling better?" the doctor asked.
"This is Captain Richard Cochrane, our leader. And
your name was Duane . . . ?"

"That's right," replied the patient, because they
didn't have to know his last name.

The man called Cochrane sat cross-legged on the
ground beside Duane, rolled a cigarette, placed it into
Duane's lips, and lit it with a match. He was clean-
shaven, tanned, his hair golden blond, and he had a
scar on the right side of his face, with a black patch
covering his right eye. Cochrane rolled another
cigarette while the doctor examined Duane's bandages.

"You're coming along fine," declared Dr.
Montgomery. "I'll check with you later in the morning." Then the doctor excused himself and departed.

Duane realized that he'd been left alone with
Cochrane by design, and a barrage of questions was
about to begin. But he'd prepared answers in advance,
and puffed his cigarette confidently.

"You've been the main topic of conversation around
here since you arrived," began Cochrane, in an educated Southern drawl. "We've all been wondering who
you are and what you've done."

Duane couldn't tell them that he was a lost wandering

cowboy, because no cowboy would stray as far as Mexico. "I'm running from the law," he confessed.

"What'd you do?"

"They say I killed a few people, but it was self-defense all the way."

"What's your last name?"

"Butterfield." The former acolyte found it difficult to look Cochrane in the eye as he told the lie. He was using the last name of Clyde Butterfield, an old-time gunfighter who'd taught Duane the classic fast draw.

Cochrane noticed Duane's facial evasions. "What's your *real* name?"

"Are you trying to collect a bounty?"

"If I wanted the bounty, I'd ride to the nearest American town and dump you on the sheriff's desk. I'm sure he'd recognize you, even if I don't."

"What about your men?"

"They do as I say. I told you my real name. Why won't you tell me yours?"

"A name is a tag they pin on you. What's wrong with Duane Butterfield?"

"I went through your saddlebags, Mr. Butterfield. I couldn't help wondering what you're doing with Niccolò Machiavelli?"

"A book I picked up in Escondido. Ever read it?"

"A long time ago. Where'd you go to school?"

"I was raised in a Catholic orphanage. How about you?"

"University of Virginia, but I left for the war in my junior year. Most of the men here are ex-soldiers, but you were too young for the war, I imagine."

"If I went to war, I probably would've got hit by a cannonball," replied Duane.

"Once, at Chancellorsville, I saw—" Cochrane

caught himself quickly and changed the subject. "That was quite a fight you put up against the Apaches. You killed two of them."

"They would've got me in the end if it weren't for you. Mr. Cochrane, you saved my life and I'll be grateful forever. Where am I?"

"Sierra Madre Mountains. We're the First Virginia Irregulars, and we're still at war. There are many more like us all across Mexico, and one day we'll have another rebellion, only this time we'll win. We're always looking for men with sand, and if you're interested in money, you'll earn plenty with us."

"What's the Apache situation?"

"They wouldn't dare bother us, and as for the Mexicans, they don't know this place exists." Cochrane placed his hand reassuringly on Duane's shoulder. "Relax, kid. You're safe now."

After breakfast, Vanessa poured a shot of whiskey into her coffee cup. Alone at the kitchen table, she felt as if her life had no point. She was rich, but restless, moody, and suspicious. She could only read so many books.

She placed the dirty dishes into the basin, then poured another cup of coffee, laced it with whiskey, and carried it to the chair overlooking the sunlit street. She recalled when she was a child, playing innocently in the boulevards of Charleston, never imagining the dark cloud of destruction on the horizon.

There was a knock on the door. Vanessa opened it and admitted Lonnie Mae, her maid. "I'm sorry I'm late, ma'am, but I'll get everything done, you'll see."

"How's your little boy?"

A broad smile wreathed Lonnie Mae's face. "The doctor said his leg is a-healin' fine."

Vanessa couldn't help feeling happy for her maid's good fortune. "I'm sure he'll mend quickly. God takes care of the little ones, they say."

"I'se sorry I couldn't help you get ready for the party. How'd it go?"

"I guess I'm too old for parties."

Lonnie Mae's big brown eyes twinkled. "You should never get too old for parties, ma'am."

"Well, it's who you're with that makes the difference."

"No nice gentlemens there?"

"None of them appealed to me."

"I can understand that," Lonnie Mae allowed. "Harold is the only man I ever wanted, and thank God I got him. Well, there's a lot to do, and I'd better get started."

Lonne Mae headed for the kitchen while Vanessa angled toward her office, sat at her desk, and sipped spiked coffee. Life is the same on both sides of the color line, she mused. A woman needs a good man, and good men don't come along every day.

She tapped her fingernails on the desk as she wondered about Duane Braddock. What if he thinks about me as much as I think about him? she asked herself. As far as he knows, I'm still the married lady who betrayed him. What if he discovered that I'm presently unmarried?

Now hold on, Vanessa, she cautioned herself. You're not thinking about actually searching for Duane Braddock, are you? You wouldn't trade this luxurious hotel suite for a smelly flea-bitten stagecoach and every night in another horrible little town. You're too old to be a silly fool, Vanessa. Settle down, girl.

Duane opened his eyes, the sun shone brightly, and a big hulking man with a walrus mustache and a peaked cowboy hat kneeled beside him. "How're you doin'?"

"Getting stronger every day," replied Duane. "Who're you?"

"Beasley, sergeant of this jolly little band of irregulars. I just wanted to say that you put up one helluva fight against them Injuns, and I admire a man who ain't afraid of a good fight. What're you wanted fer?"

"Murder, but it was self-defense all the way."

"'Course it was. And we're just a bunch of traveling salesmen." Beasley winked. "The doc says you'll be up and around afore long. We could use a good man like you, and I hope you'll jine up with us."

"Don't think so," replied Duane. "There's something I've got to do."

"Not even fer a leetle while? I mean, we can use another good gun . . . and we've just saved yer fuckin' life."

"Let me think about it," replied Duane. "When I'm stronger, I'll give you my answer."

"I've been shot a few times myself, and it's no picnic. Anyways, take care of yerself, kid. And just remember one thing." The sergeant winked. "A good run is better than a bad stand."

Duane raised a cup of milk to his lips, then replaced it gingerly on the ground. He'd never dreamed he could be so weak. What good does it do me that I've got sand? he asked himself. Now I'm stuck with a gang of outlaws who think they're soldiers in a war that ended almost seven years ago. Maybe courage is another word for stupidity, and I've fallen from the frying pan into the fire.

Dudley Swanson stood behind his desk and smiled graciously. "How good of you to stop by, Mrs. Dawes. Can I get you some coffee?"

"If you please," replied Vanessa Fontaine as she swept dramatically toward a chair, "and if you could pour a few drops of whiskey in it, so much the better."

He raised his eyebrows as he poured coffee at his small office stove, then added a healthy dash of whiskey. Vanessa sat with her back ramrod straight, because Miss Dalton had taught that a lady's back should never touch anything except her clothes. Swanson returned with the coffee, passed a cup to her, and sat behind his desk. "How fortunate we Austin gentlemen are to have the rare privilege of feasting our eyes upon that great work of art Mrs. Vanessa Dawes. What brings you to my gloomy cramped office? I can't help wondering."

She sipped her coffee daintily. "This may sound strange, but I need a bodyguard. Could you recommend somebody, perhaps a bullwhacker with time on his hands, who's got sand, bathes fairly regularly, and would respect a woman's privacy?"

Swanson appeared taken aback. "What on earth do you need a bodyguard for?"

"I'm planning a trip to Mexico."

He stared at her in alarm. "Why in the world would an intelligent woman such as yourself want to go to Mexico? Are you aware of what Mexico is? My dear Mrs. Dawes, in case nobody told you, Mexico isn't another state like Texas or Alabama. Most of Mexico is as wild as when the conquistadores first arrived, except for a few towns here and there. You'll need more than one bodyguard if you're going to Mexico. I'd recommend no less than two heavily armed and experienced men. But surely you're not serious, because, to be perfectly frank, who'd protect you from your bodyguards?"

"That's why I'm coming to you. I figured you'd know somebody reliable."

"Most bodyguards are little better than criminals themselves. Why else would a man take such a job, when he could have a safe life following any of a hundred normal pursuits?"

"Then I'll have to go myself," she replied. "It's been very nice talking with you. Good day." She rose from the chair.

"But you haven't had your coffee yet!"

She turned toward him and hooded her eyes. "If I wanted to find the toughest, most dangerous man in town, where would I go?"

"I don't think you understand what you're asking, Mrs. Dawes. You sashay inside one of those rough saloons—they'll tear the clothes right off your back."

"I'll ask you again. Where?"

"Please . . . Mrs. Dawes . . . you can't—"

She interrupted his ravings. "Where!"

He sighed in defeated exasperation. "You want a straight answer? Here it is. The most notorious saloon in Austin is the Shamrock Star. You know, I've just realized something that I never noticed before." He peered into her sultry green eyes. "You're really quite mad, aren't you?"

"Quite," Vanessa replied as she waltzed toward the door.

*   *   *

A woman drifted into Duane's vision as he reclined in front of Dr. Montgomery's hacienda. She wore an angle-length dark brown skirt, an orange blouse with the top three buttons undone, and had black hair that almost touched her shoulders. It was the sacred vision of his delirium, but in real life she evidently was riding with the First Virginian Irregulars.

"How are you doing?" she asked with a friendly smile.

"Much better," he replied, "and I remember you taking care of me. You may laugh if you want to, but I thought you were the Madonna."

She laughed as he'd anticipated, flashing white teeth. "I'm no Madonna, but I brought your rosary. You are Cathólico?"

"I used to be, but I don't know about now."

"I was Cathólica," she said as she draped the rosary around his neck, "but those priests, they drive you crazy. Some of them are very bad men, but they are so . . ." She closed one eye as she searched for the proper gringo word.

"Hypocritical?" Duane offered. "But don't forget that there are lots of good priests out there."

"Maybe, but I thought that most gringos were Protestants."

"I was raised in a Benedictine monastery. My mother was Irish Catholic."

"And you are a bandito, no?"

"Not me. I've just got into an argument with the law, and the law appears to be winning. Soon as things settle down, I'm going back to the ranching business."

She looked at his silky jet-black beard and eyebrows.

"They say that you are very brave, and they want you to join the gang."

"If I don't, will they let me leave alive?"

"I think so, if it is up to Cochrane. He is a very honorable man, although he is basically a bandito. There is only one hombre here that you have to worry about." She looked both ways. "Johnny Pinto. Do not ever turn your back on him."

"Thanks for the warning, and you can be sure I'll keep my eyes peeled for him. My the way, my name is Duane. What's yours?"

"Juanita."

"What're you doing here?"

"I am Cochrane's woman."

A hands-off sign lit up her ample bosom, and he silently swore never, under any circumstances, to make advances toward her. "How'd Cochrane get to be boss of this gang?"

"He is a hero of your Civil War. The men respect him very *mucho*, except for Johnny Pinto."

"Sounds like this Johnny Pinto is more trouble than he's worth. Is he a soldier too?"

"He is a killer, but they always need another gun. Cochrane thinks he is still fighting the Civil War."

"I guess there are some things a person can't forget."

"You talk just like him, but I am only his woman and what do I know? When he gets tired of me, he will throw me away."

She was on her feet in a sudden rustle of skirts, and the next thing Duane knew, she walked swiftly away from him. The rapidly changing moods of women never ceased to amaze him, as he admired her shapely rear axle assembly. I'm sure that Cochrane has his hands full with her, in more ways than one.

*   *   *

The *Austin Gazette* maintained files of back issues stored in cabinets set near reading tables in the basement of its imposing building in downtown Austin. Reporters came to the files to check facts, unless they were too busy, and occasionally citizens were permitted to study records, provided they had the right connections. Vanessa Fontaine had prevailed upon Dudley Swanson to pave the way, and now found herself seated at a long oaken table in the basement of the *Gazette*, studying the public career of Duane Braddock, alias the Pecos Kid.

Since she'd seen him last, he'd allegedly shot a federal marshal under mysterious circumstances in a Morellos church, of all places. Then he'd become sheriff of a tough border town, Escondido, where he'd killed at least a half-dozen other people. Reliable unnamed informants said he was part Apache, and a bloody legend was building concerning the Pecos Kid. When last seen, less than a month ago, he'd been headed for the Rio Grande with the Fourth Cavalry in hot pursuit.

It was common knowledge that anybody who crossed the Rio Grande was fair game for Apaches, banditos, Comancheros, and the Mexican Army, not to mention rattlesnakes, scorpions, and poisonous lizards. I'll need my own private army if I want to go there, and I'm not *that* rich.

Forget about Duane Braddock, you damned fool, she counseled herself. One of these days somebody else'll come along, and maybe he won't be wanted dead or alive.

*   *   *

Duane opened his eyes on the sun sinking toward rocky crags of Lost Canyon. Cooking odors wafted out of the buildings; he felt mildly hungry and reached for his cup of milk. A dead fly was in it; he spilled it onto the ground and tried to get up.

A terrible pain rent his stomach, and he was afraid that he'd opened the wound. He laboriously unbuttoned his shirt, but the bandage wasn't red. I'm holding together, he thought. He closed his eyes, relaxed on the chair, and uttered a prayer of thanks.

A man of medium height approached, dressed in tight black pants. "So you're the galoot who nearly got hisself shot by Injuns," the newcomer said.

Duane disliked him instantly. "Are you Johnny Pinto?"

The man appeared surprised. "How'd you know?"

"Just a guess."

"I was the newest man in the gang afore you showed up," Johnny said proudly. "Now yer the one who'll git the shitty jobs."

"You heard wrong," replied Duane. "I'm not joining the gang."

Johnny Pinto scowled. "Don't like the sound of that. How do we know you won't bring the law on us when you leave here?"

"I guess you'll have to trust me."

"I don't trust nobody, kid. What're you think I am?" Johnny laughed, showing yellowing teeth. He looked like a desert adder poised to strike. "Who're you runnin' from?"

"How about you?"

Johnny Pinto pushed out his chicken-boned chest. "I killed about six men, fair and square."

"I'll bet," replied Duane, unable to restrain himself.

Johnny Pinto stiffened. "What was that?"

"I'll bet you're real fast."

"Some say that I got the talent." Haughty contempt came over Johnny Pinto's deeply tanned features. "You damn near got yerself kilt by Apaches. If we din't come along, you'd be in some buzzard's belly right now."

"You saved my life," Duane said, "but don't push it."

Johnny giggled oddly, wrinkling his long thin nose. "I guess you know I wouldn't shoot a man who couldn't defend himself."

"At least not when there are witnesses around, right?"

There was silence between them, then Johnny Pinto coughed up an enormous gob of brown phlegm, which he spat into Duane's cup. "When you get better, you and me should have a little talk."

"Up to you," replied Duane.

Johnny Pinto sauntered away, his two gun grips hanging outward, gunfighter style. Duane tried to convince himself that a former seminary student should turn his cheek like a good Christian, even though his great visitation of the Madonna had just been Juanita feeding him soup with a lantern behind her head. Duane didn't tolerate insults agreeably, hated bullies, and wasn't accustomed to backing down.

For no particular reason, and without his volition, an image of Vanessa Fontaine sprang into his mind. She was standing before him, hand on her hip, looking back over her shoulder, smiling gaily. A mild throb of animal lust rocked Duane as memories of the marvelous Miss Vanessa Fontaine flooded his mind. He'd loved to look at her gorgeous face, the stage for a full repertoire of human emotions, some so compelling that he experienced powerful romantic feelings despite severe wounds.

I must be getting better, he realized as he yearned for Miss Vanessa Fontaine. They'd been perfect mates, or so he'd thought, but he'd never gaze upon those pert breasts again. Vanessa Fontaine and I were brought together by God, fate, or the devil himself, but she thought I was just another dumb cowboy. I may meet other women in my life, but there'll never be another Miss Vanessa Fontaine.

Around seven o'clock that evening, two matched black horses drew a black shellacked carriage down a narrow dirt street near the banks of the Colorado River. Mrs. Vanessa Dawes sat in the cab and gazed out the window at drunkards and bummers staggering along the planked sidewalk in front of hardware stores and blacksmith shops closed for the night. She wore a simple but dignified long black dress, black bonnet, and a long black cape, beneath which she held her derringer tightly in her fist. If anybody starts up with me, she swore, I'll shoot the son of a bitch.

The carriage stopped in front of a crude wooden structure with no signs in front, only dim light shining through one small window. The driver, a tall spindly man, jumped down and opened the door. "Ma'am," he said, his eyes pleading, "are you sure you want to go in there?"

"Out of my way," she replied.

She stepped to the ground and saw three men sitting on a bench in front of the establishment. Two were passed out cold, and the other leered crazily at her. "I shall return in approximately ten minutes," she told the driver. "If you don't see me by then, go for help."

"But ma'am . . ."

She stiffened her resolve, pushed open the door, and stepped inside the Shamrock Star Saloon. It was thick with smoke, plus the fragrance of whiskey and other odors that she didn't want to think about. The patrons were the usual crowd of drunkards and fiends, the bar was to the left, and she headed toward it forthrightly, holding the derringer in her right hand, cocked and ready to fire.

Men glanced at her curiously, some grinned suggestively, and others elbowed their companions to draw attention to the apparition descending upon them. The Shamrock Star was the bottom of the barrel in the cleanliness department, while its assorted denizens were bearded, tattooed, with scars on their faces, teeth missing, and the occasional ear partially torn off.

Everyone made way except one lanky fellow with crooked blubbery lips and bright red cheeks. "Where you goin', missy?" he mumbled angrily.

"I'd like to speak with the bartender. Out of my way, please."

He teetered, licked his lips, looked her up and down, and said, "What if I don't git out'n yer way?"

Vanessa had hoped it wouldn't come to this, but all she could do was whip out the derringer. "I'll kill you," she said evenly, aiming at his nose.

The saloon went silent as everyone stared at her. But the former Miss Vanessa Fontaine was accustomed to drunken males and knew how to deal with them. She advanced slowly toward her tormentor and his grin faltered as he gazed down the two eyes that were the derringer's over and under barrels. Finally she came to a stop in front of him and said, "Mister, your life doesn't mean a damned thing to me, and no jury would convict a lady of killing the likes of you. What's it going to be?"

Her knuckle went white around the trigger, and the crude bummer stepped out of the way, his face a few shades paler. "Sorry," he muttered drunkenly, a dazed expression in his eyes as he dropped back into his chair. The path was clear to the bar, where the man in the apron waited, a quizzical expression on his face. He wore a long handlebar mustache and a single gold earring, not to mention an old scar on his chin. "What can I do fer ye, missy?"

"I want to hire a bodyguard of good character. If you run into such a gentleman, I'd be grateful if you'd send him to my hotel." She handed the bartender a slip of paper with her name and address and a ten-dollar gold coin. "That's for your trouble, and there'll be another just like it if I hire somebody you send me. But I don't want any oafs, outlaws, or fools, do you understand?"

The bartender winked, then quickly pocketed the gold coin. "You've got yourself a deal, ma'am."

Vanessa returned to the door as saloon patrons watched her progress with awe, fascination, and lust in their eyes. One of them opened the door, and she disappeared into the dark Austin night. It was silent in the saloon for several seconds after her departure, then a butcher of steers sitting at the bar with a mug of beer in his hand said, "I wonder who she was?"

"Nothin' in the world scarier than a woman with a gun," replied the bartender.

"She looked like she knows how to use it," said a carpenter, whose hammer was jammed into his belt. "Goddamn, she was pretty, and she was a-wearin' widow's weeds, didja notice? I wonder how many times she plugged her ex-husband, and what he did to deserve it?"

Duane dozed a few hours inside Dr. Montgomery's house, but reopened his eyes at the sound of footsteps. It was a curly-headed man in his thirties, with his tan cowboy hat on the back of his head, freckles, and a toothy cowboy smile. "Howdy," he said. "Ginger Hertzog's m'name, and there's somethin' I wanted to ask you. You're Duane Butterfield, and there used to be an old-time gunfighter name of Clyde Butterfield. You kin of his?"

"Never heard of him," Duane replied. "What's he done?"

"Killed a whole lot of people. I heered that you ain't innerested in jinin' up with us."

"There's something I've got to do," Duane replied. "Sorry."

Hertzog narrowed his right eye. "You ain't a Yankee lover, are you?"

"I love everybody, just like it says in the Bible."

"If you love everybody, how come the Fourth Cavalry is after you? Did you shoot somebody?"

"What makes you think that?"

"Yer a wanted man, but you don't wanna commit yerself, eh? You know what they say about the middle of the road. All you find there is horseshit."

"All you find on the sides are varmints waiting for something to fall."

"What varmints?" A new voice intruded onto the scene, Captain Richard Cochrane in his high-topped cavalry boots.

Duane tried to speak first, but Hertzog beat him to the draw. "I din't know we had a Yankee lover with us."

"Leave him alone," Cochrane replied. "You don't argue with a man when he's been shot like this."

"Maybe he deserved to get shot. Ever think of it that way?"

"Go back to the bunkhouse and stay away from this wounded man. That's an order."

"Yes, sir." Hertzog tramped away, muttering to himself.

Cochrane waited for him to move beyond earshot, then turned to Duane. "Why'd you rile him?"

"I didn't mean to, but I guess I don't hate Yankees enough to suit some of the men here."

"You don't know any better," replied Cochrane, "because you're too young to remember. But my irregulars and I remember all too well. The damned Yankees tried to take advantage of us at every turn before the war, and they brought it on themselves. Did you know they forced us to sell cotton to them for less than we could get on the London exchange? And please don't preach to me about poor downtrodden darkies. They would've been freed eventually without the need for war, because many leading Southerners didn't believe in the so-called special institution, including Bobby Lee himself, for instance. That may be hard for you to believe, but it's the truth."

"Truth depends what side of the line you're standing on," replied Duane. "As you said before, I didn't have anything to do with the Civil War. But I knew a woman once, and she couldn't let old Dixie go either."

"Certain people in Boston and Philadelphia wouldn't let us solve our problems in our own way, at our own speed. The war was about Northern domination, not those poor ignorant darkies."

"Just tell me one thing, sir. If Robert E. Lee, the

great hero of the Confederacy, could surrender, why couldn't you?"

"Bobby Lee was sixty-seven when he signed the surrender, but he should've stepped aside and let a young man carry on the fight. A few important generals like Wade Hampton and Nathan Bedford Forrest wanted to keep going, but finally they caved in too. In my not-so-humble opinion, I consider them traitors."

Duane had become accustomed to tirades concerning the Civil War. Wherever he went, old veterans argued about this battle or that famous general. They'd been through hell's hottest furnace; it seared their lives, and Duane felt like a child compared with troopers who'd charged the mouths of cannon in the great Civil War.

"I don't know much about the war, to tell you the truth," confessed Duane. "But I understand how you feel. I've got a score to settle too. People try to talk me out of it, but they can go to hell."

"Exactly," agreed Cochrane. "It's good to talk with a man who's got feelings, unlike those who compromise their lives away. What is it that you're trying to do?"

Duane paused a moment, then impulsively spilled the beans. "Both my parents were killed when I was a baby, because of one mean son of a bitch up in the Pecos Country. Folks tell me I should forget it, but it's easy to say when it wasn't your father and mother. I'm going back to Texas as soon as I heal, and I'm settling the accounts, one way or the other, the devil take all."

"Congratulations," said Cochrane. "You and I understand each other, Butterfield. We'll get along just fine."

It was late at night, and Vanessa paced back and forth in front in her parlor, recalling her performance at the Shamrock Star Saloon. She'd even surprised herself when she'd aimed her derringer at the bummer who'd obstructed her path. I would've shot him between the eyes, no question about it, she reflected. What is death but the end of all living creatures, no matter what decisions they make, how they live, or what they say?

She gazed at the derringer lying in the palm of her hand, smelling faintly of oil, its knurled walnut grips gleaming in lamplight. She'd never fired it in anger, but the ugly snub-nosed tool of death would stand between her and threats from strangers along the journey into Mexico. I'll pretend to be a saloon singer, because I might as well have some fun while I'm at it. They'll hang posters with my name in every town, and maybe Duane will see one of them. He might come to see me one night, and we'll get back together again.

There was a knock on the door, and Vanessa jumped three inches into the air. She'd scheduled no gentleman callers, so who could it be? She stood behind the door, the derringer in her hand, and asked, "What do you want?"

"The bartender at the Shamrock Star sent me."

Vanessa put on a crimson shawl, covering the derringer in her hand, loaded and cocked. Then she opened the door on a stocky man of medium height, wearing a dark blue suit in reasonable repair, once-white shirt, and bright red-and-blue paisley tie. He carried a flaring flat-topped Mississippi gambler hat in his left hand. "Mrs. Dawes?"

"Have a seat."

She examined him through the eyes of maturity, and he appeared a scoundrel, his smoothly shaven features decorated by a raffish half grin. "My name's McCabe.

The bartender said you was lookin' fer a bodyguard, and I'm applyin' for the job."

"What are your qualifications?"

He reached into his frock coat and pulled out a .36-caliber Spiller & Burr. "I'm not afraid of a fight, and you can depend on me."

She measured him as if he were a horse she was going to purchase. He appeared fairly healthy, substantially confident, and only a scoundrel would take such a job in the first place.

"You're hired," she said, and he was momentarily startled by her decision. "Your pay is fifty dollars a month, plus room and board. The job will entail constant traveling, so go home and start packing."

"Don't have all that much to pack, ma'am. I move around a lot on my own. Where we headed?"

"Mexico."

McCabe leaned back in the chair and screwed up his eyes. "What's the purpose of this trip, if'n you don't mind me askin'?"

"I'm looking for an old friend named Duane Braddock. Ever heard of him?"

A puzzled expression came over her new bodyguard's face. "Seems I have, but I'm not sure. He must be an awful good friend."

"Correct," she replied, "and there's something you must understand. You're my bodyguard, but that's as far as it goes." She revealed the derringer with an easy twist of her wrist and aimed down the barrel. "I'm not afraid to use this either."

His face betrayed not one iota of emotion. "I'm only interested in fifty dollars per month, plus my expenses. What made you think different?"

He was a total stranger, and could be a wanted

killer for all she knew. "You've got the job," she told him. "Your first assignment is to find out when the next stagecoach is leaving for San Antone."

"Hold on," he replied. "I hired on as bodyguard, not errand boy. Maybe we'd better get that straight right now."

"Why should two people go to the stagecoach office, when one will do? If this is the way you're going to be, maybe I'd better find another bodyguard."

He raised his hand and smiled. "Don't be hasty. I was just testin' you, and you passed. Wouldn't want to work for any skeered woman."

"Are you wanted by the authorities?"

McCabe looked around with discomfort. "The damned Yankees claim that I committed a few acts of piracy during war."

"You sound like my kind of man, Mr. McCabe." Vanessa smiled for the first time since the interview began. "You may commence your duties immediately."

CHAPTER 5

DUANE PUSHED HIMSELF unsteadily to his feet, every motion carrying new agony. Dr. Montgomery handed him a crooked cane fashioned from a juniper branch. They were on level ground, and Duane was about to take his first step since he'd fought the Apaches.

An invisible monster tugged his healing stomach muscles every time he moved. He took one faltering step, paused, and then attempted another.

"You're doing very well," Dr. Montgomery said proudly. "The more you try, the better you'll be. I don't hold to those old-fashioned theories about a wounded man staying in bed all day long. Hell, that'll only make you weaker."

"And this might finish me off completely," Duane wheezed. He took another tentative step, tottered, but managed to right himself as something fragile ripped in his guts. "I opened a stitch, I think."

"Don't see any blood."

Duane probed his left foot forward. He'd lie down if he were alone, but didn't want to appear weak in front of the doctor. He advanced with great effort across the clearing, and all heads in the vicinity turned toward him.

He limped twenty feet; the pain grew severe, his left leg felt paralyzed. "I can't go on," he said in a choked voice.

"Sure you can."

"Something's going to bust at any moment."

"Nonsense."

It's not his body that was shot up, reasoned Duane as he pressed onward. "When do I get a break?"

"A few more feet. I've got a big reward if you make it, but don't ask what it is. You'll have to keep going to find out."

The irregular soldiers watched, and Duane couldn't collapse before an audience, though he was sure his vitals were rupturing.

"That's enough," said Dr. Montgomery. "Have a seat."

A chair appeared beneath Duane; he dropped onto it, and never had his limbs felt so heavy, while his chest heaved with effort. A table was placed before him, and on it was a platter covered with slabs of meat, mashed potatoes, collard greens, gravy, beans, tortillas, and a pot of hot black coffee.

"Enjoy it," said Dr. Montgomery.

Duane reached for the knife and fork. They might be outlaws, he considered, but they're good Samaritans as well, and I owe my life to them. There's decency in everybody, including outlaws. Thank you, Lord, for the bounty of this table, and also for slowing me down and forcing me to think more deeply about my ridiculous life.

Captain Cochrane approached the table as Duane finished his wedge of apple pie. "You look like a new man," Cochrane announced in his deep booming cavalry officer's voice.

"Should be able to ride soon, and hope you'll sell me a horse."

"But of course." The ex-officer sat on the edge of the table and rolled a cigarette. "If you're headed for a long trip, you'll need some money, I reckon."

"A traveler can always use money, that's for sure. What's on your mind?"

"We're going on a military operation and could use another gun. Your share would be five thousand dollars for a few days of riding. We won't be leaving for another month, so you might want to think it over."

"Thanks for the offer," replied Duane, "but I don't think I'll be going with you. As I told you before, there's something I've got to do."

Cochrane smiled thinly. "If I offered you a regular job for five thousand dollars, you'd snap it up in a minute. Let's call a spade a spade. You think we're a bunch of thieves, am I right?"

"I don't mean to insult you," replied Duane, "because you've been damned good to me, but when a man takes something that doesn't belong to him at gunpoint, it's known as armed robbery."

"We're recovering what the Yankees have stolen from us. Why can't you understand that simple concept?"

"I doubt that the federal marshal in San Antone would agree with you, and he's the one I'm worried about. Sorry, but I'm having enough trouble with the law as it is."

Cochrane pondered Duane's rejoinder for a few moments, then slowly and thoughtfully rolled a cigarette. "You and I have fundamental disagreements about what's lawful and what isn't, but I loathe any form of surrender. The tragedy of the South is that she was betrayed by her leaders. Bobby Lee became a college professor, which is what he should've been in the first place. Wade Hampton and Nathan Bedford Forrest became cheap tinhorn businessmen while everything we fought and bled for was tossed into the trash pile. It's too damned bad that Stonewall Jackson got killed, along with Albert Sidney Johnston and good old Jeb Stuart. Our best, the ones who would've fought on, were lost in the fray, while opportunists live on and get richer every day."

"I've always been curious about something," said Duane cautiously. "If the South had so many brilliant generals, and so many good dedicated soldiers, how'd you lose?"

Captain Richard Cochrane of the Confederate Cavalry Corps gazed solemnly at the horizon. "We ran out of supplies, ammunition, and horses. In the final year, we looked like gray ghosts in rags, with the missmeal cramps and no soles on our boots. All we had left was our good old-fashioned Southern pride, but we did our duty to flag and country, unaware that the worst blow was yet to fall, when we were sold down the river by our leaders."

Cochrane shook his head bitterly, his eyes watered, then he looked away and declared firmly, "It's not a happy story, but it's not over yet. The one true fact of history—and even Machiavelli realized it—is you can't hold good people down." Cochrane balled his fist, turned toward Duane, and looked him squarely in the eye. "One day, mark my words, the South will rise again!"

Well-dressed passengers boarded the Concord stage-coach as baggage handlers tossed luggage to their brethren atop the designated compartment. It was a bright sunny day, a crowd of children and well-wishers were gathered, and Vanessa Fontaine wondered if she was going out of her mind, instead of taking a stage-coach trip to San Antone with a man she didn't even know.

As if in a dream, she ascended the two steps and landed inside the cab. A salesman sat in front of her, next to a lawyer. She shifted her butt toward the far window; they tipped their hats and mumbled friendly greetings with the faint suggestions of lechery.

McCabe followed her, carrying a sawed-off dou-ble-barrel shotgun, while his Spiller & Burr .36-cal-iber revolver slept peacefully in a holster against his right leg. He sat next to Vanessa and was followed by a gentleman who looked like a schoolteacher, but could have been a doctor, perhaps even an ax murderer.

What have I done? Vanessa asked herself as the door closed. I'm going through this misery for a *man?* But I'll be fine once I get over the initial shock. After all, most stagecoaches arrive at their destinations without a scratch, don't they? If I don't find Duane Braddock, maybe I'll meet some other nice fellow.

The carriage jerked abruptly; Vanessa looked out the window and waved one last time to Lonnie Mae. A cheer went up from the crowd as the stagecoach rolled down the street. Panic broke over Vanessa, and she wanted to jump out the door and run for her life. Her stagecoach might be the one that didn't make it through Comanche territory, and perhaps she'd be taken prisoner, spending the rest of her life as some warrior's squaw.

Why am I never satisfied? she wondered, swallowing hard as clomping horses pulled the stagecoach down the street. If another woman were doing this, I'd tell her she's an utter nincompoop. They came to the edge of town, and before them stretched the vast lawless sage. Vanessa tried to feel hopeful while next to her sat a personal bodyguard wanted by the Yankees for piracy, and God only knew what else.

What have I done? she wondered again as the stagecoach of fools rocked from side to side on its leather thoroughbrace suspension. The team of snorting drooling horses pulled the ornate vehicle onto open range, and the passengers looked at each other warily, because it was possible they'd die together in the days to come. This time I've gone too far, Vanessa thought as civilization, mercy, and Christianity fell behind the rear wheels of the stagecoach. There ought to be a law against people like me.

Late that afternoon Nestor spotted a herd of wild ones in the distance, grazing on an endless carpet of grass. They were the beasts of the range who ran without bridles and saddles, and no cruel two-leggeds kicked spurs into their withers.

Nestor was shy, afraid they wouldn't accept him, and feeling lonely. He didn't sleep well, because he was food to many different creatures. It would be easier if he could cooperate with others on guard duty.

If they didn't accept him, he'd go on his way alone. Maybe he'd let some cowboys catch him, because a nice warm barn and plenty of oats were worth a certain amount of spurs.

He'd been living on grass and strengthening his instincts during the time he'd been on the loose. He could smell the herd and was certain they smelled him, too, as he loped closer, peering ahead through his huge eyes, as his ears listened for danger.

He approached the edge of the herd, stopped, and looked at them hopefully. The nearest horses stopped munching and gazed back for a long time. Then a big Appaloosa stallion took a few steps toward Nestor. Welcome, brother. We are the wild ones.

Nestor lowered his head as he advanced closer. They appeared skittish, light on their feet, with sharp glancing eyes and tremendous power radiating from their muscular bodies. Numerous pretty fillies were among them. Come join us, and be one with us.

They made way for Nestor, and he walked among them like an honored guest. They moved closer, touching him with their lips, snorting and snickering warmly. We are the wild ones, and we are on our way to the land of the sun.

Late that night the stagecoach arrived at a shack alongside a muddy trail west of Austin. The shotgun guard jumped down and opened the stagecoach door as passengers groaned, unfolded themselves from cramped seats, and headed outside. McCabe helped Vanessa to the soggy ground; it was pitch-black, and a chill was on the sage. She pulled her purple wool shawl more tightly around her shoulders.

The stagecoach stop was rough-hewn and lopsided, and its interior visible through cracks between the logs.

McCabe opened the front door, revealing scattered tables, a small bar, and a stove where a woman in a apron was flipping steaks. "Supper's ready!" she called. "Yer just in time."

"Where can I get two whiskeys?" McCabe asked. "And fast."

At the bar, a boy of fourteen upturned a jug and filled two glasses. McCabe carried them to Vanessa as other passengers stumbled into the warm dim-lit room. The aroma of broiling beef, sweaty clothes, garbage, and unwashed flesh filled Vanessa's nostrils. She sat at a table, rested her chin on her hand, and pondered, My God, what have I done to myself?

McCabe chuckled on the far side of the table, his white teeth gleaming in the light of a lamp suspended from a hook in the ceiling.

"You look plumb tuckered out, ma'am. I was just wonderin' if we're headed back to Austin."

"Of course we're not going back. We just started."

A lightning bolt rent the heavens as the cook's children served food and drink to the weary travelers; a light rain began to fall. He's right, I should return to Austin, Vanessa speculated, but do I want to spend my life lying on the sofa, reading Lord Byron, and being bored? I was made for better things, so why am I following a wanted killer to a place about which I know nothing, and sleeping in roadhouses not fit for self-respecting swine? How low I've fallen, all for the love of a man who may not even remember me anymore.

Several hundred miles away a much different meal was being served in a canyon that appeared on no official maps. Cochrane sat at one end of the table, and at the other, Juanita ladled hearty beef stew into large wooden bowls. Dr. Jeff Montgomery and Duane Braddock were guests, facing each other midway down the table.

Duane's mouth watered at the fragrance arising from his bowl, but he couldn't begin until grace had been said. I might as well make the best of my stay with this outlaw gang, he figured. About time I took me a vacation.

Captain Cochrane folded his hands and bowed his head. "Lord, we thank You for the food that You have brought forth from the earth, and please help us defeat the Yankee invader. Amen."

They proceeded to dine, their table illuminated by a hand-worked elaborate silver candelabrum purchased in Monterrey, while a framed portrait of General Thomas Stonewall Jackson hung on the wall. Duane was becoming increasingly devoted to Mexican food, and consumed his portion with great gusto as his tongue tingled with exotic Mexican spices. This is the way a man should live, he figured, instead of in saloons where a cook might spit in the soup, or a dead fly could be buried in your mashed potatoes.

On the other side of the table, Captain Cochrane watched Duane out the corner of his eye. The young man had been nearly dead, but now sat upright, his color coming back, and he appeared almost normal. "You're making quite a recovery, Duane," Cochrane acknowledged. "You must have a strong constitution."

Before Duane could respond, the doctor said, "Youth is a powerful antidote to everything imaginable. We've seen with our own eyes how it can defeat death itself."

"It was not youth that did it," declared Juanita. "It was God!"

Dr. Montgomery and Captain Cochrane looked at each other as if to say, *There she goes again.* Juanita noticed their mocking expressions, but that didn't stop her. "It is God who does everything, not us."

Captain Cochrane didn't want to argue with his acid-tongued bed partner, so he sidestepped the issue entirely. "Have you picked out a horse yet, Duane?"

"I sure wish I could have the one that I was riding when the Apaches attacked me. He was the fastest horse I ever rode, and I paid a hundred dollars for him. I wonder whatever happened to him."

"The Apaches probably got him," replied Cochrane. "That's an awful lot of money for a horse these days."

"What's a hundred dollars when the Fourth Cavalry is on your trail?"

Juanita shook her head in disapproval. "Banditos," she muttered. "How could anybody want such a life?"

"I'm not a bandito," corrected Duane. "I never stole anything except a couple of horses out of necessity."

"In other words," Dr. Montgomery said, "you're a horse thief."

"It was a matter of life and death."

Juanita interjected again. "God wants us to live at peace, but men fight all the time. That is the main *problema* in this world."

"Our high priestess has spoken," declared Cochrane jokingly. "Unfortunately, not many people can understand a great purpose. You can do whatever you like to ordinary people, as long as you give them a roof over their heads and a pot of stew once a day. That's the way the Yankees want us to live—one small cut above slaves—and I guess we're supposed to lie down and enjoy it. The Yankees are small petty men—they want to punish us for our supposedly wicked ways, and

Juanita doesn't understand one iota of it, but she provides me with the conventional point of view."

It became silent in the tiny adobe hacienda as Captain Richard Cochrane and Señorita Juanita Torregrosa glowered at each other across the table, shattering Duane's happy family portrait. Meanwhile, Dr. Montgomery chewed a tortilla as if nothing untoward had happened. It looked as though Cochrane and Juanita were going to jump over the stew pot and start punching, scratching, and biting.

Juanita tossed her hand in the air. "You can use all the big words you want, Mr. Confederate Army, but you are not fooling me one bit. You love to hate, and that is why you are still fighting your Civil War. You have fancy words, but you do not know a damned thing what you are talking about."

"Sure I don't," he replied, getting deeper into the spirit of domestic discord. "Only ignorant Mexican peasants know the truth, isn't that so? That's why Mexico is poor. God can't be a very good father if that's how he treats the Mexicans."

Duane Braddock, defender of the faith, decided to jump in with both feet. "According to theology, evil is caused by people who make free-will decisions. So don't blame it on God."

"Are you referring to the holy-boly Roman Catholic Church, which gave the world the Crusades, the Inquisition, and two thousand years of opposition to everything bright, new, and wonderful?"

"God didn't start the Civil War. It was either the Southerners who fired on Fort Sumter, or the Northerners who forced them into it, but don't blame it on God."

Duane noticed Dr. Montgomery on the far side of the table, motioning for him to simmer down. Duane had stepped into an argument between his host and hostess, thus committing a major social blunder. Should I apologize? he asked himself.

Cochrane smiled at Duane indulgently. "You're a funny kid, and you don't mince words, just like Juanita. Whatever she says, I know it's the truth as she sees it. Lying is the most terrible insult that I can imagine."

"Personally," replied Duane, "I think murder tops the list."

Cochrane gazed at him thoughtfully for a few moments. "How strange . . . you were raised in a monastery. Why'd you leave?"

"Mexican girls came to Mass on Sundays, and I started to think about getting married."

"There's a Mexican girl at the far end of the table whom I love with all my heart, and all she ever does is criticize, nag, and insult me at every opportunity."

"He is such a cold-blooded gringo," Juanita announced. "You just heard him say with his own mouth what he thinks of women. The truth is that he doesn't like men any better, but he needs them for his robbing and killing."

"We never kill civilians unless it's necessary," corrected Cochrane. "Please don't make us worse than we are."

"I should leave you, but I love you too much. That is the tragedy of my life."

Cochrane turned to Duane and smiled. "Mexican girls aren't happy unless they're tragic. It gives them an excuse to go to church and light candlesticks. They all secretly want to be nuns, I think."

Juanita turned toward him, her eyes narrowed to slits. "I do not like you doing these things, because I fear that one day you will be killed."

"You're wrong as usual," Cochrane replied.

Juanita slammed her fist on the table. "You see how he is?" she asked Duane. "Oh, what am I doing with this man? Maybe he is right, and I should be a nun."

She rose from the table and stormed into the next room, leaving the three men in awkward silence. Cochrane cleared his throat and drawled, "I apologize for my wife's behavior, but she's very excitable. If you'll excuse me for a moment . . ."

He headed toward the room into which Juanita had disappeared, leaving Duane and Dr. Montgomery sitting at the table. The doctor motioned with his eyes toward the door. He and Duane grabbed their hats and slunk away from the warring household.

"I should've kept my mouth shut," Duane admitted as he hobbled toward Dr. Montgomery's cabin.

"They were fighting long before you ever showed up," replied the doctor, "and they'll be fighting long after you're gone. Yet, difficult though it seems, they love each other. You may consider me vulgar, but even as I speak they're probably ripping off each other's clothes. It's a form of brain sickness, but who am I to criticize? Sometimes I question what we're supposed to be accomplishing here myself."

"Where do you keep all the money that you've robbed?"

The doctor looked at him askance. "You're not interested in stealing it, are you?"

"I was just curious."

"We've always suspected that one day a spy might show up. You're not he, I don't suppose?"

"I've got better things to do than spy, and I've got enough money of my own anyway. Have you ever stopped to consider what most Texans think of people like you?"

"Their stupid opinions don't matter to me in the least. And please don't ask again where the loot is hidden, because your health might suffer another relapse. I hope you won't be offended, but we live by the articles of war, and that means we're authorized to form firing squads. Have you ever seen a firing squad?"

"Never," admitted Duane.

"It's a quick painless death, from what I've seen, but the hours leading up to it are most disagreeable. If you're as smart as you seem to be, you'll stay off the ridges. Get my drift?"

The travelers were led to a small room with four inches of straw on the floor. "It may not look like much," the proprietress said cheerily, "but we sweep it every morning, then shovel in fresh straw."

How sanitary, Vanessa thought as she entered the dank, damp room. A diminutive iron stove sat in the corner, providing no discernible heat. The men inclined toward one side while the only woman headed for the other. No blankets were provided, never mind sheets. Vanessa removed the long black wool overcoat from her trunk, spread it on the straw, sat upon it, and removed her shoes. She lay on the straw, covered herself with the coat, propped her head on her purse, and wondered if one of them would try to rape her in the course of the night's events.

They all seemed honorable men, but a rapist wouldn't carry a sign announcing his intentions. Her bodyguard arranged himself on the nearby straw, providing Vanessa with a small margin of safety, although she didn't trust him completely yet. Reaching into her purse, she pulled out her tiny gold-plated derringer, then recalled Duane Braddock sleeping every night with his Colt in his right hand, ready to fire. I hope I don't shoot my toe off, she thought as she gripped the derringer firmly and closed her eyes.

Something itched her hip, probably a wayward louse, but she barely paid attention. She listened to the groans and sighs of her fellow travelers, plus other bodily sounds best not enumerated, punctuated by the steady *pit-pat* of rain leaking through the roof. Vanessa slipped down the precipitous slope toward slumber as a heavy drop of water landed on her nose and splattered over her face. But she was already fast asleep, dreaming of Comanche warriors slouched in their saddles, riding steadily across the vast unknowable sage.

Cochrane reached for Juanita, but his arms closed around an empty blanket. He opened his eyes; it was morning, and something rustled in the kitchen. A smile came over his face at the anticipation of eggs, bacon, beans, and hot black coffee.

I ought to marry her, he thought, recalling certain highlights of the night. It wasn't because she was more beautiful than other women, or more accomplished in the bedroom arts, but her raw animal passion astonished and pleased him considerably. He didn't think he could return to an ordinary woman again.

She continued puttering, but he didn't smell coffee or hear pots and pans. He rolled out of bed, wrapped his nakedness in a blanket, and opened the door. She was packing her few belongings into a bedroll and spun around as he approached. He waited for an explanation, but she turned away and continued to prepare for a journey.

"Going somewhere?" he asked.

"I am leaving you," she replied.

"How?"

"You are going to give me a horse. I have worked for you so long, I think I am worth one horse, no?"

"Why are you leaving me?"

"Because you do not love me anymore."

"How can you say that, after last night?"

"If you loved me, you would make a family with me. But I am just somebody you stick your thing into whenever you feel like it. I am going back to the cantina, because at least there the men were honest about what they wanted. It is not hard for a rich man like you to find another woman."

"But I don't want anybody else."

"One day your men will ride back and tell me you are dead. Then what will I do?"

"Fine another hombre."

She was silent for a few moments, then a tear rolled down her cheek. "So that is what you think of me. The truth has come out at last. Well, maybe I will start looking for another hombre right now. It has been nice knowing you, gringo."

She headed for the door, but he moved to intercept her. "The Apaches will get you before you go five miles. Did you know that horses are their favorite food?"

"Take your hands off me," she said in a deadly tone.

"I'm not letting you go."

She struggled to get away, and they wrestled with each other in the kitchen.

"Leave me alone," she snarled.

He was stronger and more skilled at combat, so it wasn't long before he pinned her to the wall. "Let's talk about it," he said.

"I am tired of talking with you. You can hold me as long as you want, but one day I will escape. And I will never love you again, so help me God."

Her voice was tremulous, she spoke with the deepest conviction, and the hairs stood up on the back of his head. This was no ordinary kitchen squabble. "But you know how much I need you, Juanita."

"Prove it."

He couldn't say the words she wanted to hear, because he couldn't give up the Cause. "All right," he said gruffly as he turned her loose. "Have it your own way."

She hoisted the bedroll onto her shoulder and walked out of his life. He rushed ahead to open the door while she marched outside without even looking at him.

He felt as though his heart would stop. Life without her seemed valueless, empty, and pathetic, but he tried to hold on. Hell, there are a million more where she came from. She disappeared into the stable as he watched from the kitchen window. He couldn't believe that he'd never sleep with her again. Memories of their lovemaking flooded his mind, and he felt bereft.

It wouldn't be a bad idea to live with her on a little *estancia* with children and mongrel dogs, he pondered. Maybe she's right when she calls me a cold-blooded gringo. Who'll cook my breakfast from now on? Who'll wash my clothes? When I feel discouraged, who'll cheer me up? He'd come to depend on her and never dreamed that she'd have the courage to leave him. She doesn't really mean it, he tried to convince himself. She thinks I'm going to cave in to her demands, but I'll find somebody else to cook my breakfast.

A shadow came over the door of the barn as she rode outside on the back of a horse with her bedroll tied behind the saddle. The Apaches will turn her into a slave, he evaluated, after they rape her brains out, and she damn well knows it. She's going a long way to make a point, but what the hell is it?

The answer came with stunning forcefulness. She knows that I'm in love with her, and she's playing her final trump card. Well, maybe we can cut a deal. He jumped into his jeans and ran barefoot out the door. She appeared not to notice him charging across the backyard, and when he grabbed the horse's reins, she refused to acknowledge his existence.

The horse looked back cynically, for human beings were the bane of his existence, always dragging him in one direction or another, and occasionally a poor horse would get caught in a shoot-out, with terminal results. José was his name, and he wished she'd get off his back, return to the stable, and let him catch up on his sleep.

Meanwhile, Cochrane looked at Juanita pleadingly. "Let's have a talk," he said.

She shook her head staunchly. "We have talked enough."

"We've been together nearly two years, and you've got to let me speak my peace."

"Make it fast."

"I want to go on one last raid, and then I'll do anything you say."

"Haven't you robbed enough already?"

"This is the biggest one so far. I've been planning it for a year, and can't pull out now. But when it's over, I promise you that I'll buy us a little *estancia* wherever you want, we'll have children, and be together always. I mean it." He raised his right hand and looked at the sky. "So help me God."

"You will say anything to get what you want," she replied coolly.

"If you love me as much as you say, you'd give me one last chance."

"After this robbery is over, there'll be another one, because you cannot stop—you are *un pocito loco*. A *fanático*."

"I've already raised my right hand and sworn to God Almighty. If that's not good enough for you, I don't know what I can do. Maybe you're just looking for an excuse to leave me. Well, you don't need an excuse. You can leave whenever you want."

He walked back to their cabin, his shoulders squared, erect as a soldier, noble and splendid in Juanita's eyes. The exultation of victory filled her heart, and she gave silent thanks to the Mother of God, who looks out for wayward Mexican señoritas.

She slid down the side of her horse and ran toward Cochrane, her sandals slapping against the ground. He turned around, a smile broadening his face as he opened wide his arms. They clasped each other tightly, their lips touched, and he felt the bittersweet pain of defeat mixed with the promise of new victory.

"You will never be sorry about this decision," she whispered. "I will be your woman forever, and if you die first, I will be your woman even beyond the grave."

CHAPTER 6

VANESSA FONTAINE STROLLED
down the main street of San Antone, passing an adobe barbershop, law office, and
then three saloons in a row. Mexican and American
women could be seen upon the sidewalks, and Vanessa
thought she should be buying beans and tortillas among
them instead of hunting for the Pecos Kid.

McCabe accompanied Vanessa on her walk, and
thus far he'd been a solid faithful bodyguard. He slept
close to her at night, but never attempted monkey
business. The arrangement was turning out perfectly,
and she congratulated herself on her good luck. The
stagecoach trip to San Antone had been without incident, and she wondered whether the threat of Indian
attack had been greatly exaggerated by the hysterical
Texas press.

They drew near the sheriff's office, and she said, "I'll
do the talking."

McCabe opened the door, and Vanessa entered a room furnished with three wooden desks, a Lone Star flag nailed to the wall next to a map of Texas, and a tanned lean young man reading a newspaper. He had a lantern jaw, smoothly shaved cheeks, and a badge pinned to his tan rawhide vest. "Help you, ma'am?"

"Are you the sheriff?" she asked sweetly.

"The sheriff is out of town on official business. I'm Deputy Downey."

"I'm Mrs. Vanessa Dawes, and this is my friend, Mr. McCabe. I'm searching for a certain gentleman who's wanted by the authorities, and I wonder if he's passed through the vicinity lately. His name's Duane Braddock, and some folks refer to him as the Pecos Kid."

"Rings a bell," replied Downey. He opened a wood cabinet, searched through stacks of paper, and came out with four official documents. He dropped them onto the desk, and on top was a wanted poster featuring a crude drawing of Duane Braddock, offering five hundred dollars for his capture, dead or alive. The small print at the bottom said that the Pecos Kid was charged with killing a federal marshal in Morellos. "What's Duane Braddock to you?" Deputy Downey asked, making a confidential smile.

"Friend of mine," replied Vanessa.

Deputy Downey uncovered the next document. "It says here that he was elected sheriff of a town called Escondido, where he shot six men in cold blood. It got so bad the citizenry asked for the Fourth Cavalry to get rid of him. He sounds like a real hard case, and he's a friend of yours?"

"If Duane Braddock shot a federal marshal," Vanessa replied, "the marshal probably had it coming."

The deputy looked her up and down slowly. "The judge who issued this warrant didn't think so."

Vanessa walked toward the map and looked for the town of Escondido. It was a tiny dot near the Rio Grande south of Fort Davis, approximately four or five hundred miles from San Antone. Anyone embarking on such a trip had better get ready for the Comanche homeland, followed by Apache ancestral territory. Vanessa wondered if she was up to it.

The deputy cocked his head to the side, and asked, "How well do you know Duane Braddock?"

"We were engaged once, so I guess you can say that I knew him rather well, and in my opinion he doesn't have a criminal bone in him. I don't know what these false accusations are all about, frankly, and I don't care. Have the Indians been peaceful west of here lately?"

The deputy shook his head no. "Injun depredations have been worse than ever, and there's practically no law at all once you get west of San Antone." The deputy painted a knowing expression on his face.

"Thank you for the information." Vanessa turned like a royal personage and headed for the door. She landed on the sidewalk with McCabe, and together they headed back toward their hotel. "I guess we're going west," Vanessa said. "Are you still with me?"

"Long as you keep payin' my salary," replied McCabe.

Duane could walk almost normally, but wasn't strong enough to run up and down mountains like an Apache yet. His mind was filled with new projects, such as practicing the classic fast draw. It wasn't a skill he wanted to forget, and next step was asking Cochrane for permission.

Cochrane's firm control of the camp had become increasingly apparent to Duane. Cochrane brooked no nonsense, and paradoxically, respect for the former cavalry officer hadn't decreased substantially since Cochrane had begged Juanita publicly not to leave him. Love makes fools out of us all, realized Duane.

He heard footsteps and turned to see Cochrane walking toward him, his wide-brimmed silverbelly hat slanted low over his eyes. "Don't shoot," said the captain with a mocking smile as he raised his hands in the air. "Where are you headed?"

"Just taking a walk."

"I'm having a meeting with the men tonight, after dinner. I'm going to explain our next raid in detail and thought I'd extend the invitation to you."

"No thanks," replied Duane. "I don't want to know anything that might give me lead poisoning."

"You've heard everything else about us already, so what's the difference? You might find it interesting."

"I've got my own plans. Sorry."

"I think you'd better be there."

It sounded like an order. "Why?"

"Because the men saved your life, and now it's your turn to help them."

"When I draw this Colt, it's for self-defense only."

"I wouldn't ask you to violate your principles. What kind of rascal do you think I am? The raid will be purely military, and you can care for the horses. I'll expect you at my place after dinner."

Cochrane smiled confidently, performed a perfect about-face, and headed toward his hut, leaving Duane standing alone on the far side of the canyon. Duane wanted a favor, so he ran woodenly after him, and said, "I'd like to ask you something, sir. Could I start getting in some shooting practice?"

"Sure, just as long you don't hit any of my men by mistake or on purpose. I always figured you for a gunfighter, and now the truth comes out."

"I'm no gunfighter," Duane replied. "It's just that I intend to live for a long time."

"Don't we all. Shoot all you want, and by the way, don't forget to show up at the meeting."

Vanessa was admitted to a small office in back of the Black Cat Saloon. Dan Cunningham, proprietor, sat behind his desk, a grossly obese man with a long mustache, a round flabby face, and beady eyes that looked her up and down. "What can I do for you?" he asked in a cold businessman's voice.

"Aren't you even going to invite me to sit down?"

"Sit—stand—do as you like, but I don't have much time."

She placed her fists on his desk, leaned forward, and peered into his dull gray orbs. "You behave as if you're doing me a favor, but the shoe is on the other foot. Most of your customers are Civil War veterans, and I know all the good old songs they love to hear. Once I start singing them, you'll be surprised how quickly your establishment will fill with patrons. I am Miss Vanessa Fontaine—perhaps you've heard of me—and I'm not unreasonable in my requests for recompense. What do you say?"

Cunningham narrowed his eyes, and a grin came to his lips. "Women walk into this office every day with the same story. They want to be singers, and they've got the greatest voices in the world. But what'll they do for me? That's what I want to know."

She raised an eyebrow. "What do you want them to do for you?"

He didn't reply, but the insinuating leer on his lips said everything. Vanessa was tempted to smack his face, but instead smiled and said, "Sorry, but I'm not a prostitute. You should think with your wallet for a change, sir. You hire me, plaster my name around town, and sweep the saloon, you'll sell so much whiskey you can buy all the prostitutes you want."

He puffed his black cigar. "You're a tall drink of water and you've got a big mouth. All right—I'll give you a chance. You can open tonight, and stay as long you keep bringing in the business."

A map of Texas and Mexico was nailed to Cochrane's kitchen wall as the outlaw band huddled around their leader, waiting for him to begin. Cochrane carried a pointer carved from the branch of a cottonwood tree, and stood in the light of an oil lamp hanging from the ceiling.

All the outlaws were there, and even Juanita had been invited. Duane hung toward the back of the crowd, determined not to get sucked into illegal shenanigans regardless of how they coerced him.

"We might as well begin," said Captain Cochrane, his voice businesslike and confident. "As you know, this will be our most complex raid so far, and most lucrative. It's time we made a major contribution to the treasury of the New Confederacy." He narrowed his eyes as he leaned toward them.

"On the fifteenth of every month, a wagon departs

Fort Richardson, carrying payrolls and other monies for forts throughout the Fourth Cavalry command. It is variously estimated that the monies amount to approximately a quarter of a million dollars. For the rest of the month, they drop off pay at posts and commands, and then return to Fort Richardson to prepare for the next delivery." Cochrane pointed to a region about a hundred miles south of Fort Richardson. "I propose to intercept the wagon here. It's a little-known spot called Devil's Creek, where they stop to rest and water their horses. We'll strike at sundown on the appointed day, recover the money, and be gone before the Yankees know what hit them. Your own personal shares will be approximately five thousand dollars each. Are there any questions so far?"

Sergeant Beasley raised his hand. "How many soldiers will we have to contend with?"

"Twenty to thirty troopers with rifles and pistols, plus a few Indian scouts."

Beasley shook his head vehemently. "Don't like the sound of that, especially the Injuns. They'll smell us comin' a mile away."

Cochrane smiled indulgently. "People sometimes confer supernatural powers upon Indians, but if the bloody savages are so all-powerful and all-knowing, why are they surrendering left and right all across the frontier? The Indians won't even know we're there, and don't forget that the pay wagon has stopped at Devil's Creek a hundred times, so they're not expecting anything. You know very well that small units frequently defeated larger ones during the war—I could give you hundreds of examples. Besides, the Yankee soldiers of today don't have much fight in them, and most'll run at the sound of the first shot."

"I *still* don't like the odds," Beasley insisted. "We need at least five more men. Sir, I don't want to be disrespectful, but this doesn't sound like such a hot idea."

"I understand your concerns, Sergeant, but we'll make liberal use of dynamite, and I've left nothing to chance. It'll be worth more than ten of our usual jobs, and this is the legacy that I want to leave the Confederacy."

Cochrane looked like an officer standing beside the map, and Duane imagined him in a tailored gray cavalry officer's uniform, with polished brass buttons, a yellow sash, shiny black knee-high boots, and his trusty saber at his side. Duane fantasized the other irregulars attired in the uniforms of the Confederate Army, with stripes on their sleeves and medals on their chests. Duane became aware that everyone was looking at him curiously. While daydreaming, he'd missed something.

"Well?" asked Captain Cochrane. "Haven't you been listening? I asked if you were going on the raid with us."

"I already told you there's something I've got to do."

The outlaws grumbled, displeased by the response. Dr. Montgomery stepped forward, a frown on his normally placid face. "We've placed our lives on the line for you, young man, and you can't find it within your heart to give us a hand?"

"I'm not a gunfighter or an ex-soldier, and I'm not interested in breaking the law. Sorry."

"What law?" asked Cochrane. "The Yankees have no dominion over you unless you give it to them. Do you consider yourself subject to the Yankee government?"

"I'm an American citizen," Duane replied. "That's all I know."

There was silence, then Duane heard an angry snort from Johnny Pinto. "It don't have nawthin' to do with bein' an American citizen. I think he's just a god-damned coward."

The ugly word singed Duane's ears as he turned toward Johnny. "People who say *coward* are usually the worst cowards of all," he replied.

"Easy for you to say, 'cause you know I won't hurt you. Yer so sickly and all."

"I'm sickly and you're stupid, but I'm getting better every day."

Johnny's pupils dilated. "Izzat so? Well, since yer gittin' better every day, maybe you and me ought to settle this like men afore long, all right?"

"Up to you."

Johnny turned toward the others. "You all heard him."

Cochrane broke the silence. "If you're going to be staying with us that long, Duane, you might as well come on the raid. You don't have to draw your gun if you don't want to, because God forbid that we should drag a wanted outlaw such as yourself into our sordid life of crime. You can be the quartermaster, and free up Walsh for active duty. It'd be a big help to us, and we'd really appreciate it."

"That's right," said Walsh, absentmindedly stroking the mole on his cheek. "I for one ain't afraid to fight the damned Yankees. We've done a lot fer you, boy, and you got a short memory. That day we rode to save yer worthless ass, we could've been ridin' into the whole damned Apache nation. But we took the chance to help another white man."

Dr. Montgomery smiled indulgently. "How can you refuse to look after our horses and supplies for a few measly days?"

Duane couldn't say no. After all, they *had* saved his miserable worthless skin, no doubt about it. "I'll have to think it over, but I'm not getting into gunplay, and I don't care how many times you insult me or make me feel guilty." Duane turned toward Johnny Pinto. "And I'll take care of you after we get back."

Johnny Pinto made an impulsive threatening motion toward Duane, but saw a Colt aimed at his nose. It happened so quickly, Johnny blinked in surprise, then smiled, showing teeth yellowed by tobacco. "You're not as sick as you look, eh, Mr. Butterfield? But you won't fight me hand to hand and man to man. Afraid I'll dirty yer pretty face?"

Duane aimed down the barrel of his Colt at Johnny Pinto. "In about one month you and I are going to fight, Johnny. Then we'll see whose face gets dirty."

Vanessa Fontaine applied cosmetics to her cheeks in a small musty storage area behind the Black Cat Saloon. Converted into her dressing room, it had a big framed mirror with a crack down the middle, four dented brass lamps, and a broken-down couch for her to languish upon between shows. The time neared for her opening-night performance, and Cunningham had papered San Antone with posters that said:

BLACK CAT SALOON
LIMITED ENGAGEMENT
THE DULCET VOICE OF
MISS VANESSA FONTAINE
THE CHARLESTON NIGHTINGALE

She'd devised *The Charleston Nightingale* from memories of Jenny Lind, the famous Swedish Nightingale, who'd visited Charleston during her triumphant 1850 American tour. Vanessa's parents had bought the best available first-circle seats on opening night, because Vanessa had studied music, and they wanted to show her the greatest singer in the world. The performance became the most extraordinary artistic experience of young Vanessa's life, and afterwards she'd wanted to become a great singer like Jenny Lind. She studied harder than ever, everyone told her she was wonderful, and she decided to get married to the nicest young man she'd ever known. Then the war broke out, Beauregard died at Gettysburg, the South was destroyed, and music became the only practical skill she had left. Those damned Yankees, she thought bitterly. Oh God, please forgive me for hating them so.

There was a knock on the door. "It's time, Miss Fontaine," said McCabe.

She looked at herself in the mirror one last time, satisfied that her cosmetics were perfect. Then she threw her black shawl over her bright red satin gown and opened the door. She could hear Cunningham's baritone at the end of the hall. "And now, gentlemen, may I present for your entertainment pleasure . . . the lovely lady we've all been waiting for . . . the famous Charleston Nightingale . . . *Miss Vanessa Fontaine!*"

Applause trembled the timbers of the Black Cat Saloon as Vanessa made her way down the corridor. At its end, she handed the shawl to McCabe. "I hope they don't throw tomatoes," she said.

"Just toss 'em back," replied McCabe with a grin. "Good luck."

She stepped onto the stage; the saloon was jammed from bar to doorway, and Vanessa viewed the outlines of hats worn by cowboys, gamblers, lawyers, farmers, and other forms of masculine frontier life. She waited until the clapping died down, then folded her hands together and said in her inimitable purr, "Good evening, gentleman. I know that many of you were in the war, and so was I. With your kind permission, I'd like to sing a few songs from those great days."

Without piano accompaniment, standing alone in front of them, she held out her arms, filled her lungs with air, and began to warble one of the most popular songs of the recent conflict, "The Southern Soldier Boy."

> *"Bob Roebuck is my sweetheart's name,*
> *He's off to war and gone;*
> *He's fighting for his Nannie dear,*
> *His sword is buckled on. . . ."*

Her gentle voice wafted about the smoky saloon, and men could smell magnolia blossoms, taste mint juleps, and feel the power of King Cotton surge through their veins. Vanessa transported them to the lost kingdom that existed south of the Mason-Dixon Line seven years ago, when their hearts were young and jubilant.

> *"He's fighting for his own true love,*
> *His foes he does defy;*
> *He is the darling of my heart*
> *My Southern soldier boy."*

She sang the chorus, then plowed through the first verse once more, capturing them in her memory web. It gave her a lift to know that she could still dazzle an audience, despite the stupidity of her personal life. Although they were gathered in a cheesy San Antone saloon, it felt like a ballroom on the banks of the Ashley River, or a log cabin in the Alabama piney woods. Vanessa could evoke the tragedy of old Dixie clearly, because its flames still burned brightly in her not-so-innocent heart.

Once she'd loved a Southern soldier boy, too, and he should've been a poet, but he fell beneath the hooves of federal cavalry, and something in Vanessa fell with him. Perhaps it was her heart, but the world was never the same for her after Gettysburg.

There wasn't a dry eye in the house, and that included the eyes of the Charleston Nightingale as she threw herself into the final chorus of the her song.

> *"He is my only joy*
> *He is the darling of my heart*
> *My dearest Southern Soldier boy."*

The saloon exploded with applause as Vanessa took her first bow. Coins rained upon the stage, a hurrah went up from the gang at the bar, while an enthusiastic music lover jumped up and down near the door so he could get a better look over the sea of hats before him. Vanessa knew that she could do anything with them, and God had given her a special grace, though she hadn't yet divined its purpose. She drew herself erect and scanned their nostalgic faces, searching for a certain pair of high cheekbones and green eyes, but the Pecos Kid wasn't there, and all she could do was get on the with the show. Maybe in the next town—who knows? she thought, as the crowd quieted. Then she began her next Civil War classic, "A Georgia Volunteer."

Every man in the saloon had lost a brother, friend, or comrade in the Rebellion, and together with the Charleston Nightingale, remembered, mourned, and glorified the blood sacrifices to their noble cause. A few men sang with her, others stared into space, while some were passed out cold on their tables. Cunningham stood in the shadows and rubbed his hands together in anticipation of the take at the end of the night. She can stay as long as she wants, he determined, and maybe I'll up her salary before she decides to go somewhere else. This dizzy Southern belle is going to make me dirty rotten filthy stinking *rich*!

Duane lay on his cot, unable to sleep. Against his interests, he'd agreed to participate in a raid on a Fourth Cavalry pay wagon, of all things. Now that he was alone, with time to reflect, he saw that his hosts had cleverly manipulated his feelings of guilt and obligation.

The last thing he wanted was to shoot somebody in the Fourth Cavalry, and he had forebodings of new pitfalls during the Devil's Creek robbery. There was no way he could weasel out of it, because a man was only as good as his word. He tossed and turned, but somehow the criminal enterprise loomed in his mind and kept him awake. Duane had never stolen anything in his life, except for a couple of horses, but soon would participate in a major robbery against the Fourth Cavalry. If Colonel MacKenzie, commander of the Fourth, ever figured out that the Pecos Kid was mixed up in it, Duane Braddock might have to live in Mexico until he was a gray-bearded old man.

Just when he was regaining his health, a new pile of trouble had been dumped onto his lap. No matter what he did, or how fervent his prayers, his life continued to deteriorate. He wondered if God was trying to teach him a lesson, or if he was just a dumb, wandering kid that people tended to push around.

He couldn't help recalling the certainties of the monastery in the clouds. His most serious concern had been getting to choir practice on time. Some days, while singing Gregorian chants, he'd felt transported to heavenly realms, but then the devil tempted him with pretty Mexican girls, and he surrendered unconditionally.

I have no character, always take the easy way out, and I don't stand up for my principles. The cot creaked beneath him as he tried to find a comfortable spot. Why was I born to a mother and father who got themselves killed?

The world seemed out of balance to Duane, and he'd never fall asleep unless he could think of something pleasant. He searched for radiance through the tunnels of his mind, and eventually came upon a memory of his first great love, the former Miss Vanessa Fontaine.

It soothed him to recall her long elegant body, those incredible Celtic cheekbones, eyes like chips of ice, and the naughtiest pink tongue ever devised. Duane had experienced powerful religious ecstasies at the monastery in the clouds, but they'd been nothing compared with the reality of Miss Vanessa Fontaine.

Why do I think of her so often? he wondered. We were only together about two months, and it really didn't mean a damned thing at all. I'm sure she's forgotten all about me, and she's probably pregnant, so why doesn't she leave me alone?

Vanessa Fontaine paraded past gentlemen drunkards gathered the length of the bar, and they pounded their hands enthusiastically. Like the Queen of Sheba, she headed toward the batwing doors, followed by her faithful McCabe, his hand inside his coat, fingers resting on his Spiller & Burr. Vanessa could have her pick of men in the Black Cat Saloon; the knowledge of it stoked her feminine pride, and perhaps on another night, who could say what might develop?

"Buy you a drink, Miss Fontaine?" asked a goatee and big purple cravat.

A gentleman opened the batwing doors, and his eyes said, "Please take me home with you." She gave him a wry smile as she stepped into the cool night air. Thanksgiving was coming, she was far from home, following a young ex-lover into the Apache homeland, but too late to turn back now.

A horde of admirers, glasses of whiskey in their hands, followed her back to the hotel, providing protection like intoxicated knights of the roundtable. The evening had witnessed a triumphant return of Vanessa's singing career, and any doubts she'd had about her talents were dispelled. Moreover, she truly enjoyed being the talented and charming Charleston Nightingale instead of the gloomy and morbid Widow Dawes.

But there was one fly in the ointment: the Pecos Kid hadn't shown up to see the show. She wondered if he'd seen her name and rode in the opposite direction, or maybe he was hiding down Mexico way and didn't know she was in San Antone.

She arrived at a large flat one-story adobe hotel, and her praetorian guard came to a stop behind her. She blew them a kiss, they applauded, and she bowed low on the planked sidewalk. Then McCabe opened the door; she entered a carpeted lobby and plunged into the dark corridor beyond.

She and McCabe arrived at their suite of two adjoining rooms. He'd been assigned the one in front, with Vanessa in back. It was a far cry from the Arlington in downtown Austin, and Vanessa's bed had a permanent excavation in the middle, but at least everything was clean superficially.

As Vanessa was about to enter her personal room, she heard McCabe say, "Good night, ma'am. I'd like to say that you put on a helluva show, and I never knowed you could sing so good."

His praise was genuine, and he'd never said anything complimentary before. "I couldn't have done it without you," she replied graciously, "because you make me feel safe."

She entered her room, closed the door, removed her gown, and hung it in the closet. Then she washed her face and hands in the basin, changed to her nightgown, blew out the candle, and crawled into bed.

She felt exhausted, frustrated, and doubtful concerning her sanity. McCabe's footsteps rumbled on the far side of the door; they'd spent every day together since Austin, a strange enigma sleeping a few feet away, but thus far he'd been a gentleman, and he'd even appreciated her singing.

McCabe didn't interest her particularly, like her servants back at the old plantation. He did his job and that's all she cared about. Her most compelling concerns were for the so-called Pecos Kid. Is Duane Braddock worth this effort, she asked herself, or am I just a pathetic weak woman who needs young men and public admiration to make me feel worthwhile?

One morning, over eggs, bacon, grits, and coffee, Duane Braddock asked Dr. Montgomery, "Have you ever heard of a woman named Vanessa Fontaine?"

Dr. Montgomery cocked an eye. "Rings a bell, but I can't be sure."

"She's from Charleston, and last I heard, she was married to a lieutenant in the Fourth Cavalry."

"I recall visiting a relative in Charleston once," began Dr. Montgomery, "and saw a fair number of belles. They thought the sun rose and set between their legs, and some of them were so pretty, I thought that it *did* set between their legs. If you've fallen in love with a Charleston belle, you have my deepest sympathies. They were the most spoiled women that the world has ever produced."

Duane helped Dr. Montgomery with the dishes, then the doctor left to see a sick cow. Left to his own devices, Duane filled a gunnysack with empty cans and bottles, then lined them on a plank suspended by two barrels behind the bunkhouse. He took twenty paces backward, assumed his gunfighter's stance, and prepared for his first fast draw since being shot by the Apaches.

He bent his knees, hunched his shoulders, and poised his right hand above the worn walnut grips of his Colt. Then he took a deep breath, his hand darted to his gun, and his muscles felt jerky and foreign. The lethal weapon fell into his hand, he drew it quickly, thumbed back the hammer, and fired in one smooth motion. An empty bottle shattered like a rainbow in the bright morning sunlight.

"Not bad," said Cochrane, strolling into the yard. "Where'd you get that fast hand?"

"I'm way slower than usual," complained Duane. "I wonder if I'll ever be like I was."

"I've been shot a few times, and made a complete recovery. Don't rush things and you'll be just fine. Say, do you think you can teach me to shoot faster?"

"The principles are simple," explained Duane. "It's better to aim low than high. It's not the first shot that counts, but the first *accurate* shot. Practice makes perfect. That's it in a nutshell."

Cochrane faced the bottles and cans, worked into his gunfighter's stance, but it didn't appear correct to Duane's critical eye; the officer was too stiff and mechanical. Then Cochrane reached for his Remington, snatched it out of its holster, thumbed the hammer, and fired. A can went flying into the bright blue sky.

"Not bad," said Duane.

Cochrane fired again, gunfire echoed off Lost Canyon, and a crowd of irregulars gathered to watch, among them Johnny Pinto, thumbs hooked in his gunbelt, head cocked to the side. Cochrane ran out of cartridges, then it was Duane's turn again. Duane dropped into his gunfighter crouch, his hand suddenly snapped to his Colt, and this time his muscles were oiled by recent experience. The gun leapt into his hand; he fired once, twice, thrice, and tin cans went toppling through the sky. Then he tossed the gun up, caught it behind his back, spun around, and drilled an empty vinegar bottle. It exploded into bits, he thumbed back the hammer. *Click*; out of ammunition.

The crowd applauded lightly, except for Johnny Pinto. Captain Cochrane looked at Duane with new respect. "I've never seen anything like it in my life," he confessed.

Duane thumbed cartridges into shiny iron sleeves as Johnny Pinto scuffled closer. "Ain't it strange how Butterfield can shoot like a whole man, but he ain't healthy enough to fight with his fists like a real man?"

Duane smiled thinly. "You'll get your chance before long, Johnny. Are you in a hurry to get beat up?"

A few outlaws snickered, and Johnny believed that Duane was making fun of him. "I'll rip yer fuckin' haid off," he swore.

Their eyes met, and a silent vow was made. Everybody knew that when the fight came, it would be a humdinger.

"How long till yer better?" asked Johnny.

"A few more weeks," Duane replied. "Until then, stay away from me."

"You don't tell me where to go, varmint. I go where I want."

Johnny saw the hollow eye of a Colt .44 looking at him and stepped back in surprise. Again, Duane had pulled a lightning draw. Johnny tried to smile. "You took me by surprise."

"One minute you're here," Duane replied, "next minute you're gone. Step lightly around me, cowboy. That's all I've got to say."

"You wouldn't dare shoot me in cold blood!"

Duane pulled the trigger, and lead flew through the crown of Johnny Pinto's hat. For a moment Johnny thought he'd been shot in the head, and he staggered dizzily from side to side. Then he took off his hat and inspected the bullet hole, as everyone laughed. His face turned bright red; he'd never been so humiliated in his life and wanted to choke Duane Braddock to death, but Duane Braddock still held the Colt on him.

"You owe me a new hat," Johnny said.

"Be glad you're still alive," replied Duane. "And get the hell away from me. Next time I'll aim for your heart."

Johnny Pinto considered retreat a sign of weakness, but had no viable alternative. He put one foot behind the other and backed off, holding his hands where Duane could see them. "I'm going to beat the piss out of you someday," he said evenly. "But you'll probably weasel out of that one too."

"There's no backing out, Johnny—for you or me. I'll see you in a few weeks."

Duane waited until Johnny was a fair distance away, then holstered his Colt. If there was one thing Duane didn't like, it was bullies. Johnny was the typical loud-mouthed birdbrain, but this time he'd leaned on the wrong cowboy. *He's spoiling for a fight*, mulled Duane, *and am I going to give it to him.*

Target practice continued, irregulars took turns firing at bottles and cans; it sounded like a thunderstorm in Lost Canyon. Duane noted Juanita approaching, pulling a strand of black hair from her eye. "You are some shooter, but you had better watch out for Johnny Pinto. One day when you least expect it, he will be behind you."

"Maybe one day I'll be behind him."

Juanita shrugged. "If I were you, I would kill him while I had the chance."

"Could you really *kill* somebody, Juanita?" he asked, out of curiosity.

"What makes you think I haven't?" she replied.

"I'm sure the nuns have taught you better."

She snorted derisively. "If you go to hell, don't have five mortal sins—have ten mortal sins, and make them good juicy ones."

Now Duane understood why Cochrane had abandoned the Civil War for her. She had a compelling point of view, a figure built for comfort, and saucy sparks in her dark brown eyes. *They say that when Catholics break away from the church, they really go loco.*

Gunfire echoed across the ridges as outlaws honed shooting skills. Captain Cochrane loaded his gun as he neared Duane and Juanita. "What are you talking about so earnestly?" he asked, a touch of jealousy in his voice.

"Johnny Pinto," replied Juanita. "He is the most evil man here."

Cochrane raised his eyebrows. "But he's a damned fine soldier. War has its own rules, and I'd make a pact with the devil himself if I could strike a blow against the Yankees."

"Sometimes I think you already have made a pact with the devil, Ricardo."

He looked askance at her. "What's that supposed to mean?"

She didn't reply vocally, but her expression said it all. With a barely perceptible toss of her shoulder, she turned and headed toward her hacienda.

Duane and Cochrane gazed at her retreating figure. "What a woman," Cochrane said.

"You can say that again," replied Duane.

"She always hits me where it hurts most."

"Don't they all?"

Both men chortled. "Don't get any ideas," Cochrane said, "because she's mine."

"I'm no bird dog, and I've got my own woman troubles. You ever heard of a Charleston belle named Vanessa Fontaine?"

"What'd she look like?"

"Tall, blond, kind of pretty?"

"That could describe half the belles in Charleston. You can't tell me about Charleston belles, because my mother was one of them. I truly believe that the only person I've ever been afraid of was my mother. She would've been a great general, because she was utterly remorseless in everything she did."

"Sounds a lot like Vanessa Fontaine."

"Well, you know what the old soldiers say. The best way to forget one woman is find another as soon as possible." Cochrane leaned closer. "We're going to Ceballos Rios in about a week to buy ordnance. If I were you, I'd pick out a nice religious Mexican gal like Juanita while you're there. I tell you, she'll make you happier than any spoiled ex–Charleston belle."

"Sorry, but I'm not going to any towns until I'm fully recovered. I don't take chances, as I'm sure you understand."

"You won't have to take chances because you'll be riding with us, and we'll look out for you."

"I'd rather look out for myself."

"You don't trust us?" Cochrane frowned. "I don't want you here with Juanita while I'm away. The thought of two Catholics scheming and plotting is enough to freeze my blood. Nobody'll dare mess with you in Ceballos Rios if you're with me, because I do a lot of business there. It's a Comanchero town, and I can promise you a grand time. They have some of the prettiest Mexican gals you'll ever see, so wipe that unhappy expression off your face. You're behaving as if I'm going to put you before the firing squad. I'm doing you a favor and you can't even see it."

"What if I say no?" Duane inquired.

"You won't," replied Cochrane.

Vanessa had given McCabe the night off so he could settle his business prior to departure for Escondido. She curled on her bed with a map, pot of tea, and biscuits from the local bakery. The next leg of her trip was to Fort Clark, a far more hazardous route than the ride to San Antone.

Her path led through land contested by Apaches, Comanches, and Kiowa, while the Fourth Cavalry was spread thinner than paper. But I'm sure the Indian menace is exaggerated, she tried to convince herself. Everyone knows they just use poor Indians to sell more newspapers, right?

There was a knock on the door, and Vanessa reached for the derringer on the desk. Who could it be at that time of night? She thumbed back the hammer. "Yes?"

A woman's voice came to her through the wooden planks. "My name is Rosalie Tyler, and I live down the hall."

Vanessa opened the door a crack and aimed at a short stout brunette in her late thirties or early forties standing in the corridor, a big friendly smile on her face. "I've heard that you're an army wife."

"I was," Vanessa confessed. "My husband was killed by the Apaches."

"My husband is Major Marcus Tyler, and we're staying in this hotel along with some other army people. The major suggested I invite you to have a drink with us." Rosalie placed her hand over her mouth, as if about to confide a secret. "We're going to a real saloon together, can you imagine?"

Rosalie spoke with a Northern accent, but looked like she enjoyed a good time. "Are you stationed in San Antone?" asked Vanessa.

"No, we're on our way to Fort Clark with a detachment of cavalry. They're camped on the edge of town, perhaps you've seen them about."

Vanessa recalled seeing bluecoat soldiers on the streets of San Antone. She didn't want to pass time with damned Yankees, but their destination was the same as hers, and maybe she could hitch a ride. "I'd be delighted to accompany you," Vanessa said graciously. "Let me get my shawl."

Why do I let people talk me into things? Duane wondered as he headed for the outhouse. The last thing I need is a Comanchero town. I should've insisted on my right to stay here, but that damned Cochrane bamboozles me every time.

It was after supper, dishes had been washed, and the time had come to prepare for bed. Duane neared the outhouse when its door opened and Johnny Pinto appeared.

Both men scowled as Duane unlimbered the fingers of his right hand. Johnny Pinto walked straight toward him, and Duane had to get out of the way before he was run down.

"You fuckin' coward," Johnny uttered in a low voice. "I wonder how yer a-gonna wheedle out of yer fight with me. But our trails will cross again someday, and then I'll see what yer made of."

"You won't have to wait long. I promise."

"A promise from you ain't worth a fiddler's fuck."

Personal insults felt like daggers through Duane's orphaned heart. They stared at each other, and Duane disliked Johnny with a passion as incomprehensible as love. It wasn't Johnny's unpleasant appearance, or even the foul stench arising from his body, but his hateful spitefulness toward the world. Both men dismissed each other from their presences and continued in their previous directions.

Duane returned to Dr. Montgomery's hut while thinking of his upcoming war with Johnny Pinto. Duane had studied pugilism at the monastery in the clouds, because his former spiritual adviser, Brother Paolo, had been a professional boxer prior to taking vows. Johnny was shorter than Duane, with less of a reach, so that meant fighting long range, and never clinching under any circumstances. Duane wanted to smash his fist into the middle of Johnny Pinto's face.

Why do I detest him so? Duane asked himself. Isn't it a sin to hate like this? But Johnny Pinto had attempted to intimidate Duane, and the Pecos Kid had to draw the line. Duane pressed his fingers against the scar on his stomach. It was tender, but a few more weeks ought to heal it fine. Johnny Pinto, you'll never insult anybody again after I finish with you. There's no lesson like a good whupping, and that's what you're going to get from me.

The officers and ladies walked beside the San Antonio River as lamps within adobe huts nearby lit their way. Plunking pianos could be heard from the saloon district, along with an occasional hoot or gunshot.

The leader of the expedition was Major Marcus Tyler, Fourth Cavalry, and junior officers, plus their women, hung on his words as he described the history of the region. "The Spaniards have been coming to this place since the 1600s, and in 1718, the presidio of San Antonio de Bexar was built by the Mexican Army on this very spot. It became the most important Spanish and Mexican settlement in Texas prior to the Revolution."

He referred to the Texas Revolution of 1835, not the American one of 1776. Texans viewed their state as a special country within America, because it had been independent under Sam Houston for a few brief years. Vanessa walked among the women, a black cape covering her green velvet dress. It felt strange to be with normal Americans instead of the drunkards at the Black Cat Saloon.

They headed back toward their hotel, Vanessa waiting for the opportunity to ask if she could accompany them to Fort Clark, but the amateur historian was continuing his lecture. "Straight ahead you can see the Alamo itself, where Davy Crockett, James Bowie, Bill Travis, and four hundred other Americans were slaughtered by Santa Anna on March sixth, 1836. It was the turning point of the war, for Texans fought with new determination afterward. They remembered the Alamo, and six weeks later defeated Santa Anna at San Jacinto, proving once again that the morale of soldiers is more important than mere quantity."

The old Catholic mission was shrouded in shadows, with no hint of the bloodletting that had taken place less than forty years ago. Flowers were planted on either side of the entrance, with cottonwood trees in the yard. Davy Crockett, Jim Bowie, and Bill Travis fought hand to hand and man to man against overwhelming masses of Mexican soldiers on that very spot, while the fate of Texas hung in the balance. Vanessa admired the hard-bitten heroes, and her heart swelled with pride in America. This'd be a great country if it weren't for the Yankees.

They stopped at the Zapato Viejo Saloon on their way back to the hotel, and sat at a round table in a corner. A Mexican waitress brought them a round of drinks, and the officers' wives gazed with amazement at real cowboys, vaqueros, and gentlemen in suits all talking at the same time, as a terrific din filled the low-ceilinged establishment. It featured no stage, only a chair in the corner, where a Mexican guitarist in an immense sombrero and red garters on his arms picked a lively tune.

Major Tyler leaned toward Vanessa and said sympathetically, "I understand that your husband was killed in action recently."

"Yes, by Apaches. He truly loved the army, and you lost a good officer when you lost Lieutenant Clayton Dawes."

He took her hand. "I'm so sorry, Mrs. Dawes. You must be utterly devastated. Whatever has brought you to San Antone?"

"I'm on my way to Fort Clark, and I understand that you're traveling in that direction yourself. I wonder if I could tag along."

"We're carrying guns and ammunition, and every Indian would like to get their hands on the merchandise. It might not be the best time for a trip, because Indians have been increasing their depredations as of late. I'd recommend that you remain in San Antone until the uprising dies down."

"If it's safe enough for your wife to travel, it's safe enough for me. But perhaps you don't want a civilian along."

Major Tyler smiled warmly. "You're not a civilian, Mrs. Dawes. Your late husband was in the Fourth Cavalry. If you want to travel with us, you're surely welcome. You're an accomplished singer, I've heard, and perhaps you can entertain around our campfire, to cheer the men."

"I'll do my best, although I only know Southern songs."

"Maybe we'll teach you some new ones. The war has been over for nearly seven years, and it's time to get on with building America, don't you agree?"

"Of course," replied Vanessa, because she'd say any-thing to get her way. "There are good and bad people on both sides of the Mason-Dixon Line."

The officers sipped whiskey and discussed the impending journey to Fort Clark while the women drank sarsaparilla and chattered about families, recipes, household chores—the usual women talk. Once again, Vanessa felt like an alien, her interests always different, and how could she ever explain Duane Braddock?

Her eyes roved the saloon, and she was surprised to notice McCabe sitting with a brawny, bearded fellow at a table against the far wall. They were talking earnestly, heads close together as if making a secret deal, gazing into each other eyes, and then, all at once, McCabe gesticulated in a way that seemed odd. Vanessa's heart stumbled as the truth dawned upon her. McCabe and his newly found friend drained their glasses, left the saloon, and headed for a quiet hotel room, or perhaps a walk in the sage.

Now at last she understood her bodyguard's peculiar reactions. She nearly burst into nervous laughter, but caught herself at the last moment. I'm chasing a man twelve years younger than I, who'll probably spit in my eye when I find him, so who am I to judge my body-guard? The main thing is that I've just hitched a ride to Fort Clark, and what a clever little Charleston girl I am.

CHAPTER 7

ON THE WESTERN COAHUILIAN desert, after reaching the crest of a certain hill, weary riders can see in the distance a large smoky village of adobe huts, wooden structures, and corrals of stolen animals scattered on a vast desert plain.

It is Ceballos Rios, a Comanchero town far from regular trails, out of the way of the Mexican Army. On a cloudy autumn afternoon, Cochrane led his irregulars down the busy main street, and each ex-soldier maintained his hand near his gun, ready to fire and ride hard at the sound of trouble.

But nobody paid attention to the newest gang in a town full of them, the only law provided by the Comancheros themselves. Comancheros were outlaws and renegades with mixed Indian, Mexican, and American blood, and they dealt in stolen goods among the three civilizations, speaking all languages, the perfect middlemen.

Duane scanned alleyways and rooftops for possible assassins. He'd never been in a Comanchero town, had no idea what to expect, and hoped nobody recognized him. Riding down the street from the opposite direction came a dozen Apache warriors who looked like they'd just returned from a raid, and Duane wondered whose horses they were selling, and how many dead Texans they'd left behind.

Duane couldn't tell the Comancheros from Mexicans, because they were all dark-skinned, wearing the same vaquero clothing, and armed similarly. A few American outlaws roamed about, but they were a minority. No law-abiding citizen would ever come to a Comanchero town.

Cochrane steered his white horse toward a sign that said CANTINA. The irregulars dismounted, tied their horses to the hitching post, and looked around warily. Cochrane didn't have to give commands, because each knew his part perfectly. They crowded into the cantina, and Duane followed Cochrane through the door. They landed in a large rectangular room with adobe walls. Men drank and made deals while waitresses served chili, tortillas, and a variety of beverages. The establishment was half-filled with patrons, the bar to the left, another on the right, and two pool tables in back, surrounded by men playing or laying bets. Also on the premises were a roulette wheel, a chuck-a-luck, and a few faro games. A disreputable-looking American with a gray beard, attired in a dirty frock coat, strolled among the tables and played the violin badly.

Cochrane and his men sat at several tables in the same section of the saloon, and Duane made sure his back was to the wall. His insides ached from the long ride, but he looked forward to a good glass of mescal and maybe some dancing girls later on. A few tables away, Johnny Pinto scrutinized him, but Duane had become accustomed to Johnny's hostile glances.

A sloe-eyed waitress approached the table, and she wore a long tan peasant dress, with a blouse made of clean undyed cotton. "¿Qué queres, señores?"

Cochrane spoke to her in Spanish. "Yo *quero hablar con Lopez. Me nombre es Cochrane, y el me sabe.* (I want to speak with Lopez. My name is Cochrane, and he knows me.)" Then he ordered a round of mescal for the men.

The waitress pranced toward a corridor at the rear of the saloon, and Duane noticed an elderly Mexican vaquero with a long white mustache, staring at him from his stool at the bar. Duane positioned his hat low over his eyes and turned in another direction.

His eyes fell on a portly prostitute squirming on a Mexican's lap, while another prostitute led an American toward the back passageway. It's another den of iniquity, surmised Duane, and here I am in the middle again. Duane was tempted to have a little fling with a prostitute, but he'd been with them in the past, a sordid transaction in his estimation.

"Think I'll shoot me some pool," said Johnny Pinto. He stood, hiked up his pants, and headed toward the tables in back. It was a breach of orders, they were supposed to stay together, and Duane noticed the corners of Cochrane's mouth turn down barely perceptibly.

The waitress returned and said to Cochrane, "In back."

"Come with me," Cochrane said to Duane. "Stay close and you'll be fine."

Duane checked the position of his Colt, then followed Cochrane toward the corridor. He noticed the same old white-mustachioed Mexican following his progress, then the Mexican turned and said something to the bartender, who examined Duane with renewed interest.

Cochrane and Duane came to a door at the end of the corridor. It was opened by a Mexican clerk, and Duane found himself in a large office furnished with padded chairs, while a portly man with a flowing brown mustache sat behind the desk.

"I am so happy to see you again," said the Comanchero, flashing a friendly smile. "Have a seat and let me get you some mescal."

"I want to introduce my friend Duane Butterfield," Cochrane replied.

Lopez looked a Duane, paused, and a quizzical expression came over his face. "Do I know you from someplace?"

"Never saw you in my life," replied Duane.

Lopez smiled constantly, revealing tobacco-stained teeth. He poured two glasses of mescal and held them out to Cochrane and Duane. "I have not seen you for a long time, Capitán Cochrane, and I have worry that maybe the americano army has got you."

"They'll never get me, but I need ammunition and dynamite." He unbuttoned his shirt pocket, took out a folded sheet of paper, and tossed it onto Lopez's desk.

Lopez studied the itemized list, then nodded and smiled. "When would you like it?"

"First thing in the morning, and I've got the gold in my pocket right now."

Lopez laughed sardonically. "If only all my customers were like you, *capitán*. You are a man of honor, and I try to be a man of honor, too, but you know how it is." His eyes turned to Duane. "Are you sure I don't know you?"

"Don't believe so," Duane replied.

Lopez looked him up and down, trying to place him. He saw many American outlaws, and it was hard to keep up. Lopez returned his gaze to Cochrane. "And how is Juanita?"

"Juanita and I are getting married."

Lopez appeared surprised.

"I've decided," Cochrane continued, "to settle down like a natural man and have a family. I'm not getting any younger."

"We are all marching steadily to our graves, my *capitán,* and sometimes we wonder what we are doing with our lives. Who is taking over your men—this one here?" He nodded toward Duane.

"This one isn't in my irregulars," replied Cochrane. "He's a friend."

"I think I have seen his peecture on a wanted poster." Lopez looked at Duane and grinned. "Is possible?"

"Yes," replied Duane.

Cochrane interjected, "He says that his name is Duane Butterfield, but I think he's lying."

Lopez looked reproachfully at Duane. "How can you lie to a friend?"

"My name is nobody's business."

Lopez shook his hand as if it were wet. "He must be wanted for something very bad, no?"

"Yes," replied Duane.

"I found him on the desert," Cochrane said, "and he was damned near dead."

"He does not look so dead now, but we all have certain facts that we want to conceal, eh, gentleman?" Lopez was laughing at what he considered a joke when an urgent knock came to the door. The Comanchero leader sat straighter in his chair. "Who is it?"

The door opened, and a waitress stood in the opening with a tray in her hands, an expression of consternation on her face. "*Un problema grande* (big trouble)," she said.

Lopez pulled a double-barreled shotgun off the wall, opened a desk drawer, and stuffed a handful of cartridges into his voluminous pocket. "I have to take care of a *problema*, and I hope you will excuse me."

"Hell, we'll go with you," Cochrane replied. "We wouldn't want to miss the fun."

Cochrane nodded to Duane, and Duane found himself drawn into the vortex yet again. He followed Cochrane and Lopez down the hall to the main room of the saloon, where everyone gathered around the pool tables. A middle-aged Comanchero was facing a gringo who needed a shave, Johnny Pinto himself, and both appeared ready to draw and fire.

Lopez strolled boldly between them, aiming the shotgun first in the direction of one, then the other. "What is going on here!"

The Comanchero's name was Valencio, and he glared at Johnny Pinto on the other side of the pool table. "That gringo has call me a liar, and I am going to keel him."

"Not in here you are not, because somebody else will end up with the mess. If you want to keel somebody, do it outside." Then Lopez turned to Johnny Pinto. "That goes for you too."

Johnny Pinto didn't bat an eyelash. "I don't give a damn where I shoot him. Watch my back, boys. I'm a-gonna show this greaser what pool is all about."

Johnny swaggered down the corridor, thumbs

hooked in his belt. He'd just lost a pool game, but had accused Valencio of scratching his last shot. Johnny preferred to win, and mere facts had little significance, unless they buttressed his interests. He stepped into a backyard strewn with barrels of trash, piles of wood, and a privy with a door on sagging hinges. Johnny positioned himself so that the moon would be shining into his opponent's eyes.

The crowd spilled outside, carrying his opponent with them. Valencio's chest was crossed with bandoliers of ammunition, his sombrero sat on the back of his head, and a long mustache trailed beneath his chin. He faced Johnny, spread his legs apart, and settled into his gunfighter's crouch.

The crowd gathered around, and Duane tagged toward the background, curious to see a gunfight from the spectators' viewpoint. The combatants were poised to fire, but it was difficult to discern a man's capacities from looks alone. Otis Puckett, the famous gunfighter from Laredo, had been Humpty-Dumpty in a cowboy hat.

Again, Lopez strolled between them. "It is a beautiful night to die," he said, "but foolish to die over nothing. What is this about, *compañeros*?"

"I told you he has call me a liar," Valencio said. "There is nothing to talk about, and I will accept no apology."

"You damned sure won't get one from me," replied Johnny Pinto. "You're just another no-good shit-eating son of a bitch, but you've done cheated the wrong man this time. I'm a-gonna to count to three."

The time for gentle persuasion had long past; Lopez stepped into the crowd, and the fight was about to commence.

"One," said Johnny.

But Valencio didn't feel like waiting. Instead he jerked his hand toward his gun while keeping his eyes fastened on his target. To his dismay, his target was hauling iron. Valencio had the sudden realization that he was going to die, but all he could do was go down like a true hombre. He drew his gun as a red flash appeared before him, and then a mighty roar filled his ears. Everything went blank a split second later, and he was dead before he hit the ground.

The gunshot reverberated across Ceballos Rios, and Johnny Pinto felt drenched with fire. He stood like a statue with his gun aimed straight ahead as his opponent fell at his feet. Johnny's eyes filled with tears, an indescribable ecstasy came over him, and at that moment he believed he could do anything, even fly over the rooftops of Ceballos Rios. All eyes on him, he puffed out his chest and stood a little taller. "Anybody else want to play," he asked out the corner of his mouth, "or can I put my piece away now?"

Nobody stepped forward to redeem the honor of the fallen Comanchero, and never had Johnny Pinto drawn faster in his life, in his opinion. He felt invincible, his hand had a life of its own, and he was certain that he could defeat anyone. "Shucks," he muttered as he was about to drop his gun into its holster.

Then, out the corner of his eye, he spotted Duane Butterfield at the rear of the crowd. Johnny decided the time had come to kill the man who irked him most. He knew that Butterfield was fast, but no one could be faster than Johnny Pinto on that night of nights.

He turned toward Duane and said to himself, What the hell, I'm sure I can take him. He smiled crookedly as he walked closer, and the crowd parted to make way for him. Duane saw him coming and figured what was on his mind. The Pecos Kid didn't feel up to snuff, but couldn't run away either.

Johnny came to a stop in front of him. "You think you've got a fast hand? Well, let's see how fast it really is."

"Wait a minute," said Cochrane, strolling toward them from the sidelines. "I gave Duane my word that he wouldn't have to worry about gunplay while he was in town, so leave him alone, Johnny."

Johnny snorted derisively. "That sickly son of a bitch is always hidin' behind somebody's apron strings. He talks big, but he ain't never willin' to back it up. Onc't he drawed on me when I wasn't lookin', but this time I'm ready fer 'im. Out of my way, Cochrane. This ain't yer fight."

"Oh, yes it is, Johnny. I gave Duane my word, so either walk away or get ready to draw *on me.*"

Johnny's triumph was transformed into murderous frustration. "Why is it that Duane Butterfield allus gits special treatment?" he asked. "Everybody has to fight their own battles 'cept him." Johnny Pinto pointed his finger at Duane and hollered, "Yer a yellerbelly coward and everybody knows it." Then he pursed his lips and spat at Duane.

Tiny droplets landed like acid on Duane's cheeks, and he felt visceral loathing for the killer braggart pig. Duane knew that ninety percent of his draw was back and wondered whether to accept the challenge.

Then a new voice came to him from the crowd. The speaker was the old gray-haired Mexican whom Duane had seen sitting at the bar. He looked at Johnny Pinto and said, "Señor, you do not know me and I do not know you, but I know this man here. He is very famous in Texas, he has killed many men, and I have seen him kill with my own eyes. That is the Pecos Kid, he is much faster than you, and you will die if you press this fight. I have no stake in this—I am telling you for your own good."

Johnny appeared thunderstruck by the news. He looked at Duane again and giggled nervously. "Him?"

"His name is Duane Braddock, but he is known as the Pecos Kid."

Duane's blood chilled as all eyes turned to him. Cochrane asked, "Is that right, Duane?"

Duane nodded, keeping his eyes pinned tightly on Johnny Pinto.

"To hell with the Pecos Kid!" hollered Johnny. "There's a fast hand for every whoop and holler in Texas, and I ain't afraid of nobody. Let's see how fast you are, Pecos."

Cochrane stepped forward, the patch over his eye like a hole through his head. "I've told you that I've sworn to defend this man, and he still hasn't recovered from his wounds."

"I've recovered enough," replied Duane. "Please step out of the way."

"I thought you weren't well enough to fight."

"I'm well enough to fight that scum over there, and I'd be grateful if you'd mind your own business, sir."

Cochrane opened his mouth to reply, took one look at Duane's eyes, and thought better of it. He moved back, and Johnny faced Duane with nothing in the way.

"Think it over, señor," said the old man to Johnny Pinto. "That man shot Otis Puckett, and Otis Puckett was the fastest gun alive."

Johnny's arrogance faltered, pride flew out his ears, and he wondered if he was getting carried away. Who's the Pecos Kid, and is he what everybody says?

"I'm waiting on you," Duane said.

Johnny smiled nervously as he gazed at the Pecos Kid. If Duane Braddock had shot the fastest gun alive, the conclusion was obvious. Not today, thought Johnny, but maybe I can turn this thing around. He forced a playful smile. "Mr. Pecos might be the fastest gun alive, but I'll bet he wouldn't dare take me without a gun. Right, Mr. Pecos?"

Duane couldn't tolerate Johnny Pinto's taunts anymore. He should wait another two weeks until his wounds were fully healed, but Johnny had *spat* upon him, the supreme insult. Duane was confident that he could receive a good solid punch to the guts without fainting, or so he hoped, and Johnny should be punished for his murderous ways. "Up to you," he said.

Johnny Pinto wanted to laugh with joy. "Wait a minute—does that mean yer a-gonna fight me right naow with yer fists?"

Duane handed his hat to Cochrane, then proceeded to unbutton his shirt. Johnny Pinto had his answer, and his excitement mounted as he saw fresh purple scars emerge on Duane's body. Johnny knew how to dig punches to a man's body, among other saloon tricks. He passed his hat to the old Mexican, then unbuttoned his own shirt.

The night air was cold and bracing against Johnny's sunken chest. Johnny lacked the muscle development of Duane, and looked vaguely like a lizard as he worked his shoulders and kicked his ankles. Johnny knew about the knee below the beltline, the thumb in the eye, and once he'd bitten off half of a man's ear. He raised his hands and said, "I'm ready when you are, Mr. Pecos Kid. What a dumb fuckin' name."

Duane was tempted to pound Johnny's head through the ground, but instead recalled the training that Brother Paolo had provided. The first rule was never fight emotionally, and second was a boxer must impose his will upon his opponent. Johnny Pinto's spittle still burned Duane's cheeks, the insult singed his heart, and Duane Braddock raised his fists into the high position taught him by Brother Paolo.

Cochrane, Beasley, Walsh, and the other members of the gang stood among the crowd of Comancheros. There was no referee, no ring, and no rest between rounds. Some spectators held bottles of whiskey and placed bets in rapid-fire Spanish. Johnny Pinto advanced sideways, holding both fists at chest level, wrists slightly bent. He was going to take the fight to Duane, so Duane danced lightly to the side, realizing with dismay that his speed was off. He tried to convince himself that it wouldn't impede his defense, yet Brother Paolo had taught him that speed was as important as power and accuracy of punches.

Johnny shifted direction, in an effort to block Duane's path, so Duane darted back toward his previous direction. Johnny stopped, made an exasperated expression, and said, "I thought you wanted to fight."

Duane flicked a stiff jab at Johnny's face. Johnny didn't see it coming; it caught him flush on the nose and drove him backward. Johnny raised his hands to protect his head, then Duane threw a long looping left hook under Johnny's elbow and into his kidney. Johnny muffled a scream as he stood toe to toe with Duane and hurled a solid shot at Duane's midsection. Johnny's aim was true, and his fist buried itself into Duane's belly scar.

Duane darted to the left, gasping for breath and hoping he had no internal injuries. He changed direction again, realizing that he wasn't well enough to fight, but he'd seen an opening in Johnny's defense. Johnny Pinto was the kind of fighter who lunged, so Duane bounced lightly, feinted a left jab, and threw a clean whistling right lead at Johnny's ear. It connected; Duane skipped out of the way, and Johnny attempted to hammer Duane's scar, but Duane was long gone.

Johnny realized with sinking heart that he was slower than Duane, but he always had a puncher's chance. He crowded toward Duane, keeping the pressure on, hoping to open Duane up. He'd seen Duane wince painfully after the stomach punch, and knew what to do.

Johnny jumped in front of Duane and threw a jab, but Duane kept dodging away as if he wore steel springs in his boots. Johnny tried to cut him off, but Duane launched another jab into Johnny's already bleeding nose. The blow jarred Johnny's brain, but he had the presence to hurl a quick counterpunch, which landed in the cool night air.

Johnny turned in the direction Duane had gone, when another punch landed on his nose, and it felt like a spear driven into his skull. He raised his arms to cover his bleeding proboscis, and a series of new blows smashed into his kidneys. He took a step back, threw a wild punch, ducked, and got walloped by a zooming uppercut.

Johnny's head snapped back, he lost his balance and fell onto his ass. A roar went up from the crowd, and he blinked his eyes, trying to understand what was happening. He was so dazed he'd forgotten his name.

A shirtless black-haired man danced in front of him, Mexicans jabbered noisily, and the clinking of coins could be heard. Johnny was getting the shit beat out of him, and Cochrane wore a half smile of pleasure on his face. Johnny had to turn the fight around, and the best way was get inside Duane's defense, work that belly, and cut him down to size. Call it courage or pigheaded stupidity, but Johnny Pinto drew himself to his feet.

He found Lopez standing before him, an expression of mercy on his features. "This has gone far enough, eh, *compañero*? Why don't you walk away while you still can?"

"Out of my way," Johnny said levelly.

Lopez stepped back, and Johnny advanced on Duane. His plan was to dive onto Duane, suffer whatever punishment would hit him, and wrestle Duane to the ground. Then, in the rough-and-tumble, he'd rip open those scars with his bare hands.

Duane danced in front of Johnny, flicking out his jab. Johnny dived underneath it and reached for Duane's legs, but Duane wasn't there, and Johnny landed painfully in the dirt. He spun around, covering his face with his arm, because he feared that Duane would kick him in the face.

Instead, Duane was keeping his distance, constantly in motion, chin tucked behind his shoulder, hands protecting his face. Johnny rolled to his feet and wiped dust off his jeans. "You ain't a fighter—yer a runner. Why don't you stand still and fight like a man?"

Johnny raised his hands and threw a jab at Duane's lips, but Duane moved his head three inches to the left while simultaneously hooking Johnny to the kidney. It was another painful shot. Johnny hooked back, but Duane caught the punch on his arm, ducked underneath a right cross, and threw an uppercut at Johnny's solar plexus. It connected on target; Johnny was momentarily paralyzed, and then it felt as if a horse had run into him.

Duane clobbered him across the snoot yet again, and Johnny reeled back, his lips pulped. He growled angrily and ran into another straight right. The next thing Johnny Pinto knew, he was lying on the ground, his eyelids held open by Lopez's thumbs. "Are you all right, señor?"

"Get the fuck away from me."

Johnny pushed Lopez away and lurched to his feet. He staggered first to the left and then to the right as crickets and birds chirped inside his head. He knew that he couldn't outbox Duane no matter what he did, but wasn't ready to give up. "This ain't no fair fight," he said, "'cause yer a professional fighter. But I've got somethin' right here that'll equal us out."

He reached behind his back and yanked out his bowie knife, then brought it around and held the blade straight up. "You got the sand to handle a *real* fight?" he asked.

I should quit while I'm ahead, considered Duane, but I'll never back down to this pig, and I don't care what he pulls on me. Duane had been trained in knife fighting by the Apaches themselves, and believed that he could defeat any white man easily. Clenching his teeth, he reached to his boot and withdrew his Apache knife. It had a carved wooden handle and an eight-inch razor-sharp blade.

"From now on, no rules," Johnny said.

"Now just a moment," Cochrane declared at the edge of the crowd. "Knife fights can be pretty bloody. Maybe the both of you'd better cool down."

"Nothin' to cool down fer," said Johnny. "Unless shithead over thar wants to give up. Otherwise I'm going home with his ears in my back pocket."

"You're not going anywhere," Duane replied, holding his knife in front of him and getting low.

Johnny was swelling around the eyes, his face had been busted up, and his nose flattened. He'd piss blood for the rest of the month, but Duane didn't feel sorry for him as he looked for likely openings. The Apaches had taught him that speed is everything in a knife fight.

Johnny feinted his blade toward Duane, but Duane was tense as a puma about to strike. Then Johnny shouted and shoved his knife toward Duane's belly, but Duane danced to the side and whipped his edge through Johnny's forearm. Blood spurted out, the blade had sliced to the bone, and Johnny couldn't suppress a howl. Duane saw three openings, but chose not to kill Johnny at that moment.

Tendons had been severed, and Johnny's knife dropped from his numbed right hand. Lips quivering with pain, he bent his knees and picked it up in his left hand. He didn't have to say anything—his eyes told the story. He was prepared to kill Duane Braddock or die in the attempt.

He grunted like a bull as he charged Duane, slashing his knife at Duane's face, but the Pecos Kid dodged gracefully and lopped off a chunk of Johnny's left forearm. Johnny screeched mightily, and all he could do was adopt a defensive pose. But Duane didn't attack. Blood poured out of Johnny's arteries and veins, and his torment was nightmarish. Johnny could barely see, everything spun around him, his face was pallid, and he tried to find his opponent; then his knees gave out, he dropped to the ground, and in spite of himself, a sob escaped his lips.

The schoolmaster's son struggled to hold back tears, but agony urged him onward, and his ravaged pride added the final touch. His face contorted by suffering, his body sagged, and the stump of his nose slammed against the ground as he passed out due to loss of blood.

Dr. Montgomery cut two lengths of fabric from Johnny's jeans, and fashioned tourniquets around Johnny's arms. Then he reached into his saddlebags for needles and thread. "Could somebody bring me some hot water?"

Lopez barked orders in Spanish, and Comancheros scurried back to the cantina. Duane wiped his blade on Johnny's jacket, then stuffed the knife into his boot. He felt unsteady on his feet; the fight had sucked strength away, and he still wasn't fully recovered from his wounds.

He wanted to sit, and the only place was in the saloon. He headed in that direction; the crowd opened a path, and he was joined by Cochrane. "That was some fight."

Duane made his way toward the table, sat with his back to the wall, and felt like a dirty beast. How do I get into these situations? he asked himself. I was bored at the monastery, but at least I wasn't knifing people. Why can't I turn the other cheek like a decent Christian?

Cochrane sat opposite him and shook his head disapprovingly. "It was a mistake to let Johnny Pinto in the gang. He's good with a gun, but he's kill crazy."

Lopez arrived with a bottle of mescal, which he placed noisily on the table. "I have heard of you before, Señor Braddock," he said. "The americano army is looking for you, no?"

"Reckon so," replied Duane as he reached for the mescal. He filled his glass half-full and took a swig. It went down smooth as velvet fire, warming his belly, easing his mind. Meanwhile, the crowd drifted back to the saloon, and everyone was looking at him. The irregulars returned to the table and sat in respectful silence. Duane wanted to sleep, but a perverse part of him enjoyed the attention. He held his head a little higher. "What've they got to eat in this damned place," he snarled. "I'm hungry."

He refilled his glass and took another gulp, because he wanted to escape his mind. The ex-acolyte took no pleasure in cutting a man, and always felt sick when the excitement was over. He guzzled mescal, wanting to blot out the memory of Johnny Pinto bleeding and weeping, Johnny's arms immobilized by skillfully aimed slashes. How can I do these things? Duane asked himself. Why don't I back off from trouble?

"You all right, Kid?" asked Cochrane.

Duane didn't feel like talking, and everybody in the cantina was looking at him. He felt like a celebrity as he took another swallow of mescal. If anybody deserved to get the shit beat out of him, it was Johnny Pinto, he determined. I won the fight, but here I am carrying on as if I lost. Johnny Pinto shot a man, and maybe I was God's own instrument of divine justice, although every atrocity had come from people who thought God was whispering special announcements into their ears.

The mescal glowed warm in his belly, he was starting to relax, and the cramped cantina took on a golden glow. A pretty Mexican waitress in a short dress placed a platter of food in front of him, and he gazed at cheese and beef enchiladas, chili stew, beans, and a salad of avocado pears. He picked up the knife and fork and began to dine. His stomach felt as if he were starving, and brightly colored lights popped inside his eyeballs. He often experienced hallucinations and strange visions when drinking mescal, so he refilled his glass and enjoyed a few more swallows. To the victor belongs the spoils, he concluded as word spread throughout Ceballos Rios that the Pecos Kid was in town.

Johnny Pinto lay on a cot in a small room. Both arms throbbed with pain, he was suffering the worst headache of his life, his kidneys felt as if iron spikes had been driven into them, and his lower lip had been split wide open. He'd never been beaten so badly in his life.

Afternoon sunlight streamed through the window, and someone sat beside him. "Who's there?" he asked thickly.

"Jim Walsh. How're you feelin', Johnny?"

"You can see fer yerself, cain't you?" Johnny gritted his teeth, the pain was so bad. "You got somethin' to drink?"

"Mescal."

The smooth cool mouth of the bottle touched Johnny's battered lips, encrusted with dried blood. Johnny swallowed as much as he could, then dropped back onto the pillow. Never had he taken such a pounding. He couldn't breathe through his nose, and it felt as if his jaw had been dislocated. He'd always believed that he was one rough hombre, but Duane Braddock had kicked his ass royally, no two ways about it. Johnny could make no excuses.

"I'll leave the mescal with you," Walsh said. "You'll be all right, Johnny. You just fucked with the wrong cowboy, that's all."

Walsh walked out of the room, and his footsteps receded down the corridor. Johnny was a solitary invalid in a Comanchero hotel, while the others were having a party at the cantina. The fall from grace had been merciless, and Johnny was stunned by its velocity. But Johnny's greatest hurt wasn't his shattered nose or torn forearm ligaments. Before, men had groveled before him, whereas now they rejoiced behind his back. *Probably got what was coming to him,* they said.

Johnny didn't know if he could ever hold his head up again. It galled him to admit that Duane Braddock was a better fighter, relegating Johnny to the second-class position again, as when he'd lived with his crazy old bookworm father, laughingstock of the neighborhood.

As a child, Johnny Pinto had thrown tantrums until his weak-willed parents gave in to him. He'd developed a hateful, spiteful, envious view of the world, perhaps because his father preferred books to the company of his son, and his mother was a frightened child herself. But whatever the reason, and maybe there was no real reason, Johnny Pinto was an extraordinarily dangerous entity as he lay suffering in a Comanchero hotel.

He bit his lower lip in an effort to fight the pain. Both arms felt submerged in molten iron, his ribs ached increasingly, and he believed that his kidneys would never be the same. He ground his teeth together angrily, setting off jabs of pain inside his skull. He wished he could pass out, but somehow remained fully conscious. He didn't have strength to raise the bottle of mescal to his lips. Wherever Johnny went, there'd be somebody who'd seen him get his ass whipped by Duane Braddock.

Johnny cringed beneath his light blanket. He didn't like folks to see his weaknesses, because that would give them advantages. He suspected enemies and threats everywhere, and believed most people were against him because they were jealous. That's why a man had to be strong and not tolerate horseshit.

As long as Braddock is alive, I'm a joke, realized Johnny Pinto as a tear dripped out of the corner of his eye. I'll pay Duane Braddock back for this no matter what it takes. He's not getting away with it, but I can't just walk up to him straight-on, because the same thing'll happen. No, next time I'll set everything up in advance. It won't be easy, but I'll act like a new man, and be friendly around Braddock, to put him off his guard. I could even apologize for being a rotten son of a bitch. If I have to lie, I'll be the best liar in the world. If I have to kiss somebody's dirty boots, I'll turn it into a game. I'll smile when I'm mad and be nice to old ladies and babies, though I don't give a shit about them at all. I'm going to nail Duane Braddock, so help me God. It won't be tomorrow, and not the next day either. But in a few weeks, when I can move my arms again, Duane Braddock will be a-goin' to a funeral—his own.

Johnny Pinto felt a trickle of new strength as revenge took shape in his convoluted mind. I'll come up behind him and put a chunk of lead into his dome. Or maybe I'll hide a charge of dynamite under his bunk. There are many ways to kill a man, and rat poison ain't a bad idea either. I'll be so nice, I won't even recognize myself, and then, when he least expects it . . .

* * *

An army stagecoach rumbled west of San Antone, sending up a long plume of dust. It was surrounded by a military escort of ten troopers on horseback and followed by a wagon containing guns and ammunition for Fort Clark.

In the cab, Vanessa Fontaine sat among three officers' wives conversing merrily while McCabe was silent and withdrawn as usual. The steady rattle and clank of weapons and equipment could be heard, the air was sweet and clean, and two soldiers rode shotgun atop the cab.

Vanessa's companions exchanged thoughts about children, recipes, family matters, etc., matters of little interest to the Charleston Nightingale. But she listened politely anyway, made an occasional remark, and gazed out the window at cholla and nopal extending to scatterings of bluish-gray mountains in the distance. The land appeared inhospitable, yet a herd of cattle grazed peacefully not far away.

She recalled Duane talking about the cattle business during their brief weeks together. Barren rocky west Texas had fascinated him, and he'd planned to buy his own ranch soon as he saved the money. It was the dream of every hard-drinking cowboy, and perhaps one in a thousand made it come true. Vanessa had considered Duane too young, naive, and confused to get ahead in a world dominated by ruthless business interests.

Business seemed unspeakably vulgar to the former belle, and far beneath the high standards she had established for her mind. She recalled how her father had spent long hours at his desk, trying to keep the plantation afloat, but then Sherman's army happened along. Now, almost seven years later, she was traveling through Texas with an escort of Sherman's soldiers, and felt like a traitor to the Cause.

"Too bad we never had the opportunity to hear you sing while we were in town," said Mrs. Dolly Bumstead, wife of Lieutenant Ambrose Bumstead. "Weren't you afraid of the drunkards?"

Vanessa pulled up the side of her dress and yanked the derringer out of its garter holster. "Don't you ladies carry these?"

"Heavens no," replied Mrs. Bessie Crawford, wife of Captain Dexter Crawford. "I'd probably shoot my toe off."

"What would you do if Comanches attacked this detachment, wiped out the men, and then came for you?"

"I doubt that such a thing could ever happen," Mrs. Bumstead said nervously.

"My departed husband," explained Vanessa, "advised me to save the last round for myself."

"I could never do such a thing in all my days."

The officers' wives were eager to steer the conversation back toward more congenial territory, and Vanessa didn't object. Instead she leaned back on her seat, lowered her eyes to half-mast, and peered out the window at cavalry soldiers riding alongside the carriage. It appeared that a puff of smoke was arising from atop a mountain in the distance, but it might be a hazy cloud. Only three more days to Fort Clark, and Duane Braddock may be there, for all I know, thought Vanessa. Oh Lord, wherever you are, please bring him back to me.

*　　　*　　　*

Duane polished off his last tortilla; the saloon had become jam-packed during the course of his meal, and everybody was still looking at him. He wanted to get away, but paradoxically, the attention was pleasing him.

His head expanded with mescal, victory, and the adulation of the crowd. He wondered if he should run for the Texas State Senate, although he was wanted by the authorities in the Lone Star State, or become the bishop of Ceballos Rios, despite the embarrassing fact that he'd just nearly killed a man.

The cantina blurred, and he was drunk at the center of a hallucinatory carousel flashing bright colors, with Comancheros riding gaily colored wooden horses around him. He didn't know whether to laugh or cry, for the beating he'd administered to Johnny Pinto had been exceedingly brutal, in retrospect. One wrong move and I would've killed him, Duane admitted.

A figure emerged from globules of color pulsating around Duane, and it was Lopez, the Comanchero leader, smiling as usual, sitting at the table. He leaned toward Duane, and Duane couldn't help wondering what heinous deeds the Comanchero leader had committed to become boss of Ceballos Rios.

"How are you doing, my friend?" asked Lopez, a diamond flashing on one of his incisors. Is it time yet for a fine young señorita?"

Duane felt a rise of lust attached to Catholic guilt, shame, and remorse. "Feel awful tired," replied Duane. "Got shot up by Apaches a few weeks back, and still ain't right yet."

Duane laughed at himself talking like a tough gunfighter. He was having fun, better to be a winner than a loser, and the primordial passion of blood victory brought a flush to his cheeks.

Lopez twirled his mustache as he sat at the far side of the table. "Too bad, because I have a true virgin for you. Only sixteen years old, as pure as new cotton, for you, my friend, because you are one helluva hombre." Lopez unbuttoned his shirt and showed a thick gnarled scar running diagonally across his chest. "I have seen a lot of fights in my day, and been in a few myself as you can see, but you are fast as a mountain lion."

Duane was struck by what Lopez said, because he'd been named *Lion* by an Apache medicine man during his sojourn among the People. It seemed an odd coincidence while Lopez continued to praise him. "You are a great fighter, and now I *comprendo* why you are famous in your country. But victory is meaningless without a woman, no? I know you are tired, but surely not too tired for a sixteen-year-old virgin. She will wake you up right quick, my friend. You take one good look at this girl, you will be amaze."

He's lying, thought Duane. Sixteen-year-old virgins don't become prostitutes, do they?

"You do not believe me?" asked Lopez. "Ask her yourself. I was saving her for a certain wealthy customer from your country, and I would charge *one thousand dollars* for little Maria Dolores, but I thought perhaps you have won her. Consider it a small token of my respect for an hombre with cojones, and if you want a more practical answer, it is smart to be on cordial terms with an pistolero like you, no?"

Duane was feeling perky, so he placed his elbows on the table, leaned toward Lopez, and asked, "Why is this sixteen-year-old virgin selling herself?"

Lopez appeared surprised by the question. "She needs the money—what else?"

"Why don't you give her the damned money?"

"I did not get where I am today by giving money to every poor unhappy Mexican girl who comes along. If you don't believe what I am telling you, I'll bring her to you, and you can ask her yourself. It is difficult to understand why you turn down such a juicy plum. Sometimes I have thought of paying her the money and having her myself, but my wife would keel me if she found out. You know how it is."

Every man at the table nodded solemnly. They all knew how it was. Cochrane turned to Duane. "She sounds like a gem to me, and just the thing to take your mind off Juanita, who's engaged to me."

Lopez continued to smile. "You should at least *look* at her, señor. She is a work of art all in herself. And a nice girl, too. She goes to Mass whenever the priest comes to town."

Duane wrinkled his forehead in thought. Who's this poor desperate Catholic kid, and maybe I can help her. "What the hell—all right," he said. "Where is she?"

The stagecoach parked by a stream for the night; tents had been pitched in the vicinity, and weary travelers were preparing for bed as fragrant fires of cottonwood and mesquite wafted across the campsite.

Vanessa and the other wives bathed in the stream together, guarded by soldiers ordered to look the other way, but occasionally, out of mad desperation, they broke the rules, catching distant glimpses of four women with skin like white marble bobbing up and down in the water, and the hot news spread gleefully throughout the enlisted ranks.

After bathing, the ladies returned to the campsite.

Vanessa said good night to the others, then stood in front of her tent and looked at the cloudless night sky.

Great constellations spun above her; the heavens were ablaze with light, and an owl hooted in a juniper tree. She wondered if Duane Braddock was looking at the same moon at that moment, or whether he was lying cold and stiff in a grave.

She heard a footstep behind her and spun around. It was McCabe, her bodyguard, his jaw unshaven. "You'd better sleep with a gun under your pillow tonight, ma'am, if you don't mind me suggesting it. I was just talkin' to the Indian scouts, and they said that Comanches've been follerin' us all day."

Vanessa recalled the smoke signal she'd seen earlier. "Surely we're in no danger, or are we?"

"Depends, and don't believe what they say about Injuns not attackin' at night. An Injun will attack anytime it damn well suits him. So be on yer guard."

He returned to his tent while Vanessa gazed at the vast mysterious desert. For all she knew, there were a hundred Comanches out there, heavily armed, creeping closer. She shivered, but not from the cool night air, as she crawled into her tent. Then she sat on the ground, took off her boots, held the derringer in her hand, and pulled the blanket over her.

She didn't like sleeping in her clothes, but didn't dare get naked with wild Comanches on the warpath. I'll definitely save the last bullet for myself, she thought. No Comanches will ever rape me to death.

She searched for a comfortable spot on the bare ground, and finally was forced to lie flat on her back, with her head cushioned by a pillow made from clothes stuffed inside a pillowcase. She felt exhausted by the constant strain of travel and trying to make conversation with officers' wives.

Why can't I be a normal woman? she asked herself. Sometimes she wondered if she'd gone bonkers on the night they'd burned old Dixie down. Then, in the stillness of night, she heard a faint, low guttural female moan. A blush came to her features, because apparently an officer and his wife were going at it.

Vanessa felt desolate as she imagined others making love. It reminded her of burning nights with Duane Braddock not so long ago. She wished Duane were there, but she was alone on the open sage, with strange soldiers and Comanches on the warpath. "Please come back to me soon, Duane," she whispered softly into the night. "Don't you know how much I need you?"

Lopez led Duane to a ramshackle two-story building not far from the cantina. Lights shone in windows, and the sound of a guitar could be heard from within. Steady streams of men ascended and descended the stairs, and nobody had to tell Duane that it a whorehouse. Smoke emanated from the chimney, and it looked like the devil's lair.

Lopez opened the front door, and they entered a gaudy parlor with red drapes, white walls, and illustrations of naked women in artistic poses on the walls. There was a bar to the left, a fair scattering of patrons, and the featured attractions, the girls themselves, painted like harlots, wandering around in corsets, bloomers, and other bizarre undergarments.

Duane was struck by how young they were, and a few were winking at him, touching their tongues to the tops of their lips, or taking seductive poses. A middle-aged Mexican woman made her way toward Lopez. She wore her gray hair in a bun behind her head, was fully dressed, and looked like a mother superior approaching the pope.

"Tell Maria Dolores that I have found her a gentleman," Lopez said. "Señora, this is the Pecos Kid."

An expression of astonishment came over her face. "Him?"

A glass of mescal materialized in Duane's hand, placed there by a prostitute in white frilly pantaloons. "Maria is a pretty leetle girl," she said, "but I am a real woman, if you know what a real woman is."

She was tall and lean as Vanessa Fontaine, but with long black hair and eyes slanted almost like an Oriental. I can have her, Duane thought. Just like that. Or any other woman in this place.

He let his eyes roll over their figures and caught a glimpse of heaven. Is this what it's like to be an Arab sheikh? he wondered. Billy-goat lust came over him; he'd been without a woman for a long time, he wanted them all, but Brother Paolo whispered in his left ear, *They're all poor girls who've chosen this profession rather than starve to death.*

Meanwhile, the ghost of Clyde Butterfield, his professor of the shootist arts, murmured into his other ear, *He's right, they're all poor girls, and it's your sacred duty to patronize them so that they won't starve to death.*

Lopez touched the back of his hand to Duane's shoulder. "By the way, I have been meaning to ask you something. Are you related to Joe Braddock, the outlaw from up by the Pecos River?"

Duane caught his breath. "He was my father. Did you know him?"

Lopez nodded. "We did business together a few times."

"I don't know much about him, and I'd appreciate anything you could tell me."

"We were not exactly *compañeros,* and I did not know him well. He was an honest man as far as I knew, although I had heard many bad things about him. You look something like him, except he had a mustachio."

Duane gazed into the eyes that had once focused upon his father, and felt a strange spectral connection with his heritage. In the corner of the room, half-hidden by shadows, he saw a broad-shouldered cowboy with a thick black mustache, his wide-brimmed hat slanted low over his eyes, talking with a prostitute. Duane wondered if his father had slept with Mexican prostitutes, but was ashamed to ask such a question.

"Did you ever sit and talk about life with him, by any chance?" asked Duane.

"Life?" Lopez appeared shocked by the question. "What for? No, we just talked business. As I said, we were not friends. All I can tell you is he used to drink like a man, or maybe two men."

The madam approached, a smile playing over her features. "Maria Dolores is waiting for you, señor. I have told her how famous you are, and she is very happy that you will see her. But she is a little shy, because she is so young, you know how it is. But she knows. . . ."

The madam let her sentence trail off, but Duane got the picture. What an unbelievably squalid situation, thought the ex-acolyte. Or maybe it's all a put-up job, and she's been a prostitute for twenty years. "You can be sure that I'll be careful with her feelings. Where is she?"

"The room at the end of the hall on the right."

Duane headed for the stairs, and all eyes were on the notorious Pecos Kid. They knew where he was going, every man envied him, and each prostitute tried to catch his eye. But he paid no attention, curiosity leading him up the stairs. He walked down the hallway to the door at the end, raised his knuckles, and paused a moment. *What the hell am I doing here?*

The door opened two inches, and he saw a big brown eye level with his chest. "Are you the one?" she asked.

"Afraid so." Duane removed his black wide-brimmed cowboy hat.

She looked like a little girl in a ball gown, except she really wasn't a little girl. He followed her into the room, observed her narrow waist and round buttocks, and noticed that her posture was proud. She turned around suddenly, and he saw her innocent eyes, upturned nose, broad face, pretty mouth. She was a sixteen-year-old doll, poised between girlhood and womanhood, exquisite in every way. She pulled back a long lock of straight black hair that had fallen over the middle of her face, and made an unsteady smile. "I am Maria Dolores."

"I'm Duane," he replied, "but I'm not what you think, so calm down. You don't have to sleep with me or anybody else if you don't want to. I'll take care of you—don't worry."

"But . . ."

"I know it sounds strange, but how much money do you need to get out of here?"

She appeared puzzled. "What are you talking about, señor?"

"I'm trying to save you, Maria Dolores. You don't

have to stay here any longer. Lopez told me you needed money because you're in trouble. How much?"

She shrugged. "In American money—twenty thousand dollars."

It was more than he'd imagined, and he'd never earned that much in his life. "How come you need twenty thousand dollars?"

"It is my father, but I do not want to talk about it."

She appeared a well-bred Mexican girl, and her father probably had gambling debts or was an embezzler, and the bank would put him in jail if he didn't return the sum.

"Are you all right, señor?" she asked.

Duane dropped into the chair, demoralized by the tragedy of her life. There was no way he could come up with twenty thousand dollars. "You don't have any relatives . . . ?"

"If I did, I would not be here. But why are we talking about these things? Don't you want to go to bed with me?"

She was absolutely adorable, a rare desert flower, sweet as mountain honey. "Not like this," he said. "Listen, I'm here with some of my friends, and maybe we can bust you out of this place."

"Lopez would track me down and kill me, and my father would land in the calaboose. I thought we were going to bed together and have some fun. I would rather you do it than some old ugly man. Are you a bandito?"

"Not really, although I ride with them."

She rubbed her arms, appeared agitated, and peered into his eyes. "Do you think I am ugly?"

"Of course not," replied Duane nervously. "But I've got to be in love."

She looked as if she were going to cry, and Duane

realized that he should never have gone there. He looked for an avenue of escape, but what would the irregulars say if he ran like a frightened child out of her bedroom?

"You don't like me," she said sadly.

"It's not that at all, but we hardly know each other. It takes a long time for love to grow."

"We do not have a long time, Duane. There is only tonight, and if it is not you, the next hombre might be a monster with a big belly and scars all over his face. I would rather have a famous man to remember for my first time."

She thinks like a child, he acknowledged, but there's a certain logic to what she's saying. Yet, on the other hand, I don't want to be the rotten skunk who takes her virginity. "I don't know what to do," he confessed.

"If you do not know what to do, and I do not know what to do, then what will we do?" she asked in a pleading voice.

They stared at each other in silence, then started laughing. The circumstance was so odd, it took on comical proportions in their teenage minds. She sat on the edge of the bed and buried her face in her hands while her tiny body quaked with mirth. He figured she wasn't more than five feet and one or two inches tall, and that unruly strand of hair kept falling down over the middle of her child's face as she looked up at him. "I have thought about this for a long time," she said. "It is something all women learn sooner or later. With the prices Lopez is charging, I will be out of here in six months, and no one knows anything when I return to my town."

Duane wondered what the real Jesus would say, the one who'd befriended the prostitute Mary Magdalene. This girl is in deep trouble, no two ways about it, just as I was earlier this evening. I carved up Johnny Pinto out of necessity, and she's going to sleep with men out of necessity. In a sense, we're brother and sister.

"I haven't felt well lately," admitted Duane. "I've drunk a lot of mescal tonight, and I'd like to relax for a while. Look." He unbuttoned his shirt and showed the scars. "Apaches."

He didn't have to explain, because Mexicans knew the Apaches well. She turned down the covers of the bed as he pulled off his boots. "You are not going to get under the covers with your clothes on, are you?" she asked.

"Guess not," replied Duane, "but I'm awful tired. I'll probably go right to sleep."

"Go ahead, if that is what you want. You are the guest here, señor."

"Would you mind turning off the lamp."

She turned the lever, and the room was plunged into darkness. He turned his back to her, removed his clothes, crawled quickly into bed, and rolled onto his back. Her garments rustled as she removed them, and Duane couldn't help feeling aroused. She was as lovely as Lopez had described, the exact opposite of Miss Vanessa Fontaine, but Duane was discomforted by moral implications. "Do you have anything to drink?" he asked in the darkness.

"Do you need to get drunk?"

"I don't feel right about this."

"Please do not feel obliged to do me any favors. Maybe my next customer will be even more handsome than you, but I do not think so."

She crawled into bed, brought her face closer, and touched her lips to his cheek. "Please do not speak anymore, *querido mio*. Let me do everything, at my own time. Maybe God has sent you to me, or maybe the devil, who can say? I will be a woman tomorrow morning, and we might as well have some fun while we are at it, no?"

CHAPTER 8

"**Y**OU CAN MOVE BACK TO THE bunkhouse, Johnny," said Dr. Montgomery, washing his hands in the tin basin, "but Captain Cochrane wants to speak with you first."

They'd returned to Lost Canyon two weeks ago, and Johnny Pinto had recovered limited use of his arms. He winced as he pulled on his boots, folded the cot, and placed it in the corner. "Thanks for all you've done for me, sir. I really do appreciate it."

Dr. Montgomery was baffled by Johnny's recent change of demeanor. Johnny appeared genuinely humbled by his fight with Duane Braddock, as if he'd finally seen the light. "Glad to help you, Johnny. Keep up the good work."

Johnny limped across the clearing, headed for Cochrane's cabin. He'd been kind and polite since Ceballos Rios, but his new role required unremitting effort against his natural tendencies. He could dress himself and get around, but his nose would never be the same, and two teeth had departed forever. He felt twinges in his kidneys as he knocked on the door of Cochrane's cabin; a voice within bade him enter.

Cochrane sat at the kitchen table, studying his map. "The doctor told me you were up and around, Johnny, and I thought we'd better have a talk. Take a seat."

Johnny sat meekly and flinched at continual wrenching in both arms. Cochrane rolled up the map, then sat on the other side of the kitchen table, with a small cotton bag between them. "I'm afraid you can't ride with us, Johnny," began Cochrane. "You placed us in danger when you fought with that Comanchero in Ceballos Rios, and we can't afford you anymore. When you're well enough to ride, you've got to leave here." Cochrane leaned forward, and the scar on his cheek looked like the Snake River gorge. "If you ever betray us, make sure we're all killed, otherwise we'll hunt you down like a dog. You can go to San Francisco or New York, but you'll have to look over your shoulder for the rest of your life. Do I make myself clear?"

Johnny smiled and tried to raise his hand. "But sir—"

"Let me tell you something else while we're at it," Cochrane continued. "The men held a vote, and the overwhelming majority wanted a firing squad. That's how seriously they take your little escapade. But you've served us well till now, and I've decided to overrule their verdict. We'll let you take your weapons, personal belongings, two horses, and five hundred dollars in gold"—Cochrane pointed to the cotton bag—"for services rendered."

Johnny smiled, widening his eyes innocently. "Can I say somethin', sir?"

"Make it fast."

Johnny bowed his head submissively. "I want to apologize fer all the bad I done, sir. Hell, that pore greaser weren't hurtin' nobody. I deserved to get the shit beat out of me, and I don't blame you fer not wantin' me here. I was tryin' to show what a big man I was, but Duane Braddock sure cut me down to size."

Cochrane stared in disbelief at Johnny Pinto. "I've always been suspicious of sudden conversions, young man."

"I knows how you feel, sir, but look at Paul in the Bible. He persecuted the Christians, then become a Christian hisself. God has punished me for my evil ways, but it's a blessin' in disguise. Now I can change, and as fer the five hundred dollars, you can donate it to the Cause, because one day the South will rise again, with men like you to lead her. If you've nothin' more to say, sir, I'll go back to the bunkhouse."

Cochrane was flabbergasted by Johnny's declaration and didn't know what to make of it. "Dismissed."

Johnny limped to the door, all his swagger gone, and he appeared truly broken by his experiences. Is this what redemption looks like? Cochrane wondered.

"I think he is lying," said Juanita's voice on the far side of the room, after Johnny was gone. "I would not trust that rat-faced sum of a beetch as far as I could throw him."

"He seemed sincere to me," Cochrane replied. "Don't you believe people can have a change of heart?"

She stood beside the stove, her arms crossed beneath her ample bosom. "A leopard does not change his spots."

"You state opinions as if they were facts, but you don't know whether Johnny's lying or not, or do you?"

"I would never take my eyes off that one, after what he has done. He is bad to the bone."

"But people can renew themselves. . . ."

"Not that one," she said stubbornly.

Cochrane's university logic crumbled before her Aztec intuition, and sometimes he thought she had magical powers. "I believe in the possibility of change," Cochrane insisted, "because I've changed so much myself since I've known you. I think we should at least give him the chance to prove himself. Maybe Braddock pounded some sense into his head."

"Johnny's head is too thick," she replied, "but he is very brave, and that is all you care about. I guess you will let him back into the gang before long, because you are not so smart as you think. But mark my words, one day he will make trouble again, and you will have no one to blame but yourself."

Stoop-shouldered in shame, knees bent beneath the weight of his misery, Johnny Pinto entered the bunkhouse. The usual crowd was gathered around the table, but Duane Braddock wasn't among them. Johnny shuffled toward Sergeant Beasley and said, in a respectful voice, "Can I speak with you, sir?"

Beasley scowled suspiciously. "What's on your mind, Pinto?"

Johnny bowed his head and fixed his vision on a chicken bone lying on the floor. "I want to 'pologize to you and the others fer all the trouble I've made. You prob'ly don't believe me, but I just thought I should say so."

His left leg dragged behind him as he made his way to his bunk, where he painfully reclined. His mouth tasted like ashes and he'd nearly gagged a few times, because he really wasn't sorry for anything. It was his long-range homespun revenge plot, but the black bile of repressed rage rose in his craw and his heart beat rapidly. Johnny Pinto was proud; it hurt him to grovel ignominiously, but he maintained his goal before his eyes: a clear shot at Duane Braddock's back. He tried to calm himself now that victory was within grasp.

The door opened and the bunkhouse fell silent. Johnny laboriously turned his head and saw Duane Braddock enter. Johnny's most difficult humiliation lay ahead, but he had to go through with it. He arose from his bunk, made his arduous way past the table, and then stumbled toward Duane Braddock's bunk.

Duane moved his hand toward his Colt as he watched Johnny Pinto draw closer. He was shaken by Johnny's appearance; the young outlaw seemed ten years older, and his old cocky swagger had been weakened by loss of blood. Duane arose from his bunk, examining welts and cuts on Johnny's face.

Johnny came to a stop in front of Duane, gazed into his eyes sincerely, and said, "You beat me fair and square, but I just want to say I'm sorry fer the mean things I did, and I'll probably burn in hell ferever fer killin' that Comanchero, but I'll never do it again. You taught me a good lesson, sir, and I thank you for it."

Johnny teetered toward his bunk, and Duane gawked at his back in undisguised bewilderment. He wanted to believe Johnny, but something told him that the outlaw was a sick snake and he'd bite somebody again soon. I've got to watch him closely, Duane warned himself. He killed that Comanchero like it was nothing.

*　　*　　*

The stagecoach rolled through a valley filled with grotesque rock formations and thorny clumps of cactus. It was morning, next water hole straight ahead.

Major Marcus Tyler had joined the ladies in the carriage and was rhapsodizing about Texas. "I know it looks like hell's frying pan out there," he said, gesticulating toward the window with his cigar, "but it's not as dry as it looks. One day, when we get the Indians under control, there'll be ranches and farms all over this land, with schools, churches, and army forts too."

Vanessa examined the stark landscape, trying to capture the officer's vision, but it was difficult to imagine civilization on the inhospitable land. Maybe five hundred years from now, she thought.

"If I were you," Major Tyler said to Vanessa, "I'd invest my money in west Texas right now. Between San Antone and El Paso the land is pretty much up for grabs. You could become a cattle queen, and if they ever build a railroad to San Antone, you could multiply your investments by a factor of ten."

The prospect of so much money dazzled Vanessa. "But this land is a desert."

"It might not look like much, but it grows nutritious grass for cattle and horses. There'll be a ranch on this very spot one day, mark my words, and it can belong to you, Mrs. Dawes. Can't you see the poetry in this vast empty space?"

Major Tyler had begun his next sentence when an arrow pierced his throat just above his blue collar and pinned him to the back wall of the carriage like a butterfly in a display case. Vanessa blinked—it was another bad dream—while the other women screamed

hysterically, shots were fired, and a war whoop erupt-
ed nearby. The stagecoach gathered speed. Vanessa
dived to the floor with the other women, Major Tyler's
bleeding corpse sagged on top of them, and McCabe
aimed his sawed-off shotgun out the window.

Hordes of painted Comanches charged toward the
stagecoach; soldiers fired back steadily, but they'd been
taken by surprise. A Comanche warrior broke through
the defensive line and rode straight toward McCabe, a
lance poised in his arms. McCabe took aim, pulled
both triggers, and the powerful kick jolted him backward as the Indian was blown off his charging war
pony.

"Keep your heads down!" McCabe bellowed, as he
reloaded the shotgun with steady hands.

Vanessa cowered on the floor with other women and
the dead soggy former cavalry major. Somebody
hollered atop the cab—perhaps the driver getting hit.
McCabe could cover one window, but the other was
wide open. Vanessa saw the emergency; she was terror-
ized, but didn't want to die without fighting back. She
gathered her courage, uttered a prayer, gritted her
teeth, and raised her head. "Give me your revolver,"
she said to McCabe.

"Keep down, ma'am," McCabe replied, as he aimed
at another Comanche who'd broken through the cavalry escort. McCabe pulled both triggers, there was a terrific explosion, and the Indian leaned crazily to the
side, red dots covering his chest as he toppled to the
ground.

Vanessa yanked the Spiller & Burr out of McCabe's
holster, thumbed back the hammer, and saw a
Comanche approaching the far window. She lunged
toward the opening and fired wildly. To her amazement,

the Comanche fell off his horse and bounced a few times, performing macabre somersaults. Her face drained of color; she'd killed for the first time, and a sergeant raced alongside the stagecoach, a Colt. 44 New Army revolver in his right hand. "What happened to Major Tyler?" he roared.

"He's dead!"

The sergeant veered away from the stagecoach while calling Captain Crawford's name. Somebody crashed into Vanessa, knocking her over. She turned around, and her eyes widened at McCabe, an arrow through his skull, dead as a mackerel. Vanessa raised her hands to her ears and screeched along with the other women. Blood was everywhere, guns fired close by, and an arrow missed her nose by two inches, ramming into the wall of the stagecoach. She dived to the floor, certain that death was imminent, and then something unbelievably horrible happened.

The stagecoach lurched, collapsed sideways, and threatened to turn over. Vanessa and the other women yelled their tonsils out and jumbled against each other as the vehicle tipped to its side. McCabe's corpse landed on the bottom, the women fell atop him, and the dead major landed on top, as the stagecoach slowed to a stop.

Vanessa was tangled in the arms and legs of McCabe, Major Tyler, and the other women. She fought herself loose, found McCabe's shotgun in the melee, climbed to the window, and poked the weapon outside.

Her heart nearly stopped as a Comanche warrior galloped toward her, aiming his rusty old pistol into the cab. She pulled both triggers of the shotgun, although she'd never fired one before. It blasted, she hadn't braced herself adequately, and was thrown back into the cab as the Comanche was riddled with tiny pellets. A moan escaped his lips as he eased off the bare back of his war pony and collapsed in a pile before the stagecoach.

Vanessa didn't know how to reload the shotgun, so she drew the Spiller & Burr. The Comanche lay still, limbs twisted, in front of the stagecoach. It was him or me, reasoned Vanessa, and it damned sure wasn't going to be me.

The cavalry soldiers took positions around the stagecoach while painted savages rode in a circle, brandishing their weapons and singing war songs. Meanwhile, dismounted Comanches fired bows and arrows from a distance, but the massed disciplined shooting of the soldiers was keeping them at bay. The bewildered and blood-bespattered women climbed out of the stagecoach, and Mrs. Marcus Tyler appeared in a state of shock. Vanessa forced her to kneel in the lee of the stagecoach as arrows and bullets zipped through the air over their heads. Mrs. Bumstead had recovered Major Tyler's service revolver and was looking at it curiously.

"Just thumb back the hammer like this," demonstrated Vanessa, "and pull the trigger. But make sure you don't shoot one of us by mistake."

"You women—get down!" hollered Captain Crawford. "Here they come, men! Hold steady, and fire at will!"

A dozen warriors on horseback were trying to breach the defensive perimeter, singing war songs, death songs, and anything else they could remember to pump them up for the hazardous venture.

The soldiers rapid-fired, but they were thin at that

end of the defense. Comanches fell off the backs of their horses, but others kept marauding onward. Captain Crawford glanced about nervously, fearing to weaken one sector to strengthen another, when an arrow shot through his stomach. The gallant captain tried to yank it out, then collapsed onto the ground and became incoherent.

Command devolved to young Second Lieutenant Bumstead, who'd been a student at West Point only seven months ago. "Maintain your fire!" he ordered. "Hold fast!"

More Comanches parted company with their horses, but three broke through the defense and headed toward the wagon where rifles and ammunition were stored, not far from the stagecoach. One of the younger warriors spotted Vanessa's golden hair shining brightly in the sunlight, and he decided that the white-eyes beauty would be his prize. Crying victoriously, the lust of the devil in his groin, he pulled his war pony's reins to the side and kicked its ribs hard.

The animal shifted direction and bore down on Vanessa, who was tempted to run for her life, but he'd simply scoop her up and carry her to his tipi. So she held steady, closed one eye, and aimed at his bobbing torso, looming larger every moment The warrior was cruelly handsome, but Vanessa wouldn't be taken against her will. "Yaaahhhhhh!" he screamed, reaching down for her as she pulled the trigger.

The Spiller & Burr kicked up and to the left, her ears rang with the report, and the Comanche sagged to the side. His war pony continued driving toward Vanessa, she dodged out of the way, and the Comanche fell atop her, knocking her off her feet.

She rolled over him, pushed him away, saw the ugly hole in his chest, and shrank back. It was as if time stopped; she'd killed again, and no one would ever bring him back. Everything moved in slow motion; a wave of dizziness passed over her, she examined herself for wounds, but the blood belonged the dead Comanche; it glistened in the morning sun.

The shooting diminished as disappointed howling warriors rode off to fight another day. Vanessa rose to her feet, holding the Spiller & Burr tightly in her hand. The dead Comanche lay at her feet, and she tried not to think about him. Soldiers gathered around, led by Lieutenant Bumstead. "It's all over," he said. "Are you all right, ladies?"

"I'm fine," replied Vanessa in a faraway voice. She sat heavily on the ground, shook her head in abhorrence, and burst into tears.

Duane watched Johnny Pinto hobble stiffly across the clearing that separated the cabins. He looked like a pathetic dying old man, his skin sallow, pain distorting his already disagreeable features. Duane decided impulsively that the time had come for a talk. His feet were moving before he could stop them, and it didn't take long to catch up with the invalid. "Johnny, let's you and me palaver awhile."

Johnny stopped, settled his balance, and smiled. "Yes, sir."

Duane placed his hands on his hips and angled his head as he stared into Johnny's eyes. "Are you putting on an act, or are you really sorry for what you did?"

Johnny looked down sadly. "It's hard to believe if you've never gone through it yerself."

"Gone through what?"

"To look at yerself from the outside, and see that you been a dirty, sneaky polecat all yer life. As it says in the Bible, *you shall know a tree by its fruit.* You've seen me at my worst, and that's why you can't imagine me at my best."

Flabbergasted, Duane stared at him. "To tell you the truth, Johnny, I've done a few things wrong myself, and sure wish I could change. For my part, I'm sorry about what happened between us. I shouldn't've got so mad at you and done so much . . . damage."

Johnny smiled beatifically. "I deserved it, but I'll tell you what. I'll forgive you if you forgive me, all right?"

"It's a deal."

Johnny struggled to raise his hand, but Duane took it in his own paw and shook it gently. "If there's ever something I can do for you, Johnny, you let me know, all right?"

Let me kill you, Johnny thought, but instead he smiled and said, "Sure, and if I can help you in some way, just ask. I've done enough bad things, and it's time I did some good ones."

Duane searched Johnny's eyes as though they were philosopher's stones. "You're not shitting me, are you?"

"What do your guts tell you?"

"That you're a liar."

Johnny Pinto smiled painfully and held out his empty hands as if to say, *How can I prove myself to you?*

"I hope I'm wrong," said Duane as he placed his hand on Johnny's shoulder. "Good luck."

Duane turned toward the far side of the canyon, showing his wide back to Johnny, who licked his lips in frustration. When my arm is good, we'll have another conversation, Mr. Pecos Kid. You turn around like that again—I'll plug you dead game.

Duane ambled across the yard, listening for the *click* of a gun's hammer behind him. *I damned near beat Johnny Pinto to death, and he's forgiven me? Somehow I don't trust the son of a bitch.*

He rambled into the wilderness, thinking about Johnny Pinto, redemption, and divine retribution. It reminded him of a book he'd read in the monastery, written by a French Jesuit priest named Jean-Pierre de Caussade. Its main premise was that Christians should abandon themselves totally to the will of God. *You are seeking for secret ways of belonging to God, but there is only one: making use of whatever he offers you.*

Duane reached for his Colt .44. *This is what God has offered me, for better or worse. I believe in the Bible, I studied for the priesthood, and I'm going to let God worry about everything from now on.* As Jean-Pierre de Caussade wrote: *If we are truly obedient to God's will, we will ask no questions about the road along which He is taking us.* If that was good enough for him, it's good enough for me.

Duane's Apache ears picked up sound in the foliage to his front. He froze, aimed his Colt straight ahead; somebody was there, possibly an Apache or a scout from the Mexican Army. Duane gently thumbed back the hammer. "Come out with your hands up!"

Juanita emerged from the night, wearing a brown leather jacket, her hands clasped over her breast. "Oh Duane, you must never do that again! I was just walking along, thinking about things, and you have scared me to death!"

Duane eased back the hammer and holstered his Colt. "I thought you were an Apache. What're you doing?"

"I was taking a walk, and you got to pool a gun on me?"

Duane couldn't help laughing. "I didn't know it was you. Calm down, Juanita."

She took a step back and narrowed her eyes. "What are *you* doing here?"

"I'm taking a walk too—thinking about things. Have you talked with Johnny Pinto lately?"

"I would never get near that peeg."

"But he seems so changed, haven't you noticed?"

"You and Ricardo are easily deceived."

"I'm not so sure. What about Matthew the tax collector, Simon the zealot, and all the other varmints who became Jesus's first disciples and now are the leading saints of the church?"

She moved her face closer and narrowed her eyes. "How about Judas Iscariot?"

They headed toward haciendas on the far side of the valley, and he glanced at her sideways. She was strong-limbed, with a provocative luster in her almond-shaped eyes, her skin silky and fragrant with the aroma of desert flowers. He felt a mad urge to tear off her clothing and drink ambrosia from those rich Mexicali lips. But she's another man's woman, so maintain your distance, cowboy. She moved with languid grace inside her long blue dress, her head held high, the kind of woman who'd be a big help on a ranch, unlike the prissy and delicate Miss Vanessa Fontaine.

"I have heard the men talking about you," she said. "You are one bad hombre, eh, Mr. Pecos Kid?"

"I keep getting into trouble," admitted Duane.

"You are too pretty for your own good, I think so."

"If people let me alone, I'd be fine."

"People like you are not made for this world. You should have been a priest, but too bad you like girls too much." She laughed sadly. "You should settle down; otherwise you will die with a bottle in your hand, or another hombre will shoot you."

"I have business to take care of, but then I'm getting married. I don't know who she is yet, but I'll find her someday."

"Have you ever been in love?"

"Yes, but she married somebody else."

"Perhaps she misses you, and wishes you'd come back."

"She's the most cold-blooded woman in the world."

"If she is so cold-blooded, why cannot you forget her?"

"I don't know, but I'd never chase a woman and make a fool of myself like a sick puppy dog."

"Not even if it could get her back?"

CHAPTER 9

THE STAGECOACH RUMBLED INTO Fort Clark at midafternoon, accompanied by additional reinforcements, two cannons, and one Gatling gun. Soldiers halted their duties and gazed with curiosity at the bedraggled column, battered stagecoach, wounded soldiers, and wagon stacked with dead troopers.

Children ran alongside the lopsided stagecoach filled with bullet holes and arrow scars. Four ladies sat inside shorn of cosmetics, their hair wild, clothes stained with blood, glassy-eyed and weird-looking.

One was Vanessa Fontaine, still unnerved by her recent experience with Comanches, as she rested on a bloodstained seat among the others. Unable to eat since the Indian attack ended, she'd drunk numerous cups of black army coffee and felt strangely disembodied.

Safe at last, but for how long? she wondered. Her Charleston Nightingale existence had been shattered in a split instant when the arrow had killed Major Tyler. Then she'd blown away three noble red men who'd tried to kill her. Why won't the damned savages let us live in peace among them? she asked herself.

Now Vanessa understood war veterans and their strange moods. Sudden violent death before her eyes had stripped away illusions forever. What makes the Indians think they own every square foot of Texas? They're barely above the animal level, and the only thing they ever learned to do was build a bonfire. The sooner they're killed off, the better.

She thought of McCabe, who'd died trying to save the lives of women. He could've cowered on the floor with the rest of them, but beneath his inscrutable desires he'd proven himself courageous under fire. Vanessa knew nothing about him, not even his first name, and no one would notify his family that he'd departed.

Vanessa glanced at her women companions, and they were thin-lipped, sitting stiffly as soldiers. They'd heard of Indian depredations from their husbands, but it was another matter to live through one. Nobody was going to rape them without a fight, and they'd save the last bullet for themselves.

The column came to a stop before a large building with the guidon flags of the Fourth Cavalry fluttering in front. A trooper opened the front door of the command post, and two officers strode out. One was tall, husky, with a thick dark brown mustache and missing fingers on his right hand. The other officer was of medium height, with bright red hair and mustache.

"It's Colonel MacKenzie!" declared one of the women in the stagecoach.

Even Vanessa had heard of Colonel Randall Slidell

MacKenzie, commander of the Fourth Cavalry. "I wonder what he's doing at Fort Clark?" she asked.

"Probably on an inspection tour. The other officer is the post commander, Major Brean."

Lieutenant Bumstead dismounted in measured military movements. He marched toward Colonel MacKenzie, saluted, and delivered his report while standing at attention. Lieutenant Bumstead had torn the seat of his pants during the battle, and Vanessa could see his underwear.

The stagecoach door was opened by a sergeant, and the newly widowed Mrs. Tyler stepped down. She was followed by Mrs. Bumstead, and then Vanessa Fontaine unraveled her long limbs. Colonel MacKenzie and Major Brean headed toward them, accompanied by staff officers, aides, and guards.

The officers attempted to console the ladies, and Mrs. Tyler couldn't suppress a sob. Her shoulders were bent and she appeared broken by her experience. Then Mrs. Bumstead introduced the newcomer to the officers. "This is Mrs. Vanessa Dawes, whose husband has recently been killed in action against the Apache."

Vanessa offered her hand to the renowned Colonel MacKenzie, tallest man in the vicinity, with splendid bright blue eyes and a solid, powerful physique. He squeezed her fingers gently and said in a deep, soothing voice, "It must have been terrible for you."

Vanessa saw no ring on his finger. She smiled faintly and replied, "Thank God for the Fourth Cavalry. Your men fought bravely, sir."

He heard her South Carolina drawl and his smile faltered a split instant, then Major Brean was introduced. "Lieutenant Dawes served under me for a time after he was first posted to Texas," said Brean. "He was one of the finest young officers in the service, and I deeply regret his passing."

Vanessa nodded politely. She'd heard much praise of Lieutenant Dawes's soldierly attributes, but too bad he'd been a jealous fool. Major Brean turned his attention to Mrs. Tyler, and Vanessa Fontaine let her eyes fall on the celebrated Colonel MacKenzie. He appeared bursting with energy, and possessed the rare quality known as charisma. Vanessa had read in a newspaper that he was the youngest colonel in the U.S. Army, and he'd probably become a general before long.

Her reveries were interrupted by the appearance of Major Brean before her. "Where had you intended to stay, Mrs. Dawes?"

"Is there a hotel?"

"Yes, but you might not find it to your liking. Our son is away at West Point, and you could have the guest room. Sergeant Donelson, please escort Mrs. Dawes to my quarters."

Sergeant Donelson saluted, and he was the same noncommissioned officer whom she'd nearly shot in the initial stages of the fight. "Which luggage is yours, ma'am?"

She pointed to her things, and he in turn yelled orders to a group of enlisted men. As her belongings were gathered, she turned toward Colonel MacKenzie, who'd placed his arm around Mrs. Tyler's shoulder and was escorting her to her quarters. Vanessa wondered if he were the damned Yankee who'd killed Beauregard, but now she was in Texas, it was a new world, and Colonel MacKenzie happened to be an eminently eligible bachelor. Hmmmm, thought Vanessa, as she followed the sergeant toward her new quarters.

* * *

The outlaw gang rode across Lost Canyon, heading toward the northern pass. Their saddlebags were full of ammunition and spare clothes, packhorses carried dynamite, and Cochrane rode at the head of the formation, hat slanted low over his eyes.

They rode toward their biggest robbery thus far, and tried to be of good cheer. Cochrane rocked back and forth in his saddle as he gazed at Juanita standing alongside the trail, an uncertain smile on her face. He raised his arm and performed a snappy salute, then winked like a Southern soldier boy riding off to war.

Her eyes glimmering with tears, she rushed toward him, grasped his hand, and placed something inside. "Be careful, *querido mio*. I will pray for you. Come back to me whole."

She took a step back and crossed herself solemnly. Cochrane swung about in his saddle, looking at her, a tear in his eye. He was tempted to jump down and run to her arms, to hell with the Cause, but his men depended on him, duty called, and soldierly habits were deeply ingrained.

He blew her a kiss like a true Virginian cavalier, then turned eyes front and continued to lead his gang toward the narrow passageway. He opened his hand, saw a lock of her hair bound with a red ribbon, raised it to his nostrils, smelled her scent. He might never see Juanita again, but refused to take counsel of his fears. He dropped the lock of hair into his shirt pocket, beside his black calfskin tobacco pouch and package of papers.

The irregulars rode single file through the narrow winding passageway, leaning to avoid outcroppings of ledges. About midway back in the column, Johnny Pinto sat atop his dun gelding, laying plans for the murder of Duane Braddock. Johnny was healed sufficiently to draw his Remington, thumb back the hammer, and fire accurately. He licked his lips in anticipation of future revenge, as the outlaw column emerged from Lost Canyon.

Ahead stretched a plateau covered with cholla, ocotillo, and grama grass, while a vertical sandstone cliff stood like a sentinel in the distance. Cochrane rode stalwartly at the head of the column, a tall erect figure leading them north toward the Rio Grande, while Duane Braddock brought up the rear.

Duane was responsible for two packhorses, whose reins were tied to the pommel of his saddle. Increasingly dubious about the upcoming robbery, he raised his bandanna over his nose, to hold back dust rising from the hooves of horses in front of him. The last thing Duane wanted was to kill an American soldier by mistake.

The former acolyte marveled at the chain of events that had led him to the irregulars, but they'd saved his worthless life, and he owed them. I'll do whatever I can to help, Duane decided, but I'm not shooting any soldiers, and that's all I know.

Duane shook his head bitterly at the twists and turns of fate. Sometimes he thought that he'd been born beneath an unlucky star, and nothing good would ever turn out for him. I've got to look ahead and stop worrying so much, he thought, worrying. As soon as this robbery is over, I'm off to the Pecos Country, to settle the score with the man who killed my parents, and then I'm going into the cattle business, if I live that long.

*   *   *

A group of officers and wives, plus a few distinguished guests, sat to supper in the dining room of Major Howard Brean, commander of Fort Clark. The long table was lit by candles, and everyone dressed as if in a fashionable Eastern restaurant.

The guest of honor was the renowned Colonel Randall Slidell MacKenzie, attired in a blue uniform with gold shoulder straps and highly polished brass buttons. His neatly combed dark brown mustache covered his lips, he possessed intelligent eyes, and his hair was short, parted on the side.

He looked every inch a combat commander, and had been seated strategically across from the only single woman available, the widow Dawes. It seemed a match made in heaven; the meal progressed, everyone conversed politely between bowls of soup, platters of roast beef and carrots, not to mention a variety of alcoholic beverages, chief of which was the bottle of whiskey that the officers continually passed to each other across the heavily laden table.

"What brings you to this forlorn part of the world, Mrs. Dawes?" asked Colonel MacKenzie as he shoved a chunk of beef past the fortress of his mustache.

"I'm on my way to Escondido," she replied.

"Really?" Colonel MacKenzie cleared his throat. "I wouldn't advise a woman traveling alone to go to that godforsaken place. Recently I've had to send a detachment there, to provide the semblance of law and order after a spate of shootings. Not only that, but it's surrounded by the worst Apaches in North America. Why are you going to Escondido?"

"Visiting friends," she said vaguely, for a Charleston belle learns dissembling at an early age.

A voice piped up at the far end of the table. It was giddy Mrs. Sullivan, wife of the Fort Clark quartermaster, running off at the mouth again. "Mrs. Dawes is a professional singer. Perhaps she can entertain us with a song after dinner?"

Colonel MacKenzie gazed at Vanessa curiously. "What do you sing?"

"Popular songs, such as the ones soldiers sang during the war. Perhaps you sang a few yourself, Colonel."

"I didn't have much time for singing during the war, ma'am."

She noticed the scarred stumps of his two lost fingers, and wondered what had happened to them. Colonel MacKenzie seemed friendly and wholesome, while the other officers and ladies fawned over him. Vanessa wondered why the celebrated colonel had never married, for he had everything that a woman could desire in a man. She caught him casting certain sly glances at her anatomy and doubted that he was of the late McCabe's persuasion.

One of the officers, young Lieutenant Grindle, was getting plastered on the whiskey. "I understand that you do most of your singing in saloons, Mrs. Dawes."

All eyes turned to the Charleston Nightingale, and she couldn't prevent the blush from tinging her cheeks. "Where else?" she asked. "There are no concert halls to speak of in Texas."

The table was scandalized, but Colonel MacKenzie appeared amused. "Do you enjoy your work, Mrs. Dawes?"

"My audiences are appreciative of music, but if they

don't like an entertainer, they've been known to throw bottles, chairs, and even tables onto the stage."

"What an odd career," observed Colonel MacKenzie. "Somehow I can't imagine you in a saloon, Mrs. Dawes."

"I didn't have a choice of occupations after The Recent Unpleasantness, sir. My home was burned to the ground by Sherman's army."

"But," said Mrs. Sullivan pointedly, "it was South Carolina that started the war in the first place, and South Carolina has the blood of this nation on its hands."

"On the contrary," Vanessa replied, her eyes flashing, "the war was started by sanctimonious individuals from the Northern states, who wanted to impose their will on Southerners. My family lost everything in the war, but *I regret nothing.*"

She said the last three words with a vigor that brought a smile to Colonel MacKenzie's usually dour countenance, while other diners appeared stricken by her words. The impulsive former belle realized that she'd lost control of herself yet again, thus committing another of her infamous social blunders. I'd better keep my mouth shut from now on, she counseled herself. Otherwise these damned Yankees are liable to hang me from the flagpole.

Dessert was served, and soldier waiters filled cups with coffee. Vanessa wanted to be alone, so she touched her napkin to her lips. "Excuse me, but I'd like to get some fresh air."

Across the table, Colonel MacKenzie replied, "I'll accompany you, if you don't mind."

A waiter pulled back Vanessa's chair, and Colonel MacKenzie rushed ahead to open the door for her, as officers and wives glanced at each other significantly. Vanessa stepped into cool November air, pulled the shawl snugly around her shoulders, and strolled past the darkened houses along officers' row, accompanied by one of the foremost officers in the U.S. Army. A three-quarter moon floated through a sea of blazing stars, and a light shone in the window of the command-post headquarters across the parade ground.

"I wish I could talk you out of going to Escondido," said Colonel MacKenzie, "but I can see that your mind is made up."

"I apologize if I seem overbearing, but there's something that I have to do."

"Let me tell you something about Escondido so you won't be completely in the dark when you arrive. It's on the border, and has managed, in a remarkably short time, to attract the worst scum of two nations. They're all armed to the teeth, drunk, and constantly fighting and shooting. Let's call a spade a spade, Mrs. Dawes. Rape is not uncommon among such men. What'll you do if a bunch of them break down your door at night?"

"I'll start shooting, and I won't stop until they go away. I can't stop living because some people are brutes."

"A beautiful woman such as yourself is certain to attract attention in Escondido. I wish I could give you your own cavalry detachment, but unfortunately I'm short as it is."

She raised an eyebrow. "Who'd guard me from your detachment?"

He smiled at her little barb. "Not all my soldiers are ex-criminals, and a few here and there even speak English. They fight well when led by officers who set a good example, such as your late departed husband. I met him briefly once, by the way. He had a brilliant future, and it's a tragedy that we had to lose him."

"I'll mourn him forever," replied Vanessa, and in a manner of speaking she meant it. "But I have a question of my own. I can't help wondering why an attractive man like you has never married?"

"But I am married—to the army— and she's a very jealous mistress."

"Most officers get married to women, and it doesn't seem to harm their careers."

The youngest colonel in the army winked. "Most officers aren't commanding the Fourth Cavalry either. I have no time for a family, and to tell you the truth, beautiful women like you scare the hell of out me."

She was amused by the great man's candor. "I won't harm you, Colonel MacKenzie. Women aren't *that* bad."

"They're terribly distracting, and I'll probably dream about you tonight, Mrs. Dawes."

"But if we weren't distracting, it'd be the end of the human race."

He grinned, revealing straight white teeth beneath the strands of his mustache. "Something tells me that you won't be single long, Mrs. Dawes. Who is it that you're visiting in Escondido?"

She wondered whether to tell the truth and decided to take a chance. "I'm looking for an old friend named Duane Braddock. Ever heard of him?"

Colonel MacKenzie wrinkled his nose. "Isn't he an outlaw?"

"So they say."

"I believe he was sheriff of Escondido for a spell." He looked at her with surprise. "If I'm not mistaken, he's wanted for murder."

"Unjustly, I'm sure. I saw Duane Braddock in a duel once, against a horrible man named Saul Klevins, and Klevins had to back Duane against a wall to make him fight."

"Perhaps I've got your Duane Braddock mixed up with somebody else. There are so many trigger-happy young fools in Texas, it's hard to keep up with them. I hope you won't think me presumptuous, but he must be an awfully good friend if you're going all the way to Escondido to see him. Why doesn't he come to see you?"

"You know very well why not. He'd get arrested by the Fourth Cavalry."

Colonel MacKenzie ran his finger over his mustache and appeared deep in thought. "Why don't you stop by my office tomorrow, and I'll show you our file on Duane Braddock. It might be just what you need to dissuade you from going to Escondido."

Outlaws slept in their bedrolls like caterpillars in cocoons, two guards had been posted, and the three-quarter moon waxed atop a mountain range in the distance. But Johnny Pinto lay awake in his bedroll, Smith & Wesson in hand, staring at Duane Braddock sleeping a few feet away. Johnny was waiting for Duane to turn in another direction.

Johnny was exhausted, dozed off, opened his eyes, and was chagrined to see Duane Braddock in the same place. Braddock appeared asleep, but he'd taken his Colt to bed with him, and perhaps the Pecos Kid was waiting for the excuse to shoot a certain Johnny Pinto.

Duane grumbled in his bedroll, twitched, and then turned over, finally displaying his back to Johnny Pinto's widening eyes. The moment of revenge had arrived, and Johnny savored the moment. He looked around the campsite to make sure no one was watching, then thumbed back the hammer of his Smith & Wesson. A faint *click* could be heard, muffled by his blankets, then Duane Braddock sat bolt upright suddenly. Johnny closed his eyes and pretended to be asleep.

Did he hear me cock my gun? Johnny wondered, opening his eyes slightly. Duane Braddock, Colt in hand, peered around the campsite. Then he uncocked his gun and lay down, this time facing Johnny Pinto.

Johnny didn't dare uncock his Smith & Wesson, because Braddock would hear him. But he couldn't fall asleep with a cocked gun, because now it was ready to fire. Johnny waited patiently, his finger on the trigger of the Smith & Wesson. Sooner or later Duane Braddock'll roll over again, and then . . .

Vanessa Fontaine stood with her hands on her hips and gazed at her naked figure in the mirror. The only light came from an oil lamp on the dresser, the blinds were drawn, and she'd just taken a hot bath, steamy fumes of soapy water permeating the air.

She saw a tall gawky blond giraffe with too small breasts and skinny legs, yet people always said how beautiful she was. I have a certain flair that never fails to get me into trouble, she thought ruefully.

She dropped a cotton gown over her shoulders, blew out the lamp, and crawled beneath the blankets of her bed. It felt good to be alone with her thoughts, where no men were staring at her, making judgments.

The blankets felt luxurious after the long bloody trip from San Antone. She recalled the Indian attack, and her devoted bodyguard was buried on the desert with a crude cross marking his grave. No sooner had she digested one major event, when another appeared: Colonel Randall Slidell MacKenzie of the Fourth Cavalry. Surely the great man knew that a cultured woman could be of immense value to his career, and marriage would put an end to certain ugly remarks doubtlessly uttered behind closed doors.

She recalled Colonel MacKenzie scouting her with eager eyes. If she played him like a piano, she could become queen of the Fourth Cavalry, and when he made general, they could move back east. A war hero like Randall Slidell MacKenzie could become president one day.

But she felt no deep sentiments for Colonel MacKenzie, unlike her feelings for a certain young outlaw with green eyes and the face of Adonis. Duane Braddock, when I get my hands on you again, I'll show you things you've never dreamed possible, she swore. Hugging her pillow tightly, she smiled in anticipation of their next meeting.

Johnny Pinto opened his eyes after dozing off, turned toward Duane Braddock, and saw Braddock facing away from him again. Johnny grinned broadly as he drew the Smith & Wesson from beneath his blankets. I'm going to empty this gun into you, and you'll never humiliate me again.

Johnny glanced around, and no one was watching. He raised the gun, straightened his arm, and took aim at Duane Braddock's back. The trigger moved back, the mechanism would trip in a second, then the fun would begin. I'm the man who shot the Pecos Kid, he thought triumphantly.

The trigger retreated the final sixteenth of an inch, tripping the hammer. It flew forward, slammed into the firing pin, and nothing happened—a misfire. Johnny nearly jumped out of his pants, then blankets exploded all around him as irregulars jerked themselves to sitting positions and drew their weapons.

They looked at each other, guns drawn, and Johnny Pinto was just another of them. "What the hell happened?" asked Beasley.

"Sounded like the hammer of a gun," replied Walsh. "Where are the guards?"

The three came charging into the campsite, guns in hands. "What's a-goin' on?" asked Ginger Hertzog.

Cochrane peered into the darkness. "Might be Apaches, but you know how sounds travel at night. We'd better search the area, just in case. Beasley, take charge."

The men grumbled as they climbed off the ground, exhausted from hard riding. Beasley ordered them to spread out, and Johnny Pinto walked through the cactus, feeling tiny hairlike needles jabbing through his jeans. He was pale, gasping for breath, nearly got caught in the act, but faulty cartridges weren't uncommon. I had him in my sights, fer chrissakes. Now I'll have to wait fer tomorrow night or some other damned time, because everybody's alert now. Duane Braddock is one lucky son of a bitch, but maybe I'll get him tomorrow. His luck can't last forever.

CHAPTER 10

THE PAY WAGON RUMBLED AND rolled across the trail, pulled by two horses. Ten troopers rode in front of the wagon, searching for danger, with the remaining fifteen in the rear, armed with rifles, pistols, and knives.

They were observed through an old brass army spyglass by ex-Captain Richard Cochrane, who lay on a mesa approximately one mile away. He noted that no Indian scouts accompanied the soldiers, perhaps because the soldiers considered their fast-firing rifles unbeatable. They wore blue uniforms with gold bandannas, and their tan wide-brimmed cavalry hats were bent into a variety of configurations to suit the mood or taste of its wearer.

Cochrane detested blue uniforms; they represented everything evil and foul to him. The pay wagon traveled leisurely in a southeasterly direction, unmindful that a ragtag remnant of the Confederate Army was about to pounce on them.

Satisfied that all was proceeding according to schedule, Cochrane climbed down the back of the mesa, where his horse was picketed at the bottom. The ex-officer felt splendid, the excitement and danger of war invigorated him, and he wondered how he could give it up for Juanita Torregrosa. He raised himself onto his saddle, amazed at the power she had over him. Now he understood why they called love the tender trap.

His horse cantered away from the butte as Cochrane bounced up and down in the saddle. After this battle, I'm going to be a Mexican, he mused. I'll even learn their lingo, and maybe I'll change my name to Rodriguez.

Mrs. Vanessa Dawes presented herself at the orderly room of Company B, Fourth Cavalry, and a crusty old sergeant with a bushy blond mustache and a corncob pipe looked up at her. "Can I help you, ma'am?"

"Would you tell Colonel MacKenzie that Mrs. Dawes is here to see him?"

"Yes, ma'am."

Vanessa's eyes fell on a picture of President Ulysses S. Grant hanging from a nail banged into the wall. Revulsion swept over her, for she considered drunkard Grant a cigar-smoking butcher, yet he'd become president of the United States, while General Lee lay buried in Lexington, Virginia. It was blood-soaked Grant who'd sent Sherman on his reckless march to the sea, destroying the Fontaine plantation, killing her parents, and sending Vanessa destitute into the world. The ex–Charleston belle wanted to be magnanimous in defeat—it was the decent thing to do—but she lacked the strength, courage, or whatever else was required. If killer Grant were standing in front of me right now, would I assassinate him?

The sergeant emerged from the next office. "He'll see you now, ma'am."

The colonel sat behind a desk, attired in a blue canvas shirt with gold shoulder straps and top button undone. He rose to his feet and smiled cautiously. "Have a seat, Mrs. Dawes. I was perusing the file on Duane Braddock before you arrived, and was surprised to learn that your departed ex-husband, Lieutenant Dawes, once arrested Duane Braddock in a town called Shelby. Is that correct?"

She sat before him, crossed her legs, and said, "Yes."

Colonel MacKenzie stared at her, trying to understand, but Vanessa switched the subject adroitly. "Does it say where Duane Braddock is now?"

"Most probably in Mexico." Colonel MacKenzie raised the file on Duane Braddock, then let it drop to the desk. "It's quite a story, and I can't fathom how a lady like you could befriend such a person. May I be frank? It says here that you were actually engaged to marry Duane Braddock when you met Lieutenant Dawes. Is that correct?"

"Let's just say that I knew him well," Vanessa replied, "and I persist in believing that he's no outlaw. His main problem is he won't back down from provocation."

"Evidently he gets provoked quite often," retorted Colonel MacKenzie. "He's shot approximately fourteen men that we know about, and God only knows how many others. What about the federal marshal that he killed in Morellos?"

"Duane's not friendly to lawmen, I'm afraid."

"He pumped two cartridges into the marshal, according to the report. That's more than just being unfriendly, wouldn't you say?"

"Maybe the marshal shot first and forced Duane to defend himself."

Colonel MacKenzie leaned back in his chair, scratched his nose, and appeared thoughtful. "Your defense of Mr. Braddock is sincere, I have no doubt about that, but isn't it strange how he leaves a trail of corpses wherever he goes? When he was sheriff of Escondido, he shot approximately half a dozen men in the space of a month. I guess they all provoked him?"

"Wherever I go, people provoke me too. Such as last night during supper, because I speak with a Southern accent and sing in saloons. I could alter my Southern accent to be more acceptable to the army in blue, but I'm proud of my heritage and refuse to apologize for it. I'll bet you one thing—Duane Braddock was probably the best sheriff Escondido ever had."

"At the rate he was going, he would've killed everyone in town, but not without provocation, of course."

"You wouldn't say that if you knew him. He's really an honest young man, and he'll make something of himself someday, if people would leave him alone. If he's arrested, I hope he'll get a fair trial."

"Duane Braddock will receive the full benefit of the law, and you can even appear as a character witness for the defense. Perhaps you can convince a jury that the federal marshal committed suicide, but somehow Mr. Braddock got blamed by mistake."

*　　　*　　　*

Duane sat with his back against a boulder, smoking a cigarette and watching the irregulars digging holes along the trail. The plan was to bury dynamite at strategic spots, blow the troopers to kingdom come, take the payroll, and cut back to the Rio Grande.

What warped sense of honor has brought me here? Duane wondered. Just because they saved my life, that doesn't mean I have to participate in mass murder. How can I sit with my mouth shut while they blow a bunch of poor soldiers to smithereens?

Duane became agitated as he paced back and forth on the riverbank. He glanced toward the trail where the outlaws were placing sticks of dynamite into holes they'd dug into the ground. The carefully hidden fuses trailed to a hedge where Cochrane would wait with a match. Duane's vivid imagination saw bloody arms flying in one direction, legs in another, and heads straight up into the air. The troopers wouldn't know what hit them, and then the outlaws would level withering fire into the survivors. Death on the menu, Duane felt nauseated, and an artery hammered his throat. Maybe I should jump on the best horse here and ride the hell away, but Cochrane saved my life and I can't alert the Fourth Cavalry that he's here. On the other hand, how can I remain silent while a bushwhack is being prepared before my very eyes?

Duane felt immobilized. All he could do was roll another cigarette, his hands trembling slightly. Cochrane's fighting a war that ended seven years ago, and he must be plumb loco, deliberated Duane. He decided to get the hell out of there and worry about moral implications some other time. He took a step toward Beasley's horse, when he heard the hoofbeats of Cochrane's steed. The outlaws stopped digging as their commander returned from his scout. Out of morbid curiosity, Duane joined them.

Cochrane climbed down from the saddle as Duane hung back at the edge of the crowd. Cochrane was bearded, covered with dust, wearing his old worn gray wool Confederate cavalry officer's jacket, but the brass buttons had been replaced by bone buttons, the shoulder straps removed, and there was no gold sash around his waist. He unscrewed the cap off his canteen and took a swig, then cleared his throat and said, "They're right on schedule—should be here around sundown. Continue with your digging, men. Please take my horse, Mr. Braddock."

Duane accepted the reins. "May I have a word with you alone, sir?" He nodded toward the horses, and Cochrane appeared surprised.

"What's on your mind?"

"Sir, I'd advise you to think this over. It's no little robbery of an out-of-the-way bank that we're talking about. A lot of men will be killed, and if there's a God in heaven, you're going to pay for it."

Annoyed, Cochrane stared at him. "Perhaps you've got a fever and had better lie down. I'll take care of my own horse—give me the reins."

"I don't mean to be disrespectful, sir, but *thou shalt not kill.*"

Cochrane laughed darkly. "Is this the Pecos Kid talking to me about killing? I'm fighting a war, but you just shoot people for the hell of it, right? You've even killed a federal marshal, so don't preach the Ten Commandments to me. Nobody's innocent here—not me, not you, and not those damned Nigra-stealing Yankees. If you can't perform your duties, then get the hell out of here."

"If I get out of here," Duane said, "I'm going to warn those soldiers."

As soon as the words were out of Duane's mouth, he realized that he'd made a mistake. Out of nowhere Cochrane punched Duane flush on the jaw, and Duane blacked out. When he opened his eyes, all the outlaws were standing around him.

"Sergeant Beasley, tie and gag this man," said Cochrane coolly.

"What's he done?" asked Beasley.

"He wants to inform the Yankees that we're throwing a little surprise party for them."

Now it was Beasley's turn to be surprised. "Why don't we shoot 'im?"

"Not a bad idea." Cochrane drew his gun and aimed it at Duane's head. "I execute you herewith for the attempted betrayal of my command."

Duane gazed transfixed into the muzzle. Cochrane's trigger knuckle whitened, then he paused, became pensive, and sighed. "Tie and gag him. We'll deal with this later."

The outlaws moved toward Duane, except Johnny Pinto, who held back and watched with an expression of utmost compassion. Duane loathed being tied and gagged; he glanced about for a path of escape, but was surrounded by irregulars.

"You can come the hard way," said Beasley, "or the easy way. It don't make a damn to me."

Duane tried to crash through the cordon of muscle surrounding him, but the irregulars massed in his path. Walsh lunged for his arms, but Duane cracked him with an uppercut, pushed him out of the way, and was hit in the mouth with a solid punch from Beasley. Then another outlaw came from behind and caught Duane in a headlock. Hertzog grabbed his right arm, Beasley punched him again, and Jim Walsh caught Duane's left arm. The others dived on Duane, forced him to the ground, and tied him tightly with scratchy brown hemp. Duane tasted blood and struggled with futility as they gagged him.

"Throw him somewhere out of the way," growled Cochrane, a tone of disgust in his voice. "The pay wagon is arriving directly, and when we're finished with the damned Yankees, a firing squad might be a good idea for a certain traitor named Duane Braddock."

Outlaws carried Duane's squirming form fifty yards from the bushwhack site, unceremoniously dumped him behind a thicket, then returned to their positions. Unable to move his arms and legs, Duane rolled himself around so he could see Cochrane's grand plan unfold. The dynamite had been buried, all marks erased, and the outlaws were deploying on the near side of the trail, hidden by thick underbrush, with Cochrane firmly in command.

A gag soaked with saliva sat in Duane's mouth, his hands were numb from tightened twine, and a rattlesnake could bite him easily, not to mention a poisonous spider or lizard, while a wildcat could chew off his ear. *I should keep my big mouth shut, but how can any decent person keep quiet at a massacre?*

He wrestled with his dilemma as the detachment drew closer in the distance. Then he detected a footfall behind him, and expected an Apache with a hatchet in his hand, but it was Johnny Pinto, a twisted smile on his vulpine features. Johnny glanced from side to side warily, then dropped to one knee in front of Duane, yanked out his Smith & Wesson, and aimed it at

Duane's head. "Say your prayers, shithead. You've come to the end of your road."

Duane couldn't speak with the gag in his mouth, and all he could do was make surprised gurgle sounds. Johnny reached forward, took Duane's nose in his fingers, and gave it a firm painful pinch. "Got you where I want you, eh? You done fucked with the wrong cowboy, and I'm a-gonna blow yer head off right naow."

Johnny yanked back the hammer while Duane's heart thumped with trepidation, terror, and madness. He protested vehemently through the gag, but only vague muffled groans came out. Johnny's finger tightened around the trigger, a smile creased his battered lips, and he joyfully anticipated the utter destruction of Duane's cranium. Then they heard a new voice. "What's going on over there?" asked Cochrane.

He was striding toward them, and Johnny quickly holstered the Smith & Wesson. "I just come to see how the prisoner is doin'," replied Johnny guiltily.

"Nobody told you to leave the horses. Get back there."

"You ain't a-gonna turn him loose, are you?"

"Don't ever leave your post again, you goddamned eight ball."

"Yessir." Johnny slouched toward the horses, cursing himself for not killing Braddock when he'd had the chance. *I hope Cochrane doesn't take the damned gag off him.* Johnny glanced back, and saw Cochrane talking to Duane, the gag still firmly stuffed into Duane's mouth. *Maybe I should jump on a horse and ride the hell out of here,* thought Johnny, *but this is Injun territory, and I could use five thousand dollars. No, I've got to see this thing through.*

"I'm really disappointed in you," said Cochrane, seated beside Duane. "I can't remove your gag and let you have a drink of water, because you'd holler at the top of your lungs. I thought you were a friend, but I'm wrong again." Cochrane shook his head sadly. "I've taken you into my home, we've broken bread together, and you'd give me up to the Yankee bastards? Doesn't the word *honor* mean anything to you?"

Duane tried to answer, but only feeble choked murmurs escaped the gag. He felt suffocation, and his body ached from being wrapped too tightly. He wanted to tell Cochrane that Johnny Pinto had tried to kill the Pecos Kid and doubtless would make another attempt soon.

"You've got an answer for everything," said Cochrane, "but you were going to betray soldiers who'd saved your life. I can't begin to tell you how disappointed I am, but you're young, you've never been in the war, and it's just a history lesson that you've learned from books written by Yankee professors."

Sergeant Beasley trudged toward them and saluted. "The Yankees is a-comin', sir. You'd better take yer post."

"I'll be right there, Sergeant."

Beasley returned to the bushwhack site while Cochrane lingered a few moments with Duane. "This is a very sad day for me," muttered Cochrane. "I guess nothing is sacred to some people."

Cochrane spat into the dirt, then turned and headed for his position. Duane rolled onto his stomach and rested his chin on a clump of grama grass as an ant crawled up his leg. Cochrane hid behind a tangle of benson cactus while the other outlaws were concealed deftly as Apaches.

On the horizon, the cavalry detachment rode toward doomsday. Duane struggled against his ropes, distorted himself into odd positions, but the binding only became tighter. The ant munched a certain tender portion of his anatomy, and all he could do was screech into the gag that stuffed his mouth. *God, if you get me out of this, I'll go to Mass every Sunday for the rest of my life.*

He tried to think of other subjects, such as the suffering of Jesus on the cross, mocked by his enemies. Meanwhile, the ant crawled up his back while the gag in his mouth upset his stomach. He wished an Apache would appear out of the bush and chop off his head quickly, cleanly, and painlessly.

Instead, Johnny Pinto arose out of the bush, the Smith & Wesson in his hand and a fiendish smile on his face. "Guess who's back?" he said. "It's me, Johnny Pinto, the feller you done took advantage of back in Ceballos Rios. Let me tell you somethin', peckerhead. Nobody messes with Johnny Pinto and gets away with it." Johnny holstered his Smith & Wesson, then pulled the bowie knife out of the scabbard at the back of his belt. "I'm a-gonna to cut yer fuckin' throat."

Thank God, thought Duane. He'd become delirious with pain and strain, and all he wanted was a quick exit. He closed his eyes as Johnny Pinto brought the sharp blade of knife to rest against Duane's throat.

Johnny looked around, and no one was close. His time had come, and a smile creased his face. "This is it, Mr. Pecos Kid. Bye-bye."

He pressed the blade into Duane's throat, and a thin red line appeared. Duane's eyes were closed, he appeared at peace, but Johnny had hoped to enjoy Duane squirming for his life. "Hey, wake up," Johnny said. "It ain't no fun this way."

Duane was passed out cold, skin waxen, but Johnny thought Duane might've died of fright. Johnny pressed his ear against Duane's shirt, heard his heart beating, but felt something odd. Unbuttoning Duane's shirt, he saw a rosary of crude black beads with a silver crucifix hanging from the bottom. Jesus Christ crowned with thorns, nailed, lanced, and dying on his eternal cross, gazed pleadingly into Johnny Pinto's eyes.

The schoolmaster's son shivered as he held the crucifixion in his hand. He'd been to church during his youth and recalled the sacrificial lamb of God. Duane Braddock lay helpless before his executioner, tiny dots of blood on his throat. Johnny caught a glimpse of himself as a hateful spiteful blood-soaked killer, and something told him to get the hell out of there. He stuffed his knife into its scabbard as he fled toward the horses, leaving Duane Braddock unconscious on the ground.

The pay wagon drew closer, its commanding officer riding stiffly in front of the column, next to a Fourth Cavalry guidon in the hand of Private John Jenkins from County Limerick, Ireland. The detachment neared Devil's Creek, and Jenkins anticipated his evening meal of hardtack, beans, and bacon, while hoping that his name wouldn't appear on the guard roster two nights in a row.

Jenkins was a slender florid-faced trooper who couldn't wait to get out of the army. He'd enlisted in Boston, hoping for high adventure, but instead found low hardship and danger. Some of the sergeants were vicious, while many of the officers didn't give a damn about the men. A soldier never knew when an arrow with his name on it was going to pierce his heart.

Jenkins searched the terrain on both sides of the column. The Comanche nation could be out there, aiming their weapons at him, but odds were against it. He prayed that the bacon wasn't rotten, there were no worms in the beans, and a mouse hadn't shit in the flour, for often the army received spoiled rations purchased by dishonest agents who'd bribed important politicians. Jenkins felt lost, forgotten, and despised by most decent Americans as he rode toward his rendezvous with destiny.

Duane opened his eyes, and at first didn't know where he was. He tried to move, realized that he was tightly secured, and remembered dreaming about Johnny Pinto slicing his throat.

He rolled over laboriously, propped his chin on grama grass, and was surprised to see the cavalry detachment straight ahead, approaching Devil's Creek. Duane wanted to jump into the air and shout the warning, but was unable to move. Incredible carnage would ensue, but he couldn't stop the ant crawling across his chest.

He narrowed his Apache eyes and saw Cochrane and his irregulars poised to attack the hapless cavalry detachment. Duane wasn't sure he wanted to watch, but youthful inquisitiveness got the better of him yet again. The cavalry column come to a halt at the edge of Devil's Creek, the commander raised his arm in the air, and hollered, "Detachment—halt!"

In the front rank, Private Jenkins shot the guidon straight up into the air, then brought it down just as speedily. He pulled his horse to a halt, then sat at attention, the guidon fluttering in the breeze.

"Dismount!" ordered the detachment commander.

It was the word Jenkins had been praying for during the past several hours. He took a deep breath, raised his leg, and eased out of the saddle. Lowering himself to the ground, he glanced around for signs of Indians. He thought he saw a portion of a bootprint several feet away, but was certain he was imagining things.

He slammed the bottom of the guidon pole into the ground and made it freestanding. Taking his canteen out of its pouch, he thought he heard a strange buzzing sound, but it had to be insects. He uncorked his canteen as men stretched their legs and slapped alkali off blue pants behind him. A huge cloud of dust arose in the air, and Jenkins felt as if his legs had been permanently bowed from riding the horse so long.

Thank God we're here, he thought as he raised the canteen to his lips. He took a gulp and was about to swallow another when a terrific boom came to his ears, accompanied by an orange flash. A terrible force smashed his body apart, and he went flying into the air, along with other men, horses, and official government equipment.

The explosion caused the ground to heave beneath Duane's stomach, his ears rang with the fierce blast, and the cavalry detachment was shredded before his very eyes. It was the most cataclysmic and gory spectacle of his life, and then, before the smoke cleared, irregular soldiers charged in a skirmish line, firing rifles at twisting twitching bodies clad in torn blue uniforms. Some of the troopers tried to put up a fight, but they were wounded, dazed, taken by surprise, and cut down.

Cochrane personally dispatched the commander of the detachment, shooting him once in the chest and a second time in the head. Duane closed his eyes and shuddered. He'd read of wars and vast carnage, but no historian's prose could do it justice, as shots reverberated across endless buttes and mesas. It made no sense. Duane couldn't hope to understand; it was the lowest, basest, cruelest, most sinful act imaginable, yet its leader was a noble-minded ex-officer from a family of leading scholars.

The firing stopped, and the irregulars proceeded to gather up the gold. "Whar's the goddamned horses?" bellowed Beasley. "Pinto—git yer ass over hyar." Beasley waited for a response, but there was no sign of Johnny Pinto. An expression of concern came over Beasley's face as he turned toward Cochrane for his orders.

Cochrane had an unholy glow in his eyes, his face flushed with emotion, a curl of smoke rising from his service revolver. "Take two men and see what happened to Pinto. The rest of you be on your guard."

Cochrane dropped to one knee amid the wreckage and carnage. He appeared lost in a dream, while Beasley, Walsh, and Cox made their way back to the horses. The massacre clearly disturbed Cochrane; he was uneasy, and his eyes darted about frantically. The Devil's Creek massacre was different from the robbery of a small bank with no casualties.

Beasley's voice traveled over the sage. "Johnny Pinto is *daid!*"

Everyone turned and stared in the direction of Beasley's voice. "Are you sure?" asked Cochrane.

"Looks like he shot his own damned self!"

The company commander leapt to his feet, electrified by the news. His gun in hand, he ran toward Beasley's voice, joined by the rest of his men. The horses were picketed in an arroyo shielded by cottonwood trees. Beasley perched on one knee and looked at a figure sprawled on the ground with blood and brains everywhere. A gun lay near Johnny's right hand, with powder burns on the side of his head where the bullet began its penetration.

Cochrane was aghast; it was the last outcome he'd expected, but he didn't have time to think about it. "Load the gold onto the packhorses," he said. "Let's get out of here, boys. We don't have time to bury him."

The outlaws led their horses toward the killing ground while Cochrane headed for Duane. He whipped his knife out of its scabbard on his belt, and Duane thought his throat was going to be severed neatly, as in his dream. Cochrane sliced the knot that bound Duane's legs, then unwrapped the twine. Next he untied the gag and pulled it out of Duane's arid mouth. Duane hacked, spit, coughed, and sucked in huge gulps of air. His legs were numb as he tried to stand, but he lost his balance and fell to the side.

"We'll hold you prisoner until things settle down," Cochrane said, "and then we'll decide what to do with you. If you behave yourself, maybe we'll let you go."

Duane drew himself to his feet. "I've never seen—"

Cochrane held out the gag to Duane. "I'm not interested in your platitudes. Do you want this back in your mouth?"

Duane definitely didn't yearn for the gag. Cochrane pushed him toward outlaws picking gold coins off the ground while others were confiscating weapons and ammunition from dead soldiers. The closer Duane came to the scene of destruction, the more horrific it appeared. He felt faint from the gruesome mess, and Johnny Pinto had killed himself at the height of the battle? Events were passing too quickly, and Duane felt swept along by the whirlwind.

"Do you mind if I go somewhere and sit down?" Duane asked Cochrane.

"Suit yourself, but don't go far. You should consider yourself a prisoner of war."

Duane knew that he should keep his mouth shut, but youthful impetuosity won out yet again. "What war are you talking about, sir?"

"The war against disloyal friends, and if you give me any more lip, I'm going to gag you again, because I'm not in the mood, understand?"

Beasley glanced at Cochrane. "How about that firing squad?"

"I've decided that we'll court-martial him when we return to the canyon."

"But sir, he'll be nothin' but trouble."

"I'm getting tired of back talk, Sergeant. Please carry out your orders."

I'm not in your ragtag lunatic army, Duane wanted to say, but this time managed to keep himself under control. His arms bound tightly behind him, all feeling gone from his fingers, he walked stiffly past the Fourth Cavalry guidon lying on the ground. He wanted a spot of clear unbloodied desert where he could sit and think through his latest catastrophe.

Private John Jenkins lay in a puddle of blood, only it wasn't his blood. The initial explosion had blown him into the air, and after returning to the ground, one of the other men landed atop him. Then a side of the wagon had fallen across Jenkins's legs, breaking tibia and fibula bones.

Miraculously he was still alive, although he pretended to be dead. A three-inch gash had opened on his forehead, his clothes were torn to rags, and he heard someone approaching. His greatest fear was that they'd find him alive. Why'd I ever join the army? he asked himself dazedly.

A tall man in a black shirt and black jeans approached, his black cowboy hat slanted low over his eyes, and he looked vaguely familiar to Private Jenkins. Jenkins peered intently at the youthful face, and then it hit him. My God!

Private Jenkins had been with the detachment in Shelby on the night the Pecos Kid gunned down Otis Puckett. The man in black walked past the wounded trooper while Jenkins felt a painful rack in his left leg. His bone poked through his skin, blood oozed out the wound, and the young soldier felt faint. A terrific swoosh filled his ears as he passed out cold amid the mass of corpses scattered beside Devil's Creek.

The gold and other booty had been loaded onto packhorses, the gang was ready to depart for Lost Canyon, and the last order of business was Duane

Braddock. The outlaws headed toward him, the moment he'd dreading had arrived, and he didn't know what to expect. His hands still were tied behind his back, but he managed to clamber to his feet and greet them. "Anybody got a taste of water?" he asked.

"Somebody toss him a canteen," ordered Cochrane as he pulled his knife. He proceeded to slice the knot that held Duane's arms.

"I thought," said Beasley, "that we were going to give him the firing squad."

"Everybody deserves a fair trial," replied Cochrane. "We live by the articles of war here, remember?"

"But he was going to betray us to the Yankees. I don't trust him."

"Neither do I," replied Cochrane. "We'll talk it over at his court-martial, and I'll take full responsibility for him until then. If he tries to escape, you have my permission to shoot him like a dog."

The twine fell from Duane's wrists, but he still couldn't move his fingers. Slowly, painfully, he turned toward Cochrane. "You're the one who's in deep trouble, not me. I wonder what Robert E. Lee would say about you fine gentlemen killers!"

Duane spat out the last word angrily, noticing hostility and riot on the faces of the irregulars. The Pecos Kid struggled to move his fingers, but they were rusty iron hinges.

Cochrane frowned. "Let's get on our horses and ride on out of here. We'll settle everything back at the canyon."

"But," protested Beasley, "he just insulted us. We ought to shoot him right here and naow. Hell, I'll be happy to do it myself."

"Put the gun away, Sergeant," replied Cochrane, "and move the column out. That's an order."

"I think yer makin' a mistake, sir."

Cochrane gazed at him coldly. "I'm not going to tell you again."

"Yessir." Beasley performed an about-face and ordered the men to mount up.

Nobody helped the traitor, so Duane raised his numb hand and grabbed the pommel of his saddle, then stuffed his foot into the stirrup. The column was on its way back to Lost Canyon, and Duane fell in at the rear with Jim Walsh and the packhorses.

"Duane—ride up here where I can see you!"

It was the voice of Cochrane, and Duane touched spurs to the withers of his horse. Drawing closer, Duane saw that Cochrane's jaw was set, and his eyes were steely as he peered ahead like the combat commander that he was. He loves this war business, Duane realized. The soldiers at Devil's Creek weren't real people to him, and neither am I.

"What happened to your neck?" Cochrane asked, glancing at Duane. "Looks like somebody cut you."

Duane recalled his nightmare about Johnny Pinto. "I'm not sure, but what do you make of Johnny shooting himself?"

"He picked a strange time to do it, right in the middle of the robbery. And you've sure fooled me, Duane Braddock."

"You fooled me, too, Captain Cochrane. It's been a helluva day."

"Make the most of it, young man. Because you don't have too many left."

CHAPTER 11

THE PAY WAGON DIDN'T ARRIVE AT Fort Stockton on schedule, and it was assumed that bad weather or an accident had forced the temporary delay. Concern mounted as days passed, and finally a detachment was sent to locate the missing wagon. It was commanded by First Lieutenant Arnold J. Haffner, a West Point graduate from the great state of Wisconsin.

The detachment numbered thirty men with a wagon filled with supplies and a medical officer. Everyone suspected that Comanches had waylaid the pay wagon and massacred its escort, but maybe someone had survived.

The detachment headed north, finding nothing unusual for the first four days. Then, as they approached Devil's Creek, they spotted hordes of buzzards circling in the sky, and smelled the stench of death. Lieutenant Haffner led his men across the creek, as they raised their bandannas over their noses. The

closer they drew to the slaughterhouse, the more dis-
comforting it became. Bodies partially eaten by scav-
engers were everywhere, the wagon utterly demolished,
all the money gone.

Haffner was glad that he was an officer as he turned
to Sergeant Gilhooley. "Organize a burial party."

"Yessir."

Gilhooley set to his task as Haffner rode upwind of
the disaster. The stalwart officer wanted to retch, but it
wouldn't look proper before his men. He was certain
that Indians had done it, and every warrior who refused
to move to a reservation should be exterminated on the
spot.

Something jarred the underbrush ahead, and
Lieutenant Haffner yanked his service revolver. His
jaw dropped as a ragged trooper with a crude splint on
his leg crawled out, covered with dust and blood, like
an apparition. Haffner didn't know whether to run or
open fire when the ghost said, through a cracked voice,
"Don't shoot."

Haffner ran toward the wounded trooper and held
him steady by the shoulder. "What the hell happened?"

Private John Jenkins's beard was caked with blood,
and a mad gleam emanated from his eyes. "It was an
outlaw gang," he croaked, "and they was led by the
Pecos Kid."

The irregulars locked Duane in a shed after they
returned to Lost Canyon, and he was under guard
twenty-four hours a day. They nailed shut the windows, provided no stove, and offered only a cot, blanket, and chamber pot. Duane expected to be called out
any moment and put before the firing squad.

They'd let him keep his rosary and King James Bible to provide solace in his final hours. He tried to think of life in the world to come. *Will I wear a white robe and live in the clouds, or is religion a pile of horseshit like everything else?*

Sometimes he gazed out the windows and observed irregulars going about their chores like monks at the monastery in the clouds. It didn't take long to discover where the gold was hidden, for he'd had seen the packhorses led to a certain ridge above the cow pasture. The wealth was stashed in a cave, prior to being turned over to the Confederate government in exile.

His other important discovery was the shack where they stored the dynamite. He'd never paid attention to it before, for there were many structures and lean-tos in Lost Canyon, but amazing what a man can learn if he observes quietly and keeps his mouth shut.

One answer eluded him, no matter how he tried to clarify it. Johnny Pinto had killed himself at the height of the massacre, and Duane had no idea why. Evidently the throat cutting had been no dream. Another mystery, and only Johnny Pinto knew the answer.

Circulation had returned to Duane's hands, he was fast as ever, and his health recovered almost completely. He paced back and forth inside his little shack like a caged animal, and sometimes thought of diving out the window and making a run for it. But he was unarmed, and there were guards. He wouldn't get ten feet during the day, but maybe if he dodged like an Apache at night, he could disappear into the mountains.

When he tired of pacing and looking out the window, he lay on the cot with the Bible. Hour after hour he read about the tribulations of Job, the pronouncements of Koheleth, the psalms of David, and the Song of Songs.

> *Behold, thou art fair, my love,*
> *Thou hast doves' eyes.*

He often thought of Miss Vanessa Fontaine and hoped she wasn't in bed with Lieutenant Clayton Dawes. Sometimes he prayed his rosary and tried to be philosophical. Everybody dies, and I'm just going a little early, that's all. I've tried to lead a proper life, I never killed except in self-defense, I never stole anything except a couple of horses in emergencies, and as for what occurred between Miss Vanessa Fontaine and me, nobody got hurt except us.

It was night at Fort Clark, and Vanessa was packing her bags, her stagecoach scheduled to leave at dawn. She'd questioned her motives during past days, searched her heart, and decided to proceed to Escondido, then figure out what to do next.

Vanessa didn't make sense to herself as she checked lists against personal belongings. I could be in Paris having a gay time, but instead I'm chasing a young man who probably hates me and everything I stand for. But tea parties and fancy dress balls no longer fascinated the former Charleston belle. Now she loved Duane Braddock, and love didn't come along every day.

Vanessa raised McCabe's Spiller & Burr revolver, made sure it wasn't loaded, then thumbed back the hammer and took aim at a crack in the wall. The finely tooled revolver wasn't a jeweled toy like the derringer, and she'd also inherited McCabe's double-barrel sawed-off shotgun. The only thing Texans respect is lead, she mused as she pulled the trigger, her hand steady. *Click.* Then she thumbed loads into the chambers. *I'll give them plenty if they ever start up with me.*

There was a knock on the door. "Mrs. Dawes?" It was Mrs. Brean, her hostess. "Colonel MacKenzie would like to have a word with you."

"Now?"

"He says it's important."

"By all means send him in."

The door opened and the great Civil War hero strode into her room, his posture erect, uniform immaculate, hair and mustache neatly combed, but with an air of danger and whiff of gunpowder about him. "I'm sorry to disturb you," he said, holding up a piece of paper. "But this report's just come in and I thought you ought to look at it."

Vanessa had no idea what he was talking about, but she took the paper, held it to the oil lamp, and recognized an official army communication from Fort Stockton.

I departed Fort Stockton on 28 October 1871 with my detachment, pursuant to Special Order No. 324. My mission was to locate the missing pay wagon, and I had with me one sergeant and twenty-eight troopers. On 1 November 1871, at Devil's Creek, we located what was left of the pay wagon. Every man had been slaughtered except Private John Jenkins, who miraculously survived despite two broken legs and numerous other wounds. All the gold was taken, including weapons, ammunition, and supplies. We thought it was Comanches, because they've been active in

the area, but Private Jenkins swore it was a band
of outlaws led by Duane Braddock, also known as
the Pecos Kid. Jenkins alleged that he'd seen
Braddock previously and knew what he looked
like. We buried the dead and returned with
Private Jenkins to Fort Stockton on 8 November
1871.

> *Arnold J. Haffner*
> *Lieutenant, Fourth Cavalry*

Cochrane had become moody and disgruntled since the Devil's Creek robbery. He couldn't sleep at night, fretted during the day, had difficulty making up his mind, and was nagged steadily by his future bride, who wanted him to release Duane Braddock from captivity.

Cochrane hid in the bedroom while Juanita fussed in the kitchen, because he didn't want to talk about Braddock anymore. Cochrane considered betrayal the most terrible crime of all, and the South had been betrayed enough.

But the former officer was haunted by the action at Devil's Creek. He'd seen much bloodshed in the war, but the recent carnage disturbed him peculiarly, while Duane's moral passion had shaken his confidence. Occasionally Cochrane could view the robbery from Duane's perspective: a bloody wanton massacre of innocent men.

If Bobby Lee were alive, he'd probably disapprove of the Devil's Creek robbery, deduced Cochrane. But they didn't call General Lee the Gray Fox for nothing, and if it hadn't been for old Jeb, Lee might've defeated the federals at Gettysburg.

Cochrane felt guilty about Gettysburg, although he hadn't given the order to raid into Pennsylvania. That had been Jeb Stuart's idea, and old Jeb had led the Confederate Cavalry Corps on a wild rampage through Yankee land, when he should've provided intelligence about approaching federal troops. Bobby Lee went into Gettysburg blind as a result, and lost the most critical battle of the war.

Young Lieutenant Cochrane had enjoyed the Pennsylvania raid tremendously. He'd drunk liberated whiskey, eaten liberated steaks, and even bedded a certain rambunctious Yankee farm girl. But at Gettysburg, General Lee made judgments based on inadequate information; he'd ordered General Pickett's costly charge, plus a few other vain exercises in blood, and that was the end of the Confederacy, although Cochrane and the others hadn't realized it at the time.

Cochrane was tormented by remorse, headaches, and vague glimpses of Sister Death dancing in the corner of the room. Sometimes he woke up abruptly at night and found himself looking at his hands, to see if they had blood on them. Everything had been fine until Duane Braddock came along. The former seminary student forced Cochrane to look at himself in a new light, and Cochrane didn't like what he saw.

Cochrane wanted to let Duane go, but that would be an admission of guilt. If Cochrane and his irregulars were truly soldiers, then Braddock was guilty of treachery in the face of the enemy. You either believed in the articles of war or you didn't.

There was a knock on the door, then Juanita opened it. "It is Beasley," she said, "and I think I know what he wants."

"Tell him I'll be right there, and leave me alone, please."

She closed the door, he rolled out of bed, thrust his feet into his boots, splashed water onto his face, and strapped on his Remington. He reached for the doorknob, and Beasley stood by the kitchen window, gazing toward the shack where Duane Braddock was under guard, while Juanita stirred a pot of beans at the stove. The sergeant spun around as Cochrane appeared.

"What's on your mind?" asked Cochrane.

Beasley aimed his thumb back. "The men think it's time you did something about Braddock, sir. If one of them was a-gonna warn the Yankees, you would've shot him by now. They can't understand the special treatment for the Kid."

Cochrane's face was a marble mask while thoughts spun furiously in his head. *Braddock is undermining the effectiveness of my command, and it's time to get this over with.* "All right—prepare the prisoner for the firing squad, Sergeant Beasley."

Beasley was about to reply when Juanita screamed, "No!" She stood at the stove, a ladle in her hands, fire emanating from her eyes. "He is just a boy! How can you do this thing?"

"It's none of your business," replied Cochrane. Then he trembled involuntarily as he recalled grotesque twisted bodies lying alongside Devil's Creek. "Sergeant, you have your orders."

"You don't have to show up, sir," Beasley replied sympathetically. "I can give the commands myself."

"I don't need anybody to do my work, Sergeant. Notify me when everything is ready."

Beasley saluted and marched out of the cabin. Cochrane sat at the table and wrote:

*I, the undersigned, have on this date 19 November
1871 executed Duane Braddock, born in Texas
and known as the Pecos Kid, for treachery in the
face of the enemy.*

> Richard Cochrane
> Captain, CSA
> 1st Virginia Irregulars

He was examining what he'd written when he heard
Juanita's voice on the other end of the table. "Just
because you sign a piece of paper, that makes it all
right?" she asked. "Have you finally gone loco?" Her
usual subtropical languor had transformed into righ-
teous passion, eyes popping out of her skull. "You are
going to *kill* that boy for *nothing*? Are you completely
lost, Ricardo? Robbery after robbery, you come back
with money, and I want to believe you are a great
brave soldier—but now I see the truth. You are no better than a Comanchero, and maybe worse, because
they do not pretend to be brave soldiers. You—you are
an *insult* to brave soldiers."

She slapped his face, and he recoiled from the force
of her blow. No woman had ever struck him before,
and he flushed with rage as he raised his hand against
her. She snarled like a puma, dived through the air,
and scratched five sharp fingernails across his purple
scar while he came up reflexively with a left hook,
caught her on the mouth, and the force of the blow
sent her sprawling against the wall. Her head slammed
against it, her eyes rolled up, and she collapsed onto
the floor.

It was silent and eerie as Cochrane gazed at her
sprawled like a rag doll. He touched his finger to his
scar, and blood appeared on his fingertips. Taking a

deep breath, he leaned against the table. What have I done?

It seemed that his world was crumbling around him. He rushed toward Juanita and rolled her onto her back. Did I kill her? he asked himself. He pressed his ear to her bosom and heard the steady beat. *Thank God.* A trickle of blood flowed from the corner of her mouth, and he felt ashamed. What's happened here? he asked himself. He felt as if he were losing his sanity. Did I do this?

He wiped blood from her unconscious lips and held the red smear before him. It evoked a line from Shakespeare's *Macbeth*, which he'd read at the University of Virginia, never realizing its full import.

It will have blood, they say.
And blood will have blood.

He recalled the slaughtered Yankees, and their blood had been the same color as Juanita's. What if I'm just another murderer? The concept was fearsome, he wanted to cry out, but then came a knock on the door.

He arose behind the table. "Come in?"

It was Beasley. "The firing squad is ready, sir."

"Did you gag him, because I'm sick of listening to his horseshit?"

"Wouldn't have it any other way, sir."

Cochrane followed Beasley out the door, and Beasley didn't stop to look behind the table, where Juanita lay unconscious. Cochrane felt giddy and strange, as if his feet weren't touching the ground. Beasley led him to the back of the bunkhouse, where the prisoner had been tied to a cottonwood tree, a gunnysack pulled over his head. Irregulars stood in a straight rank, at ease with their rifles, watching their commander stride onto the scene. Only the medical officer was unarmed, and he hovered to the side, holding a Bible.

"Let's get this over with," Cochrane said impatiently. "Does the chaplain have an appropriate prayer for the occasion?"

"Yes, sir," replied Dr. Montgomery.

"Let's get it over with."

"May the Lord have mercy on your soul," intoned the doctor.

"That's it?" asked Cochrane.

"That's it."

"Atten-hut!"

The ex-soldiers snapped to attention as if on guard at the Confederate White House in Richmond. Cochrane drew himself erect, hands stiff down his sides, and intoned, "Pursuant to the authority vested in me by my commission as a captain in the Confederate Cavalry Corps, I order you, Duane Braddock, to be shot to death for treachery in the face of the enemy. Carry out the execution, Sergeant Beasley."

Dr. Montgomery cleared his throat. "It is customary, in these matters, to let the prisoner make a final statement."

Cochrane scowled, because the last thing he wanted was another tirade from Duane Braddock, especially one energized by the prospect of his certain demise. "Do we have to?"

"It's traditional."

The natural conservative strain in Cochrane carried the day yet again. "Sergeant Beasley, remove the gag, please."

"Yessir." Sergeant Beasley stepped forward and pulled the gunnysack off Duane Braddock's head, tousling

Duane's black hair. Then Beasley removed the gag, untied the blindfold, and took a step back. "Have you got anything to say, varmint, before we carry out the verdict?"

Duane Braddock was pale and blinking like a newborn bird. Slowly he turned toward Cochrane and said in a hoarse whisper, "You're the guilty one, not me."

"I've heard enough, Sergeant Beasley. Put the gag back on him."

A terrible screech rent the afternoon air. Cochrane spun around and was appalled to see Juanita running toward him barefoot, skirts flying in all directions, wild fury in her eyes, blood on her lips. "Stop!" she shrieked. "You are all *murderers*!"

She appeared headed for Duane, and Cochrane moved to intercept her. "Get back!" he yelled.

"*Murderers!*" She sallied straight for him, and he realized that he couldn't punch her again. So he got low, sprang, and tried to tackle her, but she kicked him in the face, leapt over him, collided with Duane, wrapped her arms tightly around him, and hollered, "If you want to shoot this gringo, you will have to shoot me first!"

Her words reverberated off mountains, and everyone stared at her in alarm. Duane was at the outermost extremes of sanity and became an interested spectator at his own firing squad. *Hail Mary, full of grace, the Lord is with thee.*

"I'll take care of the bitch," said Beasley as he headed toward Juanita.

"Leave her alone!" Cochrane pushed himself off the ground, his bleeding nose creating a bright red mustache. He stalked toward Juanita and said, "Woman, you'd better stop interfering. Get away from here at once, or I'll slap you down!"

"You feelthy bandito!" she yelled back at him. "How could I ever think of marrying someone like you? Let me tell you something else you do not know. When you shoot me, you will be shooting your *child,* too, but we are not afraid of you. You are the one who should be afraid of *God!*"

Cochrane was feeling peculiar again. I'm going to be a father? Before Gettysburg, there was hope of glory, but now dishonor arrived from every direction. He examined Duane Braddock's perfect, unscarred face as Juanita hugged him firmly. Is she in love with him? Cochrane wondered. Maybe the child she's carrying is Duane's, or maybe she's not pregnant at all.

Cochrane brought his face to within inches of hers. "Get away from here," he growled as he grabbed her arm. But she held on to Duane more tightly, baring her teeth like a wild desert creature. Cochrane struggled to pry her loose; she wouldn't let Duane go, but Cochrane was stronger. She grabbed a handful of Duane's shirt, and it tore open as she was yanked away from him.

The crucifix gleamed in the morning sun, and Cochrane's eyes widened at the sight of it. He reached forward, tore the beads off Duane's neck, and threw them into the dirt. Juanita took the opportunity to dive onto Duane again, embracing him tightly.

The irregulars looked at each other impatiently, because they were keyed up for the firing squad. "Why don't we just shoot both of 'em together?" asked Beasley.

"Yes—why don't you?" asked Juanita. "You are all cowards, you shoot a man who is tied up, and now you want to shoot an unarmed pregnant woman. If your mothers could see you, they would be *sick!*"

Cochrane pointed at Duane accusingly. "He nearly got us all killed, and if you want to die with him, that's your choice to make."

"I hate you!" she proclaimed. "The whole bunch of you would not dare face this man if he had a gun in his hand. You call yourself soldiers? Don't make me laugh, you *maricones*!"

The irregulars blushed, while Cochrane appeared on the verge of apoplexy. Meanwhile, Duane saw a chance to live. It was a long shot, but worth one last desperate try. "She's right," he uttered hoarsely. "There isn't a man jack among you who'd dare fight me fairly." Duane looked Cochrane in the eye. "And that goes for you, too, bushwhacker. You're a brave soldier when the odds are on your side, but I wonder how you'd hold up in a real fight. It's no wonder the South lost the war, with men like you for officers."

Something glowed in the dirt, and Cochrane saw Christ lying topsy-turvy beside a clump of grama grass. Devil's Creek troubled him, his woman hated him, and the very foundations of his life had been called into question. All he could do was fall back on the customs of his people. He drew himself to attention once more and looked down his nose at Duane. "I'm sick of your insults, and I demand satisfaction. Beasley, untie the prisoner."

Beasley wrinkled his brow. "What the hell fer?"

"Because I've just given you an order."

"You lettin' 'im go?"

"In case you haven't been listening, he's challenged me to a duel."

"But he's a fast hand—he'll shoot you down."

"Do as I say."

"But sir . . ."

"I'm still in command here, Sergeant, and this is still the Confederate Cavalry Corps."

Beasley cogitated for a few moments. "Yessir." He stepped forward and roughly untied Duane, who shook out his fingers, worked his shoulders, then bent down and picked up the rosary, which he dropped around his neck.

"Sergeant Beasley," said Cochrane, "give him your revolver and holster."

"But sir!"

"Sergeant Beasley—your insubordination is starting to wear on me. Would you please do as you're told?"

Beasley grumbled and growled as he unstrapped his holster, then he passed it to Duane. Juanita stood to the side fearfully, because someone was going to die, her man or his friend. Duane strapped on the holster and felt the old reassuring weight against his right leg. "Mind if I make sure it's loaded?"

"Long as you face the other way," replied Cochrane.

Duane drew the Remington and spun the cylinder, its balance different from his Colt, but loaded and well cared for by a conscientious soldier. Duane eased it into its holster, then turned toward Cochrane, who stood gaunt and pale in the morning light.

"I'm ready when you are," declared Cochrane.

It fell silent behind the bunkhouse, and the irregulars looked at each other in alarm. Events were taking an unpredictable course, and soldiers aren't the most flexible people in the world. Juanita stood uncertainly, one fist near her mouth, astonished by the results of her uncontrolled ranting and raving. She wanted to stop them, but felt drained, conflicted, and pregnant with life itself.

Duane had become his old self now that a gun rode

on his hip, but he didn't want another killing on his record. "You don't have a prayer against me," he told Cochrane. "Why don't you let me ride out of here, and let's forget the whole damned thing?"

Cochrane listened impassively. "You're not riding away from treachery, and you're not getting away with insulting an officer. If you won't draw, you'll force me to make the first move. Is that what you want?"

Duane peered into Cochrane's eyes across the space of ten feet. "You want me to kill you, right?"

Cochrane felt uneasy as he noticed the crucifix dangling at Duane's throat. Something told him every word Duane said was true, because he couldn't live with himself any longer. He glanced at Juanita, saw pity on her face, and felt like a fool. The contradictions and compulsions of his past overwhelmed him like a tidal wave, and with a mad laugh, Cochrane went for his gun.

Duane was unwilling to kill him, but had no alternative. His famous fast hand whacked out the Remington, and he fired as Cochrane was thumbing back his hammer. The Remington exploded, and the round socked Cochrane in the chest. The company commander appeared surprised, took a step backward, and looked at Duane whimsically. Duane was wearing a blue uniform; they stood on the battlefield at Gettysburg, cannon fired, and soldiers grappled around him. A smile came over Cochrane's face; he dropped to his knees before Duane, and tried to raise his gun for a final shot. "I have always done my duty as an officer," he whispered.

Then he fell onto his face and lay still. Juanita sobbed, dived atop him, and rolled him over. The front of Cochrane's shirt was covered with blood, his eye closed, scarred face finally at peace. Tears flowed down Juanita's cheeks as she wailed uncontrollably.

The strength drained out of Duane's legs; he sank to his butt on the ground, an expression of awe on his face. He'd just killed again, this time a former friend, and felt as if he were choking on blood and gore.

"Get him, boys!" said Beasley.

The remaining outlaws drew on Duane, but Duane rolled out swiftly as an Apache, lead splattering dirt and grass in all directions. The Pecos Kid dodged and fired two quick shots, striking Beasley and Walsh fatally. They toppled to the dirt; the other irregulars flopped onto their bellies, and Duane ran zigzag toward the bunkhouse. The irregulars fired wild shots at his receding figure, then he fell out of sight around the corner.

The irregulars looked at each other questioningly as their commanding officer and first sergeant lay dead in their midst. Accustomed to following orders, they didn't know what to do. Cochrane sprawled in Juanita's lap, and her lips moved imperceptibly as she prayed for him, tears running down her cheeks. Meanwhile, the Pecos Kid was at large in the vicinity.

Ginger Hertzog, who'd served under General A. P. Hill, turned to Cox, who'd fought in the famed Laurel Brigade. "He's on his way to the stable, and maybe we can head 'im off."

They were soldiers to the core; their commanding officer had been cut down before their eyes, and their path appeared obvious. Hertzog assumed command and ran with Colt in hand toward the corral while the irregulars followed him between the bunkhouse and a storage shed. At the end of the alley, they spread into a skirmish line and proceeded cautiously toward the corral, searching for the Pecos Kid in every cranny and crevice of the backyard.

"I wonder whar he went?" asked Hertzog, sniffing the air. "You don't think he'd try to get away on foot, do you?"

A bundle of long tan-colored dynamite sticks flew around the side of the bunkhouse, and the irregulars dropped to the dirt. Dynamite exploded violently, flinging Hertzog through the air. Before he landed, more dynamite fell upon the outlaws; powerful thunder rocked Lost Canyon, then rolled across the open desert.

Duane crouched behind the bunkhouse as dust and smoke cleared. Irregulars lay still in and around holes blown into the ground, similar to soldiers they'd bushwhacked in Devil's Creek. Duane advanced toward them, gun in hand, and saw a few bodies twitching on the ground, while others would never move again.

Duane was aghast at the carnage he'd wrought. He dropped to a sitting position, felt nauseated, and wondered whether to put the Colt to his head and blow his brains out. I'm no better than they, he surmised, and who am I to judge them, but is it wrong to defend myself? Again, he recalled the words of the old Jesuit Jean-Pierre de Caussade. *If we are truly humble, we will ask no questions about the road along which God is taking us.*

Dr. Montgomery shuffled onto the scene, carrying his little black bag full of surgical implements. Silently he dropped beside Hertzog and examined his wounds. "Dead," he muttered.

Duane had to get away from the bodies. Like a sleepwalker, he returned to the yard where Juanita wept over Captain Cochrane's pale and stiffening corpse. The sorrows of the world sat heavily upon Duane's young shoulders, and he wondered how to continue living. At least Captain Cochrane didn't have to face ambiguities anymore.

Duane felt like crying, because Cochrane had been a friend of sorts. He wanted me to kill him, because he couldn't live with twisted honor. Duane recalled the former company commander striding about Lost Canyon, a sterling example of a military man, but loyal to a fault, perhaps. Duane admired and disapproved of Captain Richard Cochrane, but Cochrane had turned Duane loose in a roundabout manner, then gone down like a soldier.

Captain Cochrane had taught Duane one valuable nugget of soldierly wisdom, and Duane would never forget it. No matter how severe the opposition, or how confusing the battlefield, a soldier keeps advancing toward his objective. But a man must make certain beforehand that his objective is just, and therein lay the rub. There was always a rub, unfortunately. Duane took off his hat, wiped his forehead with the back of his arm, and looked around. "We'd better get the hell out of here. Where do they keep the shovels?"

Juanita stared blankly into space, rocking Cochrane's corpse back and forth in her arms like Michelangelo's *Pietà*. Dr. Montgomery appeared around the corner of the bunkhouse, carrying his black bag. "I can't do anything for them," he said in a lazy singsong voice, as if he'd taken leave of his senses.

"Maybe it's time to do something for yourself," replied Duane. "Let's bury the captain and hit the trail."

"There's nothing for me in the Yankee world," muttered Dr. Montgomery gloomily. "I'm not going anywhere."

"You give up now," replied Duane, "Apaches will get you. They'll tie you upside down on that wagon wheel over there, and light a fire underneath your head. If you can't stand Yankees—and to tell you the truth, some of them are awful pains in the ass—why don't you find another band of guerrilla soldiers? They say that Mexico is full of them."

Dr. Montgomery smiled ruefully. "I ought to shoot you, but you'd beat me to the draw. Or maybe I should do nothing, because you gave the captain a fighting chance. Possibly you're right, he wanted to die. Devil's Creek was too much for him, and perhaps I should put a bullet through my own head, too, because it's what I deserve. You're young, but at least you've got the courage of your convictions. Do you understand any of this, or have I gone completely mad?"

"We don't have time to go mad," replied Duane. "The Apaches will be here before long, and we've got to bury the captain so that coyotes don't get him. Where are the shovels—and Juanita, you'd better pack any supplies we might need. You can make your novenas on the trail, and while you're at it, say a few for me."

CHAPTER 12

THE OLD CONCORD STAGECOACH traveled west from Fort Clark, escorted by a dozen cavalry soldiers and a Gatling gun bolted to the floor of a wagon. The lone column passed through a mountainous region with crags and bluffs that could conceal Indians, but the troopers stayed alert at all times.

Vanessa sat in the cab with other travelers and passed her time dozing and thinking about Duane Braddock. The Devil's Creek Massacre had undermined her faith in him, but she'd decided it was a case of mistaken identity. Unfortunately, the U.S. government didn't agree, and was negotiating with Mexico about sending an expeditionary force south of the border to hunt down the Pecos Kid.

Sometimes Vanessa guessed that Duane was the worst thing that ever happened to her, except for the Civil War. She tried to plan ahead, but fretted over

Duane fleeing across lawless Mexico. The Fourth Cavalry would shoot him on sight, but Mexico was a big country, and Duane spoke Spanish fluently. Maybe he could elude them.

McCabe's Spiller & Burr rested in a new custom-crafted black leather holster on her hip, like a piece of exotic jewelry. The derringer was poised in its holster attached to her garter, while the sawed-off shotgun lay on her lap for special effects. I don't want to be an old lady rocking in my chair in some moldy hotel room someday, with a comical little dog to drool on my carpet. How could I look at myself in the mirror if I abandoned love?

She had money to finance the journey, and for the first time in her pampered Southern-belle life, felt confident about her ability to survive Texas. Maybe I don't have swift answers, but I know all the good old songs, and any decent Southern gentleman can be expected to help a lady in distress, I think.

Duane Braddock, I'm on your trail. Mexico is immense, but I've got plenty of time. One of these days I'm going to find you, and I wonder what you'll say when you see me next time around?

In the Sierra del Tlahualilo, not far from the Rio Grande, Tandor the Apache sat alone on a cliff, gazing intently at a herd of mustangs running wild across the valley below. One seldom saw such a spectacle, hundreds of horses at full gallop, and Tandor figured it was a horse religious ceremony, for why shouldn't the animals have their own mountain spirits to guide them?

Tandor leaned forward, shielding his eyes with his

hand, and focused his bright eyes on a big russet stallion with a black mane at the head of the stampede. In the past, the warrior had observed wild horses fighting among themselves with hooves—that's how they chose their leaders, so the horse leading the pack had defeated his rivals the hard way. The brave warrior saluted the horse from his perch in the sky. *Enjuh*. It is good. The animal appeared vaguely familiar, but Tandor couldn't place him, though their paths had crossed not long ago.

Brave Nestor now carried no saddle or rider as he sped along gloriously, his great heart thundering with the power of the universe. He reached his long legs forward and propelled himself rapidly over a carpet of delicious food.

Sometimes Nestor recalled his old cowpoke friend, the one who'd brought him apples and raisins, but the friend was gone to the shadow world, and Nestor had become horse king. Perhaps we will meet again in epochs to come, thought Nestor as he charged onward, exultant with freedom, tail flickering in the slippery wind.

The herd raced past a row of cottonwood trees, while beyond them, in a small clearing, the bleached rickety bones of a man gleamed in bright sunlight. His clothing had been taken by Apaches, and numerous creatures winged and furred had feasted upon his gristle. He had no headstone, and no one to mourn for him. Here lies the remains of Johnny Pinto, the man nobody loved.

It was night in the desert south of Bustamente, and all was still except a lone man and woman riding deeper into Mexico. They drooped in their saddles, struggling to stay awake, traveling only after sundown, hoping to avoid Apaches, banditos, Comancheros, and the Mexican Army.

The man rode three lengths ahead, hat low over his eyes, peering through moonshadows for the flash of an Apache's eyes, and listening for the clank and clamor of cavalry while cradling his Winchester in his arms, loaded and ready to fire.

He was sinewy, bearded, with an expression of determination on his youthful features. He looked like a fox, or maybe a black panther with rosary beads, as he led the way to Monterrey.

The woman also was young, with a white shawl over her head and shoulders, and she was with child. This gave her contentment as she dozed in motion while the little creature swam within her secret sea. "Your father was a great man, and you will be great, too, someday, my beloved child," she whispered gently, then raised her eyes devoutly toward the heavens. "Lord, please shower your mercy on the spirit of dear departed Capitán Ricardo Cochrane. I admit there was much he did not understand, but he was a good man deep down, and none of us ask to come here in the first place. Ricardo Cochrane did his duty as he saw it, but I bow to Your will, *Padre mio*. Let we who call upon you never be put to shame."

The weary horses plodded onward, while above them glittered a star brighter than all the other constellations, like the star of Bethlehem. It guided them across tractless desert wastes, as choruses of insects sang madrigals, and a raven flew past the face of the moon.